THE LOST TR

By Be

Without a measureless and perpetual uncertainty, the drama of human life would be destroyed – Winston Churchill

CHAPTER 1

THERE IT WAS AGAIN.

A haunting cry shot from the dark belly of the woodland, unlike anything Danny Rawlings had ever heard. He felt the skin tighten over his forearms and the back of his neck, pricking the tiny hairs.

An odd mix of curiosity and conscience urged him to drop anchor, reining in Salamanca. As if able to smell danger, the strapping eight-year-old became lit up, choosing flight over fight. Yet the panic didn't spread to Danny's assured hands tightly gripping the reins as they slowed from a canter to a trot to a walk to a standstill.

Although it cut through the woods on the Samuel Estate, the path was also a public right of way. Danny feared it was a lost rambler in some kind of trouble. He slid off to land softly on the earthy path and tied the reins round the nearby stump of a beech. Salamanca was still blowing.

Heavenly fingers of light escaped thick canopies above. Danny peered past an embrace of jutting trunks, wrapped by a breathless tangle of brambles and ferns, like the matted teeth of a hairbrush. Beyond was black as a crypt.

He simply couldn't ignore that cry for help but didn't rush, perhaps holding back while he came up with some excuse, an easy way out. As if on cue, there was another keening wail. Though it didn't sound human, neither could he put an animal to it.

Sometimes, idly clicking on Google Earth, he'd float over these woods. Looking down, it didn't seem real somehow, more like bright green model-railway trees. He'd been curious, but never that curious, to know what lay beneath. Now he was about to find out.

Not long after, he'd worked his way deep into the darkening wood. He kept lashing away with his whip until his arm felt heavy and face tingled with sweat. His fleece kept snagging and his waterproof bottoms were torn.

Everything else told him to turn back. It was probably animals fighting over a kill.

'Hello?!' he shouted, voice pinballing off the trunks. Only silence came back. 'Hello!'

The quiet noise of the woodland was disrupted by the heavy rustle of leaves and chorus of cawing rooks. Perhaps Salamanca was right. Could there be something in those tales of ghosts and secrets kept by these woods, he feared.

'Bullshit,' escaped his dry lips, as dismissive as the first time he'd rubbished them. A shudder crept up on him, as if to shed his crawling skin. At some deeper level, he clearly wasn't as convinced.

He'd never admit to fearing the dark. Male pride would see to that. But his breaths were now trembling as much as his hands. He felt hot and cold. Was this a panic attack?

Dots of light above, like stars in the night sky, were playing tricks with the shadows. He could sense movement in the dark. Flashes of *The Blair Witch Project* came to him.

He was about to concede defeat, head back to the beaten track, when another ear-aching screech travelled right through him, much louder this time. Sounded like something in the last throes of life. It came from somewhere beyond a mess of knotted weeds, creepers and branches facing him.

An angry swipe of his whip and he'd parted that heavy green curtain. Danny squinted as he peered through the tear he'd made.

He was primed to call upon the karate lessons he'd taken to ward off bullies at school.

He looked out on to a circular clearing, no bigger than a circus ring with deep brown grass and brambles bleached by the morning sunlight. There was no sign of life, just a few darting flies. Certainly nothing that could create the unearthly cries that brought him here. He then stepped into the light. He felt like an explorer discovering virgin territory.

He soon came across a pile of scattered and broken animal bones.

A glint among the tall grass made him stop. He dropped to one knee and ran a hand over a smooth, cool something. He tugged it from the dead grass and ran his fleece over what appeared to be an old timepiece.

It was way too big for a strapless watch head. Was it a pocket watch?

He then saw the sixty-second dial on the circular enamel face and a single hand. This was a stopwatch. It filled his glistening palm nicely and looked like silver.

Danny punched the mushroom button on top but nothing happened. He then turned that winding crown several times and pressed again. As the hand began to turn, second by second, he beamed a smile.

They don't make them like this anymore, he thought, and flipped it over. Engraved on the silver case were the letters H.M.

Danny pocketed the find and prepared to leave.

Despite the soothing warmth on his face and neck, he shivered again. He felt a weight of eyes upon him and spun. Four green dots were staring back, round and unblinking, like headlamps in the night.

Danny gripped the whip tighter. Was it dogs? Foxes? He suspected foxes, as he'd seen plenty darting for cover at dusk since the hunting ban had been enforced. Had they been fighting and were now about to turn on him? He'd always been told they were shy creatures, afraid of humans. He hoped he'd heard correctly. He wasn't that keen to hang around and find out.

They were still and hushed, probably thinking they were safe, shrouded by darkness. It was then he noticed at the edge of the clearing a mutilated carcass of some woodland creature, little more than a mess of flesh and bones.

He turned and made quicker time retracing his own trampled path back to the nodding shape of Salamanca, standing steadfast by the beech stump, surprisingly subdued. Perhaps the dark had messed with his body clock. As he remounted, he made a mental note to take the longer route skirting around the woods from now on.

CHAPTER 2

'WHAT'S MY ODDS?' she asked.

Danny wanted to look away from her playing with that waterfall of blonde ringlets framing a face sweet as her scent.

I've just closed the book, he felt like saying, but there were others to see. 'I'll be in touch.' He looked closer at her CV. 'Megan.'

'Sorry about the writing. Would've printed it out but it's bust, well, the ink cartridge's gone dry. No joke, right, but they cost as much as a new printer and I'm skint.' She rolled her eyes. 'That's not why I'm here, well, partly, but I love horses see, I'm light and, forget all this–' her finger drew a circle in the air to frame her portrait. 'I'm no girly girl. I'll get my hands dirty.'

'I'll be in touch.'

'I've gone too far, said too much, knew I would, nerves it is. Only I want this, need this so bad. Parents doing my head in and they need space, we all do. Don't know who's climbing the walls fastest. Even our dog Rufus is moody.'

'Don't be nervous,' Danny said and smiled. 'I like your energy, the rest you can learn. Keen to create a lively atmosphere for when owners drop by. Morale can dip when the yard fails to snap a losing run.'

'I've heard loads about Samuel House.' Which Danny took as: I've recently glossed up on Samuel House.

'We punch above our weight,' he said, directing her lagoon-blue eyes up to a gallery of mounted photos of races and presentations colouring the oak-panelled walls.

'I'd charm them silly,' she said.

'No doubt you would,' Danny said, now shuffling papers, like newsreaders once did, before they started sitting on their desks.

'Are we finished?'

Danny nodded. 'You know the way out?'

'Yes,' Megan said. 'Pleasure to meet you, Mr Rawlings,' she added, trying to end on a more refined note, though sounded more like an unfinished Eliza Doolittle.

As she walked out, he afforded a glance at her petite, yet curvy figure and pert arse in those skin-tight Levi's. More out of admiration that lust, like absorbing a thing of beauty, a sculpture in a gallery, one that was strictly not for touching, yet still appreciated. He quickly switched back to her CV. Guilty for being a lech, however innocently.

Happily married man, he thought, well, married man. Sara's for keeps.

Since marrying three years ago, he hadn't had eyes for anyone else. But he couldn't remember the last time he'd enjoyed sex, had *any* sex for that matter. Just the odd quickie and, 'don't wake Jack,' she'd say, which kind of spoilt the mood. She seemed to treat it as a fortnightly chore, like putting the bins out, to appease Danny's primal needs. Lie back and think of Wales, Danny swore she whispered once. But this wasn't the Sara he married. Danny could understand time changes people but this was like she'd had a lobotomy. Perhaps that's the reason for his wandering eye.

He sighed more than his air-cushioned chair as he sat back and laced his fingers behind his head. He then found a moment to pull from the top drawer that stopwatch. His hands skated over the smooth rounded glass, not even a hairline crack, and then the flawless silver case. *Scrubbed up well*, he thought. Outwardly it looked as new.

He clicked the mushroom button and still marvelled that the second hand quietly made its way round. *And the innards at least worked.* It was clearly waterproof and built to last.

He hadn't needed encouragement to look it up on some internet auction database and the closest match was a Webster's design from the 1920s. Guide price: two hundred to two hundred and fifty pounds. Come in handy out on the gallops, he reckoned, timing morning workouts.

He once again came back to what intrigued him most - the engraving: H.M.

Her Majesty. Nah. A previous owner of Samuel House. Possible.

Samuel House wasn't nearly as grand as it sounded. Something like three-bed trainers' cottage would be on the estate agent's particulars but how would that attract new owners to the yard? He had to somehow get an edge over rival stables down-valley.

When he heard Megan's Fiesta rev away, he locked the office door behind him but soon stopped on the landing.

Beyond the bathroom door, he heard a succession of coughs, splutters and a groan echoing around the toilet bowl. It made him want to retch too. He then heard someone spit and blow their nose, then a flush. Why on earth was Sara being sick this morning? He feared the answer was in the question. He'd always welcome another Rawlings into the world but it was the timing. Right now, he simply couldn't afford a fourth mouth to feed and then there was Sara. The stress would send her over the edge. The mere thought made him back away from the door. *Hear no evil and all that.*

Danny moved on to something he could deal with: the horses.

Passing the lounge, he heard the TV blaring away. Sara had left it on, perhaps to drown something out – it was impossible to be sick quietly. Upstairs, Jack was lying low with a bug, hopefully one of those twenty-four hour things. Danny rushed into the room to turn it off before he heard crying. But he just turned it down, holding fire for the local news reeling off the headlines. Lead story was a murder in the Ely district of Cardiff. The newsreader continued: 'Leading high-street retailers fear a double-dip recession after poor sales in the second quarter, there's a man missing off the coast of Pembrokeshire feared drowned, with the rescue mission already called off.'

Danny's finger hovered over the standby button as he waited for the happy 'and finally' story they'd sometimes wrap up with to end on a lighter note, as if to tell viewers it's not all bad out there. 'And finally, the BBC's *Antique's Heaven* rolls into town next week. So get rooting in that attic to see what hidden gems you might find.' It failed to lift Danny's mood. The most valuable thing in his family was his mum's gold wedding band and even that had been bought on the never-never, he'd later found out. He needed relaxing, so he headed out through the kitchen door towards the stable block – thirty boxes framing a paved courtyard. Kelly was hosing it down. Her pale skin shone in the weak morning sun.

'Nice to see a smiley face,' Danny said. 'Know something I don't?'

'Must be the weather,' Kelly replied, hooking black strands of hair behind her ears. 'Or that I'll be head-lass come Monday. Fancy, didn't even make the shortlist for head-girl at school.'

'This won't be an excuse to boss people about.'

'I know, I know, but head-lass, eh?' That flashy smile returned. 'Mam was in floods when she heard. Don't know who was proudest after that.'

'But it's just a job title,' Danny said. 'The shit will still need shovelling.'

'There's more to it than that, no?' Kelly asked, smile morphing into a frown. 'Responsibility?'

'Ignore me,' came out as a sigh. 'Didn't mean to rain on your parade.' He walked over and lowered his voice. 'It's just been a rough few months.'

'Is Sara okay?' Kelly asked. 'It's only, was riding out just now … I saw her walking in the upper field, she was chewing her hair and blanked me.'

'Like I said, it's been a rough few months.'

10

'Oh, right,' Kelly replied and bit her lower lip. 'I took four out for a spin first thing, hosed them down. Turnabout looks smashing, really come in his coat.'

'He's up next,' Danny said and turned to resume inspecting his twenty-eight inmates, like he always did first thing. He couldn't relax until he'd checked them over and would *never* leave for the track until finishing the rounds. Sara said it had become an OCD thing.

'I'll finish up here, and then nip back to Rhymney, left my phone at home.'

'Fine,' Danny said, 'And Kelly, you'll make a great head-lass.'

'Thanks,' Kelly replied, more spring in her step as she resumed washing away muck and straw.

Danny was most anxious about looking in on Salamanca, who had made box one his home for the past two years. Danny dusted down the laminated sheet by the stable door. It read: 'Name – SALAMANCA, By – Anchor's Away, Out of – Sally's Game, Foaled – 16/5/2003'.

The gelding was standing calmly fetlock-high in a thick bedding of shredded paper. It was a blessing to care for such a quality steeplechaser but with it came a whole new set of fears. Since the spring, he'd had a recurring anxiety dream where he'd enter and, through the morning gloom, would see Salamanca cast in his box, lying like an upturned turtle, unable to right himself. It was only then Danny would awake, heart in mouth, forehead and palms shiny. Each time he wouldn't even bother trying to get back to sleep. He'd just make himself a hot chocolate and check the CCTV camera showing internal shots of box one from his study. Mind rested, he'd often go back to bed and try to get a precious half-hour before he was up again to pull out the first 'lot' on the gallops.

Right now Danny was only nine boxes down when he was stopped by a question. Then who was being sick?

11

The loud clap of a door made him turn again. Rhys had emerged from the kitchen and was standing in shade. He flicked his long blond hair back, as if auditioning for a shampoo ad. He then looked down as if checking his sleeveless shirt was straight, or perhaps clean. Why would the stable jockey hurl up his breakfast?

Was he ill? Hung-over? Weight problems? None of them were good news.

CHAPTER 3

AS DANNY sat, perched on the edge of the rumpled quilt, he could almost feel the air thicken. He also felt Sara's eyes looking down on him. 'What?!'

'Want a list?' Sara snapped, face turning funereal.

'No, but I'm sure I'll get one!'

'Aside from you being emotionally crippled,' Sara said. 'Let's see: the way you leave the toilet seat up, stubble in the sink, overflowing bins, too long to get ready, thought that was a woman's prerogative.'

'Why stop there, Christ, you said my breathing had got on your tits the other day,' Danny argued. 'And while we're at it, when do you switch the lights off as you leave a room?'

'And don't you let me know it – you should've added "turn the lights out behind you" to our vows, bloody parrot.'

Danny had hoped she wouldn't link all this to some crappy metaphor on the state of their marriage.

She then threw the TV remote across the room, missing Danny, who'd ducked, but hitting the middle panel of her vanity mirror. Both were silenced by the shatter of glass, now a cobweb of cracks.

She then shrieked, 'Now look what you made me do!'

'Fan-fuckin'-tastic,' Danny cried. 'That's my fault too.'

'Well you're gonna clean it up, it's your mess.'

'Not the only thing that's cracked,' Danny muttered.

'What?!' Sara said.

'You heard.'

Sara looked away, anywhere but Danny.

'I didn't mean that,' Danny said, 'It's just … you keep talking to me like I'm Jack's age.'

'Can you blame me?'

'Sara,' Danny said, softer, as if trying to defuse this before one of them said something they'd later really regret. 'You've changed and I don't know why? Is it sleep-deprivation?'

She turned. He noticed his wallet in her hand. 'It's *your* deprivation.'

'Eh?'

She tossed the wallet on Danny's half of the bed. He shook his head.

'Go on,' she said. 'It's yours, open it.'

The subsequent silence made Danny feel like a stand-up who'd just told a dud. His brain was cramping with all the possible things he might find: old betting slips, receipts from the off-licence, his new casino pass. But all that faced him was Megan Jones' face in a passport photo taken from her CV. He shook the wallet but nothing else fell out. 'You've been going through my things.'

'For good reason,' Sara said. 'Who is she?'

'It's not what it looks like.'

'Never is,' Sara fumed. 'Am I no longer pretty enough, so you trade me in for a younger model?'

Soon after Jack came into this world, Danny couldn't help but notice she'd stopped taking pride in herself, losing interest in her clothes, yoga, friends and husband. Was it because she'd already got her man?

'I love you for what you are,' Danny said.

'What?!'

'Who! I meant, who!' Danny said. 'Don't trap me all the time. My head's about to burst, can't take this. All I'm saying, you seem to have lost some zest in life, I hate seeing that.'

'So you want me to put the slap on again. Is that it?'

'No!' Danny said. 'Just want you to respect and love yourself as much as I do.'

14

'So I live up to the competition,' she said.

'Lord, give me strength.'

'Since when have you been religious?'

'Think I'll turn born again,' Danny said. 'Need someone on my side.'

Sara parted the curtains, letting some grey light into the room. Danny went over and rested a hand on her shoulder but was shaken off, a withdrawal that felt much more than physical.

'Like I haven't got enough on my plate, you dish up this as a side order,' Danny said. 'What is it? Tell me, think I have a right to know, a hangover from the post-natal blues, the kidnapping or Jack going through the gruesome twosomes.'

'I've always asked why you never carry a picture of me and get the same answer.' Danny shook his head again, thoughts still lingering on why the hell he'd left that in his wallet. She continued, 'Got a photographic memory, you'd say. Why would you need to look at my image when it's already in there?' She pressed an index finger against her temple. 'Well?'

'You're always jumping in without thinking,' Danny said. 'Choosing hysterical over rational.'

'So that's the best you've come up with. You must have known I'd find out and had plenty of time to concoct an excuse.'

'If you no longer trust me,' Danny said. 'I don't see any point in making a case. I'm clearly guilty.'

'It's even got her phone number on the back.' Her brow creased. 'How can I trust you?'

'You don't believe in our vows at the altar then.'

'I did.'

'Did?' Danny cried. 'She tried for the stable-lass vacancy if you must know. Replacing Kelly, who's now head lass.' Her frown dissolved and the air then thinned of tension though Danny suspected this was the eye of the storm. He offered the photo back. 'You can feel the shape left by the paper-clip. It was fastened to her CV.'

'Name?'

15

'Megan.'

'I'm guessing she got it.'

'She impressed me,' he said. Sara looked away arms crossed. 'Not like that.'

'But that doesn't explain why her number is on the back.'

'I'll be phoning her this afternoon with the good news. Can listen in if you like? And if you're gonna read something into *everything*, I'll happily take the guest room for now. Sleep on the bloody couch if it means a quiet night.'

'But take her out of it and I'm still not your first love.'

'Of course you are,' Danny said, 'what else can I say or do?'

'I'll always come a distant second to the horses.'

'It's my job,' Danny cried.

'And you're married to it.'

'I do it for you and Jack, how many times—' Danny sighed. 'I came up here to build a future for *us*. Soon Jack can try out the ponies for size.'

'It never ends,' she cried and made for the door.

'And be quiet with it,' he said. 'You'll wake Jack.'

'Perhaps then I'll get a sensible conversation round here. And she better turn up as the new stable lass or I'll break more than that mirror,' she said. 'I'll be in the spare room, stay here.'

He returned the photo to his wallet, more out of spite. He'd done nothing wrong, so why should he throw it?

Having been woken several times by Jack and got up at 5.30 AM – some five and a half hours ago – Danny wished he could also go back to bed but he wasn't afforded that luxury. Sleeping on the job would soon have twelve individual owners and seven syndicates asking awkward questions.

'And while you're here, fix that,' she added, stood in the doorway pointing at the mirror. 'Want to look good for visitors.'

'But you haven't seen anyone for months,' Danny said. 'Look, it was never going to be easy moving up here in the wilds, we both knew that, you're a city girl at heart, you've got more friends than me, proper friends I mean, not just racing acquaintances like mine who'd happily stab me in the back for the next wonder-horse. It's a hell of a shock to the system once the novelty of rural life wears off, I know.'

'I'll be in bed,' she said, squeezing her pillow under one arm.

'Now?' Danny asked. 'It's the afternoon.'

She glanced at the bedside clock. 'It's 11 AM'

'That's afternoon to me.'

She left with a theatrical huff. The clap of the door behind her set Jack off again. He was in his cot, still nursing the tail end of that bug.

She was depressed; Danny didn't need letters after his name to see that. He'd become tired trying to get Sara back to the doctor's. He'd seen her take something soon after Jack arrived, but she didn't pick up her repeat prescription and had been in denial ever since. Danny had yet to take it personally, preferring to blame it on upping sticks to the countryside from city living in Cardiff. Although she was initially as keen as Danny for the move, it proved more of a culture shock for her. Many are romanced by the thought of bracing walks, stunning scenery and clean air but that fades once the long, cold, dreary winter nights set in and the pungent nostril-clearing smell of manure is carried downwind from farms up-valley. Test driving country living took more than a week or two at a holiday cottage.

Since moving to the wilderness of the Welsh valleys, they'd become remote in every sense.

Sara's visits to friends in Cardiff centre and the bay had become less frequent and so came the inevitable drift apart from them, with fewer things in common and excuses to 'make it another date', or 'got so much on right now, but be sure to catch up soon.'

He no longer felt tired and he began to methodically peel away the triangular shards of glass that was the vanity mirror. Focusing on anything but his marriage was kind of therapeutic, a brief escapism. He only wished he hadn't drunk the last of the lagers the previous evening.

He was about to stop picking at the glass which was coming away in large slices and go check on Jack, who was still making himself heard, when he stopped.

He flicked the lamp switch on the dressing table next to Sara's eyeliners and blusher. Seeing what lay behind the mirror, he was now a good deal more careful removing the final few shapes of glass. He looked closer, could this be the end to all his financial woes?

Behind the middle panel providing a spine for the mirror was a painting. Danny went to the kitchen. With the sharpest knife pulled from a wooden block, he began to prise the edges of the board away from the seam. He turned on the main light and then allowed himself to marvel at what lay beneath. He shook off the smaller fragments of glass, falling to the carpet like tiny diamonds. He placed the board on the quilt and stood there, looking down, captivated. His marital troubles were pushed away for those moments as he stared at the find.

He always reckoned the mirror didn't fit this old cottage but never said anything. Sara seemed to like it and that was enough.

He tried to recall when and where it had come from but nothing came to him. He hadn't helped Sara's parents carry it in and it certainly wasn't from his half of the family, which meant it was left here, along with the Welsh dresser and some white goods, when buying Samuel House with the help of a huge mortgage some three years ago.

His fingers ran over the thick layers of oil paint, the tiny ridges of the glossy swirling brush strokes and the hairline cracks that came with age. It depicted a racing scene with five horses in full flight; literally for one of the runners, which was captured midway clearing the only fence in the painting. Even to Danny's green eye, the jockeys and their silks were naively painted, with no obvious facial features. He wasn't sure whether this was intentional or just showed up the artist. The colours were still vivid, no damage from the sun, seemingly having been hidden away for much of its life, which had to be in its favour. His eyes darted to the bottom right corner of the board for a signature. He'd seen enough of the BBC show *Antique's Heaven* to know the name of any artist would always add value, something about provenance.

He then turned to see the smaller scalloped-edged panels either side of the gap in the middle. Danny knew as little of styles or fashions as the next man but he could see some art deco in this. The sort of thing he'd seen on *Poirot* as a kid after bath-time on those depressing Sunday evenings, dreading what both the teachers and pupils had in store for him the following morning.

If the largest panel had been hiding this, perhaps there was something behind the other two. At the right edge of the middle panel he'd noticed a shadow on the grass, which suggested there was also a runner on the right panel.

He cut and then prised the mirrored glass away. The right panel was indeed a continuation of the same racing scene. But that shadow on the ground led to a patch where the paint had been removed, leaving an off-white square.

He knew damaged goods wouldn't fetch a king's ransom. He dropped the panel beside the other. He did the same to the left panel and out fell the missing piece of the painting which showed a couple of stragglers in the race, jockeys stood up in the saddle, as if they'd already written off any chance of winning the race.

Perhaps he could sell the two good panels but then thought who would want just two panels of a triptych.

He pulled a chair from under the dressing table and sat there. Who would hide a painting after defacing it?

CHAPTER 4

CLICK.

Danny straightened, eyes peering over his *Racing and Football Outlook.*

A briefcase, battered and brown, something like the budget box, had been pushed across the red bookies' counter in Raymond Barton Turf Accountants, as if this was some kind of saloon.

Danny shut the paper silently. *This could get lively.*

'Not interested,' he read cashier Harry's lips say, 'whatever you're selling.'

The owner of the briefcase wasn't a regular. Danny would recognise him. He looked about Danny's age, early thirties, with a swarthy angular face that was impossibly handsome and he appeared to know it. He could have been a catalogue model in a former life, with a confident jaw-line, beneath a full head of foppish coal-black hair, sleeked with products, or grease. There wasn't a strand out of place, same as his moustache. He flashed a brilliant white smile, showing a regiment of square teeth bright as sun-kissed snow. He wore dark shades indoors, like a poker player.

He lifted the lid to show Harry, whose eyes then lit up as if seeing a lost treasure. He stood from his swivel chair and grabbed the phone. His other hand ran over his cropped brown hair, clearly under some pressure.

Danny felt like standing too as he watched Harry thumb a number.

No doubt Head Office. Dirty money, I bet.

The stranger then produced what looked like a betting slip from a leather jacket that went with his hair and shades. He smiled. 'Now you're interested, yes?'

By now a wave of rich aftershave had reached Danny, who glanced over at Stony, but his friend was busy studying form, face as solemn and soulless as a passport photo.

Harry was now talking down the phone, back turned from prying eyes and ears. He was there for what seemed like an age, clutching that betting slip. Danny was about to return to his newspaper when the thirty-something cashier came back, the phone no longer in his hand. He nodded to the stranger but was no longer smiling as he ran the slip through the till and then the scanner which timed the bet and sent an image of it to the traders at Raymond Barton Headquarters. But he didn't hand the slip over, not yet.

'May I,' Harry said, hands hovering over the briefcase. He then shiftily eyed the four men and a dog on the betting floor before carefully removing the wads of notes, each held by red paper bracelets noting that each had been bank counted as a grand. Danny watched as Harry reached for the thirtieth and final bundle of twenty-pound notes.

Thirty big ones, Danny thought, what I'd do for that. It now explained the shades. This was a high-roller, one of a dying breed. The same question kept coming back to him: what was worth risking that kind of money? Back came the same answer: a stone-cold certainty. But there wasn't such a thing in this game, or any other for that matter. So when the man had left, briefcase swinging a good deal freer than before, Danny sidled over to the counter, leaving a bin bag containing the three panels of the painting on the table. Harry emptied his lungs and didn't know what to do with his hands. 'Did you just see that?'

'That's why I came over.'

'It's easily the biggest bet I've had to take, ever! I was bricking it, make a mistake putting something like that through, my job would be smoke,' Harry said, voice shaking. 'Just amazed the head honchos at HQ gave the green light. Thirty large ones!'

'On?'

'Come on Danny,' Henry said. 'You know I can't say.'

Danny knew a bet that big could sway the market, shortening up the odds, following the simple laws of supply and demand. It stands to reason the punter would want to take a fixed price to guarantee a set return if he won. He looked over at the monitor showing the odds on offer. Harry lunged forward and flicked it to screensaver but he was too slow. *Turnabout. Evens.*

Danny took a step away from the counter. 'That's one of mine.'

'Fuck, Danny,' Harry said. 'Wish you'd said, could of got the low-down before I'd put the bet through. Should I join the gamble?'

Danny was no longer listening. He called upon a photographic memory to see the briefcase man in his mind's eye.

'Did you know him?' Harry asked. 'One of your placers is he?'

'I don't bet anymore,' Danny snapped. 'And wouldn't need to get others to place wagers for me if I did.'

'Cos you always lost,' Harry said and swivelled to face the coffee machine.

'Less lip,' Danny said.

'Only messing with you.'

'Well, don't,' Danny said and returned to the tatty bin liner, which he hoped would help deter the bookie-dwellers from sniffing around its contents, but it clearly hadn't work with a regular's Jack Russell. He shooed the inquisitive dog away, not wanting any distractions as he speed-dialled Rhys, who by now ought to be, with a clear run, approaching the Severn Bridge and about to veer off to Chepstow Racecourse with the yard's only runner in tow – Turnabout.

Being the trainer with no travelling head-lad to assist, Danny would normally drive the horsebox to the track but he had something to do this afternoon and Rhys seemed, for once, keen to steer home the van and then the horse. While he waited for an answer, he glanced at the stacked boards.

After three rings, the call went to messages. Danny suspected something other than driving had stopped Rhys from picking up. And he'd also wager *that* something had to do with the briefcase man.

'Keep an eye on this Stony, cheers.' Danny killed his phone and walked to the sideboard, pretending to study form. Should he even bring it up next time he saw Rhys? Someone was significantly more confident in Turnabout than his trainer, who knew the horse was well, but not well enough to justify putting a small house on.

The four-year-old was unbeaten in two starts as a hurdler but that meant he had to shoulder a double penalty. He was effectively carrying a stone more than his rivals. That was no easy task, particularly for such an inexperienced hurdler. Perhaps he'd jumped the gun and Rhys wasn't a mole in the yard. What had Kelly remarked the other day? 'Turnabout looked stunning.' Or perhaps there was no mole and this was just an eccentric millionaire that got some kick out of seeing the fear in a bookie's eyes – the punter's enemy.

Danny turned. He wasn't going to try Rhys again. He'd watch the race with a keen eye and then play it by ear, depending on the result.

'Cheer up, Stony.'

'I'm ecstatic,' Stony said and forced a smile. 'That's the third bloody time I've been told that today. It's my hound-dog face, born with it.'

Danny smiled. 'It's more a lived-in face.'

Stony snapped, 'By squatters.'

'What's wrong?'

'I've had it up to here.'

'Where's all this come from?' Danny asked. 'I want the old Stony back.'

'This is the old Stony, just dared to face reality that's all.'
Danny smelt the air. 'You been drinking.'

'Believe me,' Stony said, and grabbed Danny by the arm.
'I've never been more sober in my life.' He'd never seen Stony
scowl. He was strangely distant. He looked sick with sadness. 'Do
you know, Danny, think I stepped out of life years ago.' Stony
looked down at the *Daily Mirror*. How long has it been since I
had a laugh? A proper one, where your sides ache and eyes run.'
Danny shrugged. 'Thought you might know because I don't.'

'You think too much, you need to get out of this place, a
distraction,' Danny said. 'Perhaps get a part-time job, supplement
your benefits.'

'Always fancied being a long-distance trucker,' Stony said.
'A free spirit out on the open road, Dire Straits blasting from the
speakers, crackin'. Except there's the driving, would play havoc
with the new hip. Take the driving away and there you have my
ideal job.'

'But that's ... that's just sitting down, listening to music,'
Danny said. 'Didn't have you down as a traveller anyhow.'

'I'm a man of the world,' Stony said.

'Yeah, if that world is Cardiff, more specifically this place.'

'Think I'll stick with hand-outs from the Injured Jockey
Fund.'

'Come to the yard,' Danny said.

'I don't need pity.'

'It's not pity I'm offering, been meaning to ask you to come
up for ages, see The Tank.'

'What kept you?'

'Just got loads on my mind.'

'Sara?'

'And the rest,' Danny said.

'Oh, I dunno,' Stony said. 'Don't want to put you out or
anything.'

'Nonsense,' Danny said. 'That's arranged, say Thursday.'

'Thursday it is. I'd like that. And we'll keep this little "chat" to ourselves, right.'

'What chat?'

Stony smiled. 'How is the old boy anyhow?'

'Salamanca?'

Stony nodded.

'A1,' Danny said, knocking the wooden table. 'Earmarked the Summer Plate at Market Rasen and then it's off to the legendary Czech Pardubicka.'

'No Cheltenham Gold Cup?'

'Can't see it,' Danny said. 'That'll attract more stars than the Hollywood Walk of Fame. Don't get me wrong, Salamanca's got class, but he's got even more stamina.'

'Anything else for the notebook?' Stony asked.

'Nearly forgot,' Danny said. Stony closed his newspaper. 'We've got a new addition to the yard.'

'Oh yeah,' Stony said, 'talented?'

Danny opened up his wallet and removed Megan's CV photo. 'You decide.'

'Expecting moths,' Stony said and then held it.

'What?' Danny smiled as he waited for Stony to stop laughing and explain the joke.

'Sorry,' Stony wheezed, 'Danny's Angels.'

'It's not like that,' Danny said. It was worth taking some stick, just to see Stony back on form.

'Got a proper harem going on up there,' Stony added.

'She got the job on merits alone,' Danny said. 'Willing to get her hands dirty.'

'Bet she is,' Stony said and smiled again. 'Don't imagine there are many stable *lads* or *older* lasses up at yours.'

'Most leave after time, crap pay and hours. And there's Rhys knocking about the place,' Danny reasoned.

'Only pulling your leg, son,' Stony said, wiping his eyes. 'What's in the bag? I told you not to bother.'

'Oh, nothing,' Danny said

As Danny made a move, regular Basil the handyman – a nickname because he was handy with a brush – had entered, parking his bike against a Fixed Odds Betting Terminal. He then whistled and, as always, warbled, 'What's it all about, Alfie?'

'I've told you not to call me Alfie,' Danny said, smiling.

'All right, Danno, my man. How's it hanging?'

'Not so bad. You and the wife well?'

'Aye,' Basil said. 'It's our anniversary tonight, the big twenty, seems like more. Got the best table booked and everything.'

'Nice touch.'

'Just hope she likes snooker.'

Danny laughed though suspected Basil wasn't joking.

He brushed by Top Jock, who was crouched on a chrome seat, whipping his backside with a rolled-up *Racing Post*, eyes fixed to a screen showing a race from a matinee meeting in the French provinces.

This place needs padded walls, Danny thought, which made him wonder why he felt at home there. He stepped out into harsh daylight on Greyfriars Road and made the short walk to the drawbridge of Cardiff Castle where he queued to be registered for *Antique's Heaven*.

After what seemed like hours waiting in line within the castle walls, Danny was parched and felt like quitting for a pint at the Castle Keep. Almost as if sprayed on, the thick gruel of soft cloud that hung low in the sky made it even muggier. He pulled on the collar of his shirt and longed to change into something airier but he was representing the yard and first impressions count, particularly as millions would be watching when this went out. That was if he would be picked out as worthy of filming which appeared unlikely having nosed around the competition. What he held in that ripped bin liner was hardly a Ming vase.

He thought the edited programme was slow but this was like being stuck in a traffic jam on a humid, breathless day.

Never again, he thought. He began to wish he'd gone to Chepstow to see Turnabout. Even now, he considered giving up and heading for the track but feared he wouldn't get there in time for the race. He would also miss out on this evaluation and a much-needed plug on TV for the yard, making it a wasted day all round.

He'd already counted the crenels on top of the curtain wall and the lines of tables, each with an expert, and probably had time to get through the blades of grass of the castle lawns by the time he'd be seen. He was in fact trying to escape the awkward pauses in a stop-start chat with a white-haired couple next in line holding what they hoped would be their retirement plan, a hamper of porcelain wrapped in brown paper. His mum always swore he was a bit autistic. He was never quite sure what she meant by that. Which bit: the hand? Mind he'd rarely met a socially adept bloke.

Danny was gearing up to say his goodbyes and good luck to those he'd befriended when he was approached by a member of the production staff with a laminated BBC pass hung from his neck, alongside an expert, who looked over the painting. The assistant seemed more interested in Danny, asking all manner of details. Who owned it? Where did you get it? Danny felt like he was back down the police station again.

He was plucked from the line as part of the 'local interest' segment of the show and soon found himself waiting awkwardly across from that same expert called Michael, a suited sixty-something with a round, ruddy face beneath a comb-over. A make-up artist was powdering his rouged cheeks, shining like waxed fruit, and then preened his moustache. He was probably a household name, just not in Samuel House. The three panels were displayed an easel beside a blue banner with *Antique's Heaven*'s emblem in capital letters, with the crossbar of the A sharing that of the H.

When the production member's arm fell, which signalled the cameras were rolling, Danny's stomach turned over and pulse quickened like Dancing Brave. He'd done TV interviews on the

27

racing channels both as a jockey and trainer but this was something different. There were millions more watching and he didn't know what he was talking about. He had strayed far from his comfort zone.

Michael opened with, 'It's always nice to come across an object local to the area. What we have here is an oil racing scene over three panels, known as a triptych.'

Danny forced his best photo smile, all the time trying to suppress the nagging question: What's the bloody thing worth?

'Tell me, is it yours?'

'Yes,' Danny said mouth dry.

'Then how did you come by it?'

'It came with the house, job lot.'

Danny hoped for the reply: well, aren't you the lucky one.

'I'm sure you cannot have missed that there is no signature, but I'm just as sure it's by a local artist. You can see Caerphilly Mountain in the distant background,' Michael said as his finger ran along the faint hills that met the sky.

'How can you tell?'

'There are the conical spires of Castle Coch on the hillside, nestled among trees.' Danny had suspected it was generic landscape, so hadn't looked that close. 'Which leads me nicely on to age, well, it's not dated, but given the castle was built in the 1870s we have a guide there. And the fact some of the hooves are touching the turf suggests it was painted after the invention of photography. That's because until they could take stills of a horses galloping action, remarkably no one actually knew whether all feet left the ground together in one motion, or if the feet connected with the ground one by one. Once this was proven, artists were able to portray these majestic racing animals with a fair degree more accuracy. All things considered, I'd say this was painted in the nineteen twenties, maybe early thirties.'

'What about the H.M. on the back?'

'This stamp is most likely the initials of a past owner,' Michael said, turning over the panels. 'Either way, it's not a particularly good example, probably commissioned by an owner, maybe to celebrate one of the horses here in the picture, or even a race sponsor, looking to promote their feature race.' His fleshy hand now ran over the eight battling horses, legs outstretched. Unless the expert was teasing the viewers and onlookers and was about to tee up a last-minute twist, Danny could sense where this was heading. 'And it has seen better days too, with the paint cracked and even peeling in places, but the colours are still strong, we have that on our side.' He paused to smile. 'Has it been hidden away from sunlight?'

Danny didn't elaborate about the mirror as he wanted this to end as quickly and painlessly as possible. 'Yes, well hidden.'

The expert leant forward with sympathetic eyes, like a doctor about to deliver a terminal prognosis.

'Do you want to hear the good news or the bad news?'

Danny shrugged.

'Well, it's good that the painting has been kept in the dark,' the expert said. 'But unfortunately, it looks like it was painted in the dark too.' Danny's smile masked a sinking feeling inside, as if he was being roasted by a comedian in the front row of a gig. Once the laughter simmered down, the expert continued, 'A painting is a living and breathing thing, and, speaking for myself, in time, it can begin to deteriorate with age.' The laughter returned. Danny gave up feigning a smile. It would only look as false as the expert's hairstyle. 'And it's the same with oils, cracks and pealing occurs quite naturally, as we see here and over here.' His hand once again skated over the rippled paint. 'That is of little concern to me but, what is, and I'm about to mention the white elephant in the room which none of us can get away with ignoring and that's this monstrous square revealing white primer in the right panel, where I suspect another horse had been.'

'What makes you think that?' Danny asked.

'You can see the faintest skeleton of a rather crude pencil outline the artist had sketched before applying the layers of paint. Somewhere along the line, I'm afraid to say, someone has tried to restore it with turpentine, right down to the tanned board beneath and has been, shall we say, rather ham-fisted. I do hope it wasn't you.'

'Not guilty,' Danny said, smiling.

'It is now, ironically, beyond restoring, as I feel there's simply too much work to do. I mean, this needs more than a retouch and you wouldn't recoup the costs. But one thing I cannot answer, the track remains a mystery, perhaps Chepstow.'

Danny knew it wasn't and thought it a good opening to flag up the yard. 'I've struggled to place it which is a bit frustrating as I'm a trainer at Samuel House up in the valley.' He found himself talking with a posh accent, trying to fit in, he supposed.

'How quaint,' Michael replied. 'If you can't recognise the track, remind me never to send a horse your way.'

Whether it was the heat of these enclosed lawns or the pressure of being on camera but Danny wanted to rip off Michael's bow-tie – the colour of his pink face – and stuff it down that smug gob. *So much for the desperately needed plug.*

Danny's face now hurt. He hadn't forced a smile this much since he'd discovered Sara's parents were coming to stay at Samuel House for five weeks while building work was being carried out on their semi in Wiltshire.

'Put it in a general sale, given the lack of provenance, it would likely fetch no more than one-hundred to one-hundred and fifty pounds tops I'm afraid. But it might be worth doing some research to see if that reveals anything about the race as, it may be worth more to a collector of the sport of kings or ancestors of those who owned these racing colours.' Aware of the cameras, Danny hoped his face hadn't fallen as much as his heart. He knew this would be on film forever quite literally, as in this digital age, with all the new channels, these shows were repeated almost on a loop.

As if picking up on the disappointment, Michael added, 'Well, I dare say, you'll cherish it nonetheless.'

'Condescending bastard,' Danny felt like saying but actually chose, 'Wouldn't sell it for the world, no way. And it cost me nothing.'

But after all that, it was worth little more than the fuel bill to take runners to Wincanton and back.

He signed the show consent forms and handed over his details. He trudged back over the drawbridge. The three wooden boards felt heavier now he knew their value. It seemed the financial future of the yard weighed squarely on the broad shoulders of Salamanca.

He glanced at his watch. He'd missed the opener at Chepstow. His brow creased. He'd have to watch a recording of the race back in his office and hope he wouldn't stumble upon the result beforehand.

When he'd finally got back to the cool, airy kitchen of Samuel House, Megan was rinsing her coffee mug.

'You seem to be settling in well,' Danny said.

'Home from home,' she said and beamed a smile over her shoulder.

'Morning gallops go okay?'

'Yep,' Megan replied, 'and how was *Antique's Heaven*?'

Danny flicked the kettle on and groaned, 'Hell.'

'It wasn't some masterpiece after all then.'

'Good job we're short on firewood.'

'That bad?'

'Expert as good as said it was worthless, which probably means I'll be on the cutting room floor. That's a shame, always wanted to look like a complete mug in front of the nation.'

'So where is it going, the bin?'

'It's a racing scene,' Danny said. 'So probably keep it, there's a space that needs filling on the landing wall.'

'Coffee?' she asked, raising her mug.

'Yeah, ta. Where's Sara?'

'Gone back to bed I think.'

Danny's concern for Sara had grown day by day. Something wasn't right, whether it was physical or mental; he didn't know which would be worse.

'Did you see the race?'

'Don't tell me! I've got the afternoon racing on timer record, like to watch it without knowing the result.'

'Go watch it then.'

As Danny flicked on the widescreen in his office, he analysed what Megan had said. Would she say that if it had won? Encourage him to see it sluice home as the briefcase man predicted. Or was she bluffing, to hide the fact it had flopped.

The only way of knowing was by pressing 'Play.'

He watched as Turnabout bagged the early lead, flicking over the timber with the fluency of the legendary Istabraq. Rhys had sat confidently from flag fall, steering clear of any trouble out in front. Danny could hear his heart as he watched Rhys kick on turning for home, in a matter of strides extending the lead to eight lengths on the also-rans. Rhys then glanced over both shoulders to assess whether he needed to ping this final hurdle. By now he found himself in splendid isolation, so astutely slowed on the approach.

'Steady, Rhys, no heroics,' Danny whispered, knowing this was the only potential stumbling block. 'Jump!'

The trailblazer popped it nicely. Danny breathed out. 'Good boy!' He'd seen too many come a cropper when asked for a big one at the final flight, an unnecessary risk. It was one of the most confident and proficient rides he'd seen from Rhys, whose faltering career had really turned a corner in recent months.

Danny punched the air. He then turned the volume up. Rhys was now busy releasing the breast girth and removing the saddle from Turnabout, whose lean belly was barely moving. An on-course reporter for Racing TV had grabbed the winning jockey before going to weigh in. Rhys was summing up the race but Danny had already mentally tuned out; a figure in the background was proving a distraction. He paused the recording. It was the briefcase man.

Danny stared at him on the frozen screen. The black shades were on but the leather jacket and briefcase were gone. Danny could understand why the stranger had gone to see 'his' horse run in the flesh and was now lurking by the winners' circle. There was nothing odd in that, Danny reckoned, but the same couldn't be said for his clothes or demeanour. The man was now wearing a buttoned-up three-quarter length coat and a deadly serious face. Why would he change into winter clothes? It was hardly a fashion statement and Chepstow had sheltered stands and those around him wore t-shirts. Danny barely recognised him from the bookies that morning. Maybe that was the idea. He certainly hadn't looked the type to suffer from low self-esteem, enough to hide behind clothes.

And what was with the face? He'd just won thirty grand, yet he looked like the horse had done a Devon Loch on the run-in. He was shifting his weight, like a cheetah waiting to pounce. Perhaps he was working off some of the adrenalin coursing his Latin veins. Danny wouldn't like to have seen him if Turnabout had lost. He suspected Rhys would need to hire a bodyguard. Danny would be beaming from ear to ear if he was the one who'd just doubled his money. He found himself admiring the man on the screen for showing such composure under pressure. It was inside every successful punter's armoury, an ability to think and act coolly when others lose their heads. A steely outlook ensured no rash decisions were made, no losses were chased and no winnings were played up on a whim. Perhaps that's where Danny's punting career went wrong.

His face was now hovering inches from the screen, close enough to see the beige pixels making up the man's coat. The punter's hands were buried deep in those big pockets, probably thumbing yet more wads of notes. The racegoers stood nearby would have no clue that this blandly dressed man appeared to be one of the biggest gamblers in the land. It was nearly always the quiet ones, the ones that blend in. Plunder the money then quickly retreat back into the shadows.

Danny used his remote to save the recording under: 'Keep until I delete.'

Although Turnabout had done the stable proud, he felt uneasy about the result. He hoped that his fears were merely paranoia. He knew the racing game can quickly mess with the mind.

CHAPTER 5

THURSDAY, 8.06 AM.

When others were thinking about getting up, Danny had already watched at least half of his string do a serious workout. He was stood in front of the sink, staring blankly out of the kitchen window over to the stables. He wasn't looking at anything, just too tired to move. He snapped himself out of it. With the dregs of a diet cola, he washed down a multivitamin pill and then brewed a strong coffee. When a top apprentice jockey on the Flat as a teen he'd lived on similar, just about surviving off caffeine and fresh air to keep sharp and light.

Weight ruled his life back then, along with most of his colleagues, part and parcel of the job. When it was imperative to make the correct weight for each ride, Danny couldn't afford to snack between races, not even a sneaky Mars Bar to stoke up the fire during a busy book of rides.

Since taking out a trainer's licence he still kept a close eye on the scales. He needed to keep trim for the sake of his regular ride on Salamanca. He didn't want to become a porker like so many jockey-turned-trainers, who suddenly found themselves able to eat more, move less and not be out of a job.

Back then Danny had to keep at least twenty pounds below his natural weight of ten stone, which lead to stomach cramping and dehydration from sessions in the sauna, just to get enough riding fees to pay the bills. He lived with a constant hunger as his body craved a return to its default weight, not good when expected to steer and coax along a half-ton animal.

If he'd repeatedly turn up for rides carrying overweight, even a few pounds, once-steadfastly loyal owners would soon look elsewhere to one of the countless 'short-arsed featherweights' – which is what Danny used to see them as through green eyes – hovering like vultures to mug your riding fees. Even a mere ounce extra could make the difference between a horse winning or losing in this high-tech age where photo-finishes could be separated by a mere pixel.

Danny recalled turning up for a ride in the colours of Pete Wentworth, bleary eyed from a heavy drinking session the night before, banking on being dehydrated enough from a thumping hangover to make the weight. But his hazy memory forgot the large kebab he'd drunkenly devoured like the cookie monster just hours before. He duly weighed out three pounds over and never got another ride with that stable again. Mercifully, for him, random breathalyser tests hadn't been introduced back then.

Pressures to get regular rides to cover board, keep and travelling costs tipped many over the edge. Desperate times call for desperate measures. Many would ram fingers down their throat between rides to bring back up what little they'd eaten that morning. As if in some kind of denial, those were known as 'flippers' in weighing room slang, bulimia to the wider world. That appeared the least risky option to many, with others turning to drink and drugs. No coincidence that Newmarket, the home of British Flat racing has the highest suicide rate in the country.

He blew the surface of the big mug of coffee and wiped the steam wetting his top lip. When Stony's taxi pulled up Danny put the mug down.

First thing Stony did was hand over a rather sorrowful bouquet of yellow flowers. They smelt faintly of petrol and charcoal.

'Didn't think you cared,' Danny said.

'They're for Sara,' Stony said. 'She around?'

'Taken Jack to see her parents. They'll dote on him, soon be right as rain.'

'Everything okay there?'

'Put it like this, the way I was breathing was getting on her tits yesterday,' Danny said, but regretted the words soon as they were out. Stony frowned. 'Forget I said that, I'll let you know.'

It's as if Stony sensed he was approaching a gate marked NO ENTRY and did an abrupt turn. 'Nice weather for it.'

'Yeah.' Danny smiled. 'Nice weather.'

Danny led the way up a grassy slope to Kelly, who'd already tacked up Salamanca and one of the stable hacks whose quiet temperament would help ease Stony back into the saddle after all these years.

Danny turned alongside the schooling ground to check Stony had kept up when he froze, as if someone had yanked his arm. Near the gates of Samuel House, he could see two men. They were talking. He guessed it was Rhys in that white floppy beanie hat, which he'd only part with on sweltering days or if riding out. It was like Jack's comfort blankie. The other was wearing a grey three-quarter length coat which hid his hands and most of his body. His face was shaded by a black Burberry cap. It was the briefcase man. He appeared to be following Danny around like a bad smell. Perhaps he'd dropped by as a prospective new owner. After all he'd picked up sixty grand from Raymond Barton the other day. But if that was the reason for this cold call, why hadn't Rhys welcomed him over?

Danny felt a sudden disappointment stir the pit of his stomach. 'Wait here,' he told Stony.

He'd barely taken a few strides when the talking had stopped and Rhys was now walking up the snaking shale drive, alone.

Danny's suspicions went up a notch. Perhaps his stable jockey had feared more hairdryer treatment for slacking on the job. Fears of a double-dip recession meant they all had to muck in or, in this case, muck out. But a pro jockey like Rhys, even after years of underachieving, could still hold delusions of grandeur.

He looked on through narrowed eyes as Rhys steered a wide berth and went from view in front of Samuel House.

'What's wrong?' Stony asked.

'I don't know, yet,' Danny replied distantly.

When they reached Kelly, Danny was now buzzier than the horses. It wasn't the black coffee but the growing sense that something wasn't right along with the pressure of giving his pension fund a serious workout.

Just days after the Grand National exertions, he'd never forget that moment he'd led Salamanca back to the yard after a morning gallop. When he ran a calming hand over Salamanca's face and nose, his palm had turned blood red. It was a broken blood vessel. He blamed himself for asking too much too soon of his monster chaser.

With that memory sure to be fresh in both their minds, Danny had concerns whether Salamanca would think twice about giving his all again, fearing he'd feel the same pain. To pass that pain barrier, a horse needs both courage and a jockey he can trust. It's a two-way partnership – if asked for more, his mount must trust his jockey it won't hurt.

'I'll take Salamanca,' Stony said and smiled.

Danny eyes flitted between Salamanca and Stony; his two best friends. 'Go on then.'

Stony's smile had halved. 'I was joking.'

'And I'm calling your bluff.'

'I couldn't, it's been fifteen, twenty years.'

'You've told me it's like riding a bike.'

'And I'm a bit wobbly on that, as it goes,' Stony replied.

'But you were every bit as good as me in the saddle,' Danny said, showing the reins. 'It'll be a good experience for both of you. Just sit on him, walk him around, nothing fancy. I'll give you a leg up.' Danny was now like a man on a mission and wouldn't take no.

Stony's smile had now gone. 'Oh, I dunno.'

'Live for the moment,' Danny said. 'When will you have a chance to get on a beast like this?'

Danny could hear the rustle of the trees down by the lower field where Silver Belle was stood idly grazing. 'Relax, he picks up on nerves.'

'And saying that to calm me?'

'I trust you.'

'I'm honoured,' Stony said. 'I know you treat him like one of your kids. In return, I might have something that'll interest you.'

Danny tried to act nonchalantly but couldn't help but try to mask an interest. As the bookies' was Stony's second home, he'd built up an enviable list of contacts, able to get cheap goods, whether they were knock-offs or illegal imports. He'd be a popular prisoner, Danny always thought. He now wondered what something this might be.

'Want you to meet someone, a new friend. Well, friend of a friend.'

'Oh, aye,' Danny said. 'What's he want?'

'Don't know exactly,' Stony said. 'Keen to meet you, though.'

'I'm busy,' Danny said.

'Nothing like that,' Stony said. 'He dresses smart, and says it's worth your while, seems like he's a fan of yours.'

'Have we met?'

'Not yet.'

'I'll see what I can do,' Danny said. 'Now, enough stalling for time. Shall we get down to business?'

He gave Stony a leg up. The ex-jockey shifted his weight – a good deal more than he had the last time he'd sat on a horse – awkwardly in the saddle, trying to get comfy as he could be this far up on a wild beast whose mind was as strong as his athletic frame.

Stony's smile had barely resurfaced when the partnership turned sour. Danny looked on in horror as Salamanca started to buck and kick. Stony held on grimly like a rodeo.

Salamanca spooked and began to whinny, baying to the crowd. He then reared up on his haunches, unshipping Stony, who fell clumsily onto a cushion of lush turf. Danny let slip the reins and tried to gather them up again but they were flapping around Salamanca's neck like a lasso. Salamanca reared again.

Danny backed off, fearing half a ton of horseflesh would fall his way. When he dared look up again, Salamanca was bolting into the distance, full-tilt towards the woods and glen beyond.

Danny knew his horse was a stupid bugger at times, acting more like an eight-year-old child, not a mature adult horse of that same age, and only hoped he'd have the sense not to career into something harder than himself.

He didn't want to look on, as he couldn't help if he did. But he needed to know which way his chaser had chosen to give him any chance of finding the brute once he'd worn himself out.

'Shit! You okay?' Danny asked, fearing the answer.

'I'm fine, honest I am,' Stony said shakily, walking off as if his laces were tied together.

'You're staggering like a new-born foal,' Danny said, suddenly very awake. 'I shouldn't have made you do it. What was I thinking?'

'No, it's all my fault,' Stony cried.

'Give over,' Danny said, 'I got carried away, shouldn't have put you up, don't even let Rhys on him.'

'Go get him before it's too late,' Stony cried, 'I couldn't live with myself if he's speared himself on a fence or snapped a leg.'

'But what about you?'

'I'll live,' Stony replied. 'It's another tale to tell down the bookies'. Now eff-off and catch him!'

This was the last thing Stony needed, Danny thought, must feel so flaky right now.

He pulled a pair of compact zoom binoculars from his fleece and swept the green landscape left then right. Thick white cloud, like shaving foam, had moved in and darkened his view, as if the lenses of the binoculars were tinted. Up here the weather could change without a moment's warning.

'Stupid sod will surely stop for some grass.' Danny dropped the bins. 'You're shaking more than me Stony, go see Megan – she'll give you a coffee or something stronger.'

Danny thought about taking the van but knew he'd have to dump it as soon as he met a wall or a fence or a line of trees.

He'd now scanned the open spaces. But there was no sign of him. Salamanca was a creature of habit, so Danny retraced the hunting path they'd follow religiously most mornings in full training.

He began to sprint up-valley.

'You've spotted him?' Stony called after.

'No,' Danny replied, looking back. 'That's why I'm running.'

Danny jogged upslope to the highest point on the estate. To his left was dense woodland.

Unlikely he'd want to go back in there, Danny reckoned.

He'd searched for a good mile or so rounding the woods. There was the low brick wall they'd clear with ease during each morning round but no sign of the eight-year-old. He thought about ringing Megan, perhaps Salamanca had the sense or homing instinct to canter back to base, but he suspected the gelding would feel safest charging this now familiar route.

Danny pressed on, darting between the two established oaks and down slope to the brook.

'Salamanca!' he kept shouting, voice bouncing off the banking valley walls, speckled with grazing sheep and rocky outcrops on farmland either side of the estate.

He wasn't sure if his horse would hear the cries or even obey them. Perhaps it would all be a game and night would fall before Danny had rounded him up. It reminded him how glad he was when the RAF Tornados and Typhoons had stopped screaming by on their low-flying sorties around these parts. Otherwise a few of the more highly strung, flighty individuals at the yard would surely be sidelined with an injury by now.

'Salamanca!' he shouted again, voice strained. His alert eyes followed the snaking brook until stopping. 'There is a god.'

41

There was the runaway, standing on the bank of the stream, not a care in the world.

Descending the V in the valley, his stride was short and stuttering. He then crept slowly, silently, not to scare Salamanca, who peacefully lapped up the fast-flowing water, as if he'd burnt off the aggression that threw Stony off. The gelding looked up, as if to say, 'Oh, it's you, what's all the fuss about?'

Danny couldn't deny he felt ever-so-slightly choked. 'Worked up a thirst have we? Supposed to jump it, not stop for a bloody drink,' Danny whispered in those big ears. 'What am I gonna do with you?'

Salamanca flashed his tail and a fore leg scratched the earthy ground.

Danny felt disappointed that Salamanca had chosen the well-trodden path over something different.

Horses for courses, he guessed, time to experience new sights and smells. The Czech assignment would come as a massive culture shock to Salamanca, whose closed mind needed broadening.

As the Pardubice's water jumps were more like water features, he asked Salamanca to splash downstream for a good furlong,

They then galloped higher ground, instead of branching down to the road on the circuit back to the stables.

He'd never ventured up this way as he felt the steep slopes might put stress on a horse's conformation.

Salamanca trotted upslope willingly. It appeared the horse was ready for a new challenge and only briefly fought against Danny's urgings.

They were now skirting a smaller copse the other side of the ridge. The ground flattened here, allowing Salamanca to pick up some speed. For those precious moments Danny felt completely free, the warm summer air brushing over his cheeks, running wild in the wild.

Suddenly Danny was broken from this endorphin high. Salamanca's stride had shortened markedly, yet they hadn't changed gradient or surface. Danny instinctively pulled on the reins. Had Salamanca gone lame? If so, every stride they'd take with Danny on his back could add irreparable damage.

As soon as they'd slowed to a trot, Danny hopped off and landed running in tandem, until they'd stopped. 'What is it boy?'

He led Salamanca in circles, studying the fluid movement of those sturdy chestnut legs. Danny breathed out. Salamanca didn't look to be feeling anything, certainly not to the naked eye. He stopped. All four of Salamanca's feet were planted on the floor. He then ran a hand down each leg. Salamanca didn't flinch, not even a flicker. He was showing no distress whatsoever.

Danny knew he'd dodged a bullet and made a mental note that, if he was to gallop new ground, best to walk it on foot first.

What made Salamanca change his legs and shorten his stride so abruptly? If nothing had gone wrong with the horse, then some false ground needed cordoning off.

Danny retraced the hoof-prints made in the soft grass. He needed to drag Salamanca, who seemed disappointed that the gallop had been cut short. He suddenly stopped. He'd felt and heard a sudden change in the ground underfoot. The turf had turned from spongy to jarring, as if he'd moved from soft to firm ground in a stride, a bigger risk to injury on the racetrack than jumping.

Danny looked down. The grass was balding and darker here, threadbare in part. Possibly it was sheltered from the rain. Danny looked up but the reach of the overhanging canopies fell short. Even the briefest glimpse into those dark woods made him squirm.

He held the end of the reins tightly and knelt. With his free hand, he swept away loose earth, leaves and a layer of dust. Tufts of grass and sprouting weeds tickled his calloused palms. His eyes widened as if his confused brain requested to see more. His fingers were now tracing over a harder surface, as cold as stone. What the hell?

Danny stood to see the bigger picture. There was an expanse a shade darker than the slopes behind him; perhaps two, maybe three tennis courts in size. He stepped forward and pulled at the weeds and sparse grass. It was stone. He wrapped his knuckles on the rough surface, making a dull thud. Solid stone.

Just how big was this thing? He set about counting twenty-two paces away from the woods where the ground turned greener and his boots were cushioned by thicker grass. There were about forty paces of stone running adjacent to the woods. A stone plateau forty yards by twenty-two. Was it a bunker or air raid shelter left over from the war?

He dropped to his knees again and began to paw away soil from the edge of the stone. Like a digger, his hands scooped up the flaky earth matted with grass roots. By now he'd dug a few inches and broken a nail, questioning whether his multivitamin pills contained any calcium or zinc.

This was hopeless, he then thought. They'd certainly done a good job of filling it in after the war.

He tried several places along the edge of the stone, each time pulling Salamanca, who was now breathing normally. He wasn't sure what he hoped to find but he didn't want to leave until he'd figured out what the hell he'd almost literally stumbled upon. Perhaps he'd meet the top of a door frame, or an opening.

Further along the stone ridge, Danny felt something and pulled what looked like a medal from the ground. His thumb ran back and forth over the dull bronze. It was a four-pointed star topped by a royal crown and had two swords crossing the centre of a wreath. It felt heavy and important, perhaps dropped by a general visiting this place. Could be a war room, Danny reckoned, safely away from the heavy bombing in cities like Swansea, which was flattened in the blitz.

Whatever it was, Danny was hooked.

44

He suddenly looked ahead. From the heart of the nearby woods, came a shriek. He then swore he glimpsed something beyond the trunks, a ghostly face. It was a man, skeletal white, black holes for eyes. Danny froze. He couldn't move if he tried. He stood there, staring, as if trying to confirm whether this was for real. Perhaps it was a trick of the light, but there was no light between those trees. Or was it some hallucination. No, there it was, staring him down.

'Who are you?' Danny called. Unlike at the clearing, he was glad to be on the outside looking in.

With a blink, the face had gone. He blinked again. But this was a separate bunch of trees from the woodland where he'd found the clearing. Was the whole estate haunted?

He shivered and whispered, 'Shit.'

He wasn't sure why he spoke quietly. Perhaps scared there was a pinch of truth in those ghost stories of former trainer Roger Crane at the yard's late-night soirées. Danny then shook his head, as if to rid those fears of the unknown.

Was a fever doing all this to him?

He wasn't going to run until convinced this was just a trick of the mind. Otherwise that long, mournful face with narrow nose and thin lips would haunt him for nights to come.

Were the woods trying to warn him off?

The very notion made him smile. Perhaps he could sell haunted tours to tourists as a second income. Though he'd have to employ one of the stable-hands to take them round, as there was no way he was going back in there.

He turned his back on his fears and looked over the expanse of deepest green to the road at the bottom and the round-shouldered hills beyond. He took in the breathtaking view, a timely reminder why he put up with all the rainy mornings, the mucking out, the whining owners and hours stuck in traffic on race-days.

Beyond the hills, he made out the silhouette of a glider against the cloud, soaring silently on the thermal updrafts from the slopes of a neighbouring valley. He could live up this part of the estate.

CHAPTER 6

TWO MONTHS LATER

DANNY FOUND a quiet backstreet to park up, away from hoodies, drawn like moths to light from the only bus shelter.

He looked up. It was as if a dimmer-switch had been turned; the closed sky was now grey as St Paul's dome.

He followed the same path his father had once trod a thousand times, homing in on Rhymney Miners' Club. He passed stone row-houses, grey and solemn and clinging to the hillsides, just as he remembered. But it was the fine drizzle that made it. He once thought the roof slates were naturally that shiny.

The town that time forgot. Except now the Chapel lay derelict, waiting for some developer to save the day, and the 'For Sale' signs could be mistaken for the latest fashion item, as commonplace as the satellite dishes. Cursed by an obsessive compulsive character, he was just relieved he'd broken away – unlikely many of his schoolmates – before being offered a free sampler of crack to hook him in, as his brief spell housebreaking would have turned into a vocation.

Leaving for a placement at a Lambourn yard on his seventeenth birthday helped break the downward spiral. Moving away wasn't easy though and feeling homesick, he came back to the nest, tail between legs, getting on seventeen and a half. His dad was furious and fumed, 'Two years saving up for you to quit because it's too tough. Go on then, quit! End up like me, slaving all the hours god sends. I'm forty going on fifty, no prospects, is that what you really want?'

The following morning Danny was on the train back to Lambourn and that summer he'd finished runner-up in the apprentices' title. He knew even then, one way or another, horse racing would be his job for life.

Between the rooftops, Danny caught glimpses of the slag heaps he used to bike between on his granddad's reconditioned Yamaha. Even back then, he knew he had the balance and touch to become a jockey. It's what gave his dad the idea to turn Danny's stunted growth into a plus rather than just fodder for the bullies.

He stopped beneath a backlit sign: Rh m ey Min rs Cl b - even the 'h' was wonky. It was no more than a pebbledash box, only set apart by steel-plate doors and matching bars, less than a brick's width apart, guarding the windows.

Across the road, he saw two elderly men in brown and grey raincoats lost in banter. It was the people that made this place – a community where everybody knew everybody.

Once the school bell rang out, he'd often rush to press his face between the black railings of the colliery gates, waiting, willing to see the halo of light from his dad's orange helmet lamp as he emerged on those cold, long evenings.

His dad let Danny cling to his grimy overalls on his way here for a swift 'livener' to forget the gruelling shift. Danny was allowed a pint of orange squash and a packet of cheese and onion Hula Hoops. The smoke was something else, like a blanket of smog, and caught the back of his tiny throat.

As a kid, he simply didn't question the rights and wrongs. And the language was even thicker. He was told to ignore the effing and blinding. But he was at that impressionable age and a whiny 'fucking hell' once slipped out when he was dragged in by his mum from playing footy in the street, even though there was still a good half-hour of light left. He wasn't allowed to watch their only telly for a week. He didn't swear in that house again.

Dad used to rush past the shower cubicles and sinks on his way out from the pit, squinting eyes blinkered on the gates and little Danny. He was desperate to get away after each shift, Danny had later heard from his mother. Understandably he hated doing the work but knew it had to be done. This was the Eighties and he was only thankful he had a job. Up and down the country, pits were shutting their gates for the very last time.

Danny could still remember the dirt and grime on his dad's face and neck when they stepped in to 'The Club' as he used to call it.

'Thirsty work, lad,' he used to say, before explaining mum wouldn't understand, so best keep it their secret. That made Danny feel good, special. It was their secret.

He recalled one time when leaving this place his dad was streaming with a bad cold, would be called man-flu these days, but still gave the umbrella to Danny. It didn't matter as he could step between the raindrops, he said. Only being a nipper, Danny wasn't to see through those tall stories. Much like the time he'd convinced Danny that the ice cream van only played its tune when they'd run out of ice cream.

Winter was hard. His father would go down the pit before daybreak and emerge after sunset. Danny often wondered why a set of three prints showing some tropical islands hung in their tiny living room, probably to remind him what the sun looked like. All that graft and suffering just to keep a roof over their heads and food on the table.

Weird and a bit sad that Danny knew it was now just the silent relic of a pit head, one of many rusting tombstones left from mining in The Valleys, but the coal slag that had once badly scarred the landscape were now green with grass and shrubs; a past gone, but not forgotten.

Danny could understand why the service sector was now South Wales' bread winner, with many up here drawn to the big cities of Cardiff and Swansea to find their way.

He buzzed the intercom and had barely stepped back when the steel wall split in two.

'Fort Knox got nothing on this place,' he muttered.

He stepped into a modest hallway with a glass and wooden booth on his left, clearly for checking members' passes back in better times.

Danny's leather soles slapped the shiny tiles. He caught a glimpse of a notice board, pinned with sheets, mostly club league tables for snooker, darts and skittles, and a raffle poster.

He pushed a door marked *Club Lounge* but it wasn't half as posh as it sounded. Dark wood chairs, scarred and stained, were scattered around Formica tables and a cushioned horseshoe of tan-plastic seating faced the bar. It was just the same as the last time he'd dropped by, all those decades ago. Though there was no smell of smoke now, just some sickly sweet air freshener. Danny wasn't sure which was worse.

A white-haired couple were staring blankly at a TV hogging a dusty alcove in the corner, showing Jeremy Kyle on mute. A bank of sporting photos, mostly of rugby teams, alongside individual players wearing international caps, was covering the wallpaper.

Danny swerved a man perched on a barstool, his bloated red face all grizzled and bristly, and rotund belly propped by the battered mahogany bar, or was it the other way round. A wonder of the body's survival mechanisms to be still upright, just, probably after years of necking pints of Brain's Best and god knows what else. He seemed happy enough, comfortably numb, and smiled as Danny brushed by.

'The sights you see when you haven't got a gun,' Stony muttered, sat the other end of the bar. 'Glad you could make it.'

'It's been a while Stony, been so busy,' Danny said. 'Good to see you've made a full recovery.'

'Bruises are long gone, only wish I'd fallen as well at Catterick, might have squeezed another few years out of my career. Only glad you caught him in time.'

'Wasn't a scratch on him,' Danny said, unzipping his padded jacket. 'I would've called you myself, it's just, that wasn't the only thing I found up there.'

50

'Glad you didn't. Megan kept me updated, it's been long time since a young lady's called me,' Stony said. 'She's a keeper, that Megan, a proper find.'

'She sailed through her trial period, no complaints yet from me or the owners. Mine is it?' Danny asked.

'Now you mention it.' Stony supped on his near-full pint of real ale as if already playing catch-up and wiped away the white moustache.

'Another of those,' Danny said. 'And a lager for me, and make that one for yourself too.'

'Ta, lovely,' the forty-something stewardess replied while teasing her peroxide hair.

Danny glanced down at a name necklace hung from her long neck. 'Cheers, Brenda.'

He gulped down a third of his pint, relishing the cooling sensation. He sighed. The distant rumble of a skittle alley out back somewhere barely registered. 'This better be good. What *something*'s that important?'

'Not something,' Stony said. 'Someone I'd like you to meet.'

'No one dodgy,' Danny said, handing a crumpled tenner over the bar.

'A friend of that lad at the yard.'

'Rhys?'

'Well, saw them talking by your gates as I waited for the taxi to finally show, you were off looking for your horse still.' Danny's ears pricked up. 'Keen to get a tip, I reckoned. So I moved in, friendly chap he was. Soon as I mentioned you, he was keen to meet, seems you're a bit of a *name* these days.'

'Seems so,' Danny said. 'I blame Salamanca. Did *he* give a name?'

'Chowbutt.'

'Eh?' Danny said, now funnelling loose change and a fiver into his jeans pocket. 'Chinese fella?'

Stony now looked lost. 'Welsh-Italian, I think.' His gaze brushed over Danny's shoulder. 'You can ask him.'

51

Danny turned on his heel. He was rarely good at placing faces but did this time. Stood before him was the briefcase man. He laid his raincoat over the back of a barstool. When that realisation suddenly struck home, Danny struggled to keep his tiny facial muscles relaxed. The more he thought, *look normal*, the more they tightened. He was pretty convinced he was now scowling. He found himself knitting a damp beer mat between fingers too.

'Caio, butt,' greeted the man.

'All right, butt.'

'Franco's the name.'

'Danny.'

'I know.'

'What can I do you for?' Danny said, hoping for an innocent explanation of why he was lurking around the yard and, more worryingly, the stable jockey. And why the hell was Franco keen to meet up? Surely a successful punter wouldn't want to risk blowing his cover, or raising his profile. Like a loss adjuster, the pro punter's life is all about assessing risk, and Danny reckoned approaching a trainer would be one too far. How could Franco ensure Danny wouldn't go squealing to the authorities?

Perhaps he was getting greedy and, having yet to be blackballed by the bookies, arrogantly wanted to expand the business by fixing the Samuel House runners ridden by jockeys other than Rhys. Even if his stable jockey was on the make, doesn't mean the whole yard's at it. But he kept that thought exactly that, a thought.

'My friend, it's more what I can do for you.'

'Nature calls, again!' Stony said. As soon as he'd negotiated himself off the barstool and walked off to the gents out back, Danny was eyeballed by Franco, who whispered, 'I hear you are giving your stable jockey a hard time.'

Danny sensed a palpable shift in the atmosphere and felt like zipping his jacket back up.

'Who told you that?' Danny asked, mind turning over as he brushed off the heavy hand on his shoulder. He swelled his chest.

'Friendly word to the wise: back off, unless you want him to disappear.'

'Threaten me all you like,' Danny said, clinging to his composure. He hadn't seen this coming and, later that day, was sure to think of a million better things to come back with.

'I have more influence over Rhys' career than anyone, including you.'

'Whatever I say to Rhys is private,' Danny said. 'And he'll get another bollocking for grassing to you. And while we're at it, I don't want you sniffing round the yard. Okay?'

'Are you like this with all potential new owners?'

'New owner, you?'

'Rhys gave me a guided tour.'

'Telling you which ones are bouncing, I bet,' Danny snapped.

'I don't follow.'

'We're not a gambling yard,' Danny said. 'So if you're looking for a horse to buy, go to one that is.'

'Don't tangle with me,' Franco growled. 'It'll be easier if we're on the same side, join my inner circle.'

'Didn't you listen? We don't moonlight by betting on our horses.'

'Is that because you're a reformed gambler, three years clean?'

He'd only confided something that personal to Rhys and Stony. He now knew for definite who was feeding this leech the inside scoop.

'Count me out. And if I see you at Samuel House, I'll be on to the police and the BHA quicker than you can say, "thirty grand on the nose".'

Franco stepped forward to cast a shadow over Danny's face. 'You're bluffing.'

'Why should I?' Danny said. '*My* conscience is clear.'

He glanced over at the white-haired couple. They seemed hypnotised by the telly.

53

'Well, it looks like I'll need to follow you as closely as your horses,' Franco said and stepped back. He then glanced over Danny's shoulder. 'Yes, we'll have to do that some time.' As quick as a mime artist, his face changed from serious to happy.

Stony was back. 'Everything okay, lads?' he enquired, as if picking up on something.

'Just saying to Danny here I'm thinking of dipping into ownership,' Franco said.

'You couldn't find a better man than this one,' Stony said, hand on Danny's shoulder.

For once, Danny hadn't welcomed such a ringing endorsement. 'I was just telling Franco there are better things to spend his money on.'

Stony looked at Danny as if he'd spilt his pint. 'Then perhaps he could buy that painting of yours.'

'Tell me more,' Franco said. 'I'm interested.'

Stony said to Franco, 'It's a racing scene, like that one.' He pointed at the wall of photos.

But it was Danny who led the way over. His eyes scanned over the gallery until stopping at a black and white photo though it had become faded and milky with time, now more yellowy-brown. It wasn't the colouring that transfixed Danny but the setting. It was the same as the triptych. The horses were more spread out in this action shot but there was the clump of oaks in the background and the distant conical towers of Castle Coch. He skirted a table in the way to get up closer. Printed on the cardboard surround was: 1936 Cardiff Open Steeplechase won by The Whistler.

Danny could sense Franco looking over his shoulder. 'I hope the colours are more vibrant in yours,' he said.

'It's an oil painting, of course it is,' Danny snapped.

'Relax, Danny,' Franco said. 'We're among friends.'

Speak for yourself, Danny thought. 'It's not for sale.'

'I'll pay good money, if I like it.'

Danny didn't want to receive cash made from that bet. 'You won't.'

'But where there's a deal to be made,' Franco said, 'there's also money to be made.'

'You don't seem to be taking the hint, you're not welcome at my yard,' Danny said. 'That clear enough English?'

'Danny?!' Stony said. 'What the hell's up with you?'

'I've decided on keeping it.'

'Friend, why are you being like this?' Franco asked, gesticulating wildly with his hands, making his gold bracelets jangle.

'Friend?'

'Any friend of Stony is a friend of mine.'

Danny hadn't the time or space to back away as Franco grabbed his hand, lunged forward and planted a kiss on both cheeks.

Stony laughed, presumably at Danny's look of shock. 'Think he likes you.'

'Come, Stony, my friend. There's a large vanilla ice cream and amaretti biscuits with your name on.' Franco beamed. 'Trust I'll see you there.'

Stony nodded obediently, like a dog after a treat.

'And my new friend, Danny?'

'No, ta,' Danny said, 'watching my weight.'

Franco's sparkly brown eyes clocked Danny's pint. 'So I see.'

'Well, if it's a contest between beer and dessert.' Danny took another gulp. 'There's only one winner.'

Franco look turned sour as if to say 'wrong answer'. 'Arrivederci.'

'Right you are, butt.' Stony supped up the frothy end of his bitter. 'Thought you'd warm to him, friendly chap isn't he.'

'Bit too friendly,' Danny replied, wiping spit from his cheeks.

'Smart boy, too. It's a wonder he's not got a woman.'

'Probably got one for every night.'

'Mind now, jealous … Trust I'll see you in the bookies' sometime?'

'It's a date,' Danny replied.

Stony limped off, leaving Danny and the fat man either end of the bar.

Danny looked across. It was hard to tell if he was nodding off or he just had puffy eyes.

The man said, 'Yet to know Franco well enough, I see.'

'Why say that?'

'You're still talking to him.'

Danny slid up the bar. 'Tell me about the real Franco?'

'Cost you.'

Danny suspected he knew the man's favoured currency and waved a crisp fiver at Brenda, saying, 'Pint of Best, cheers.'

'And a whisky chaser,' the man added. 'Mike, it is.'

'Danny Rawlings.'

'Good god, no. Peter's kid? I remember you.'

Danny couldn't say the same.

'Helluva boy, he was. Still miss him, this place went a lot quieter when … well, when he left us. Many a night he could drink me under the table, and that's when I could knock em back.' Mike managed to look Danny up and down. 'He'd be proud of how you've turned out, kid.'

It was good to meet this link with his dad's past though he suspected Mike's memories would be fuzzier than for Danny from the drink and right now there were more pressing concerns. 'Well?'

'They say Franco's like a getaway car,' Mike said.

'Fast?'

'Reliable,' Mike replied, 'but rarely up to any good.' His smile soon dissolved.

Suspect there's some history between the pair, Danny thought, perhaps a grudge. Best treat any character assassination with a degree of caution.

'What's his business?'

56

'Officially, the ice cream parlour down the road,' Mike said.

'And unofficially?'

'Well, ice cream's seasonal, see, and summer normally happens on a Tuesday up here. Besides, most prefer chips in their cones,' Mike took another gulp and shifted the freshly poured pint into place. 'Let's just say, he's diversified to make ends meet, spread his muck.'

'And that muck is?'

'What's it to you?'

'Caught him lurking around the yard acting all … well, he wasn't there for the fresh air and views.'

'What's the time?' Mike asked.

Danny reckoned Mike's watch must've stopped. He glanced at his wrist and then felt it, as if not believing his eyes. Panicked thoughts rewound and then spun through that day, until he pictured himself looking at his watch entering this place.

'Think I've answered your question,' Mike said, eyes almost as pink as his round face.

'Thieving bastard!'

'Wouldn't say that to his face.'

'Say what I frigging well like,' Danny growled. 'That was a gift from the wife. Wish you'd bloody said something.'

'It's just a party trick of his,' Mike said.

'Remind me never to go to his parties.'

'Let it go,' Mike said, turning to his beer. 'Another of life's lessons.'

'Why?' Danny said. 'Part of the valley mafia is he?'

'Whatever it's worth, it's not worth it. Pays to keep on side with some folk.'

'And he's one,' Danny said.

'That's why I kept zipped, least until he was gone. Even the police turn a blind eye to Franco, the Don Corleone of the valleys, offers them gifts.'

'Like watches.'

'You're catching on.'

Danny skinned his knuckles on the bar. His hand now hurt as much as his pride. He couldn't fathom how he'd fallen for those classic diversionary tactics, caught off-guard by the kisses. That was the first thing he'd learnt from a veteran on a stretch inside. 'So he's a petty thief, pickpocket.'

'Not for me to say but-' Mike shifted his bulk. 'He most definitely *didn't* steal from my *left* coat pocket at the last Christmas do here.'

'But he dipped the right pocket.'

'Your words not mine.'

'Has he done time?'

'Doubt it, but would probably treat it as an occupational hazard if he had. Nothing scares him.'

'Thanks for the heads up,' Danny said, slapping his glass on a bar tray.

Mike said, 'Off to the bookies after these, got any tips?'

'Salamanca in the Summer Plate, next week,' Danny replied.

'Certainty, is it?'

'Trust me, no such thing pal,' Danny said. 'Which way is Franco's?'

'Turn right up the hill half a mile or so, and it's on your left, can't miss it.'

'Cheers, Mike. Will pop back soon, have a proper catch up then.'

Mike nodded, glass apparently stuck to his mouth.

As the heavy metal door clunked back into shape, he began to run up the hill, removing the crumpled fiver he'd been given as change. Franco had held back for Stony. Danny quickly caught the pair up.

'You left this Stony?' Danny said between breaths. He handed over the note.

'Did I?' Stony asked. The confused look seemed genuine.

'Yes, you did,' Danny said firmly, 'on the bar.' He knew his friend wouldn't pass up a freebie and it was worth it, just to have a viable excuse for chasing after them.

'Well, if you say so.'

'And sorry about the frosty reception back there, Franco,' Danny said and leant forward to embrace the man. Give him back some of his own medicine, Danny thought, as he deftly slipped his hand in Franco's deep raincoat pocket. No sign of a watch at the bottom, just a great tear in its seam. He carefully removed his hand so as not to touch Franco's midriff, like those buzz-wire games he'd play at the village fetes as a kid.

Franco had got enough set aside to put thirty grand on Turnabout the other month, yet couldn't afford a new coat. Surely his glaring vanity would've seen that tatty old thing in the bin years ago. Perhaps the coat held some sentimental value, or was it to fool bookies into thinking he was a mug punter though he chose to wear a leather jacket at Raymond Barton's.

Something wasn't right. Perhaps the lumpy bet wasn't Franco's money, as the briefcase was as stylish as this coat. Perhaps he was just a 'placer' putting bets on behalf of a big-hitting successful pro punter, who'd got more chance of getting laid in a convent than at the bookies. These thoughts only served to stir up his suspicions.

CHAPTER 7

DANNY POKED HIS HEAD around the lounge door. Sara was staring at the TV.

Jack was lying on his belly by the fireguard. He had inherited Danny's blue eyes and fair hair, which had later darkened with age. It was like looking at himself thirty years ago. Jack was even playing with the same Star Wars figures from Danny's own childhood.

'I'm off out, give Salamanca a spin.'

Sara looked over, face screwed up. 'You always do this.'

'What?' Danny cried.

'Keep it down,' she said and glanced at Jack. 'When there's something important, you go AWOL. Don't know how many times I've shouted "food's up" or "we're leaving now" and hey presto, you vanish.'

'It's a TV show.'

'But you're in it. Aren't you bothered?'

'Bothered they'll make me look like a complete mug. The painting's worthless, remember, can only hope I've been cut out.'

'Oh, go play with your bloody horses.'

The expert came on and was introducing the triptych, a cue for Danny to leave.

'Why do men grow moustaches?' she asked. 'Disgusting things.'

Danny sighed as he tugged on his boots in the kitchen. He opened the doors under the sink. Behind grimy dishcloths, sponges, shoe-polish and colourful plastic bottles, he saw the triptych wrapped in black bin liners. He thought about shoving it up the loft. Out of sight, out of mind.

Since taking over the freehold, he had yet to venture up there, preferring to hoard disused white goods and toys, like clapped-out fridges and microwaves with the rest of the crap in an outbuilding, until the day he'd have time to sort it for the rubbish tip and charity shop.

For now the sun was out, he thought, shame to waste it. Why he felt the need to justify going for a spin, Danny wasn't sure.

He cantered Salamanca upslope towards the awesome stone plateau. He felt strangely drawn to the place, like a druid to Stonehenge, as if it contained some mystical qualities. He slowed as they neared the darker expanse of level ground. He steered around it and once more urged Salamanca down the steep gradient, all the way to the road at the bottom. Mindful of the various steep banks on the Pardubice course, he wanted to teach Salamanca a valuable lesson, prepare for when they tackled the real thing at racing pace.

The fields of dusty plough would also be alien. Danny had therefore lined up a workout on one of the beaches west of Cardiff.

When they'd reached the broken hedgerow hiding the road at the bottom Danny ran a reassuring hand down the gelding's neck and said, 'Good boy,' as if to send a psychological trigger. At no point did he feel Salamanca lose balance or change his stride pattern on the descent and he wanted this positive experience to sink in at some level. He then completed the full circuit of the hunting course, back over the brook and the wall. That route was strictly out of bounds for others in the yard.

He felt the extra homework would make Salamanca man-up, something he needed to do given his temperamental past.

Danny's boots slapped the concrete as he led his charge, who'd barely turned a hair, back to the stables. He sponged and towelled down Salamanca and then let him cool off.

Ribbons of steam rose from his long back as he stood there patiently. Although Danny had a list of more pressing things to do, Salamanca wouldn't allow anyone else near him.

Like the retired mare Silver Belle down there in the field, most jumpers were out in the paddock getting fat over the refreshing summer recess until back in full training for the autumn campaign. Salamanca, however, looked a picture at fighting weight, chestnut coat gleaming in the July sun. His noble and lean head swept gracefully to a thick muscular neck and strong sloping shoulders. His large liquid eyes were bold and expressive, full of life. His silky tail and mane shone in the sun, black as an oil slick.

Led by Megan, he strutted around as if on springs, saying 'look at me.' There was a presence about him. He didn't need to tell the gelding he was the star turn in this yard. He hailed from a long line of game and talented jumpers, ready and willing to lead home a cavalry charge. He was bred to stretch those massive lungs to fill a colossal chest cavity more than twice a second in full flight. They fed a heart as big as his neck that serviced the rippling hind quarters driving him on.

Next week's Summer Plate at Market Rasen couldn't come soon enough.

He turned and there was Franco. 'I thought I made myself clear in the Miners' Club.'

'I suspect you will change your mind. I'm here for Rhys.'

Danny was surprised when he saw Sara come over. She'd normally stay away when visitors came.

'Well, he's not in today,' Danny replied, 'I'm surprised you didn't know that.'

'Shame.'

Danny turned to Sara. 'It's okay, love, just business.'

Franco smiled. 'This must be the enchanting Mrs Rawlings.'

'Well? Introduce me to your friend,' she said. It was the brightest she'd sounded all summer.

Better not go for the cheeks, Danny thought. 'This is Franco, ice-cream man.'

He planted a kiss on her hand. Oh, please! Danny thought, slimy twat.

'I own a chain of shops.' He glanced over at his gleaming Porsche 911. 'Trade is up.'

Sara smiled again. 'So I see.'

'What did you want, love?' Danny asked.

'That's no way to speak to a lady,' Franco said.

Sara's eyes lit up.

Danny didn't rise to it. He wanted Franco gone.

'I think we've said enough for one meeting.'

'Then you leave me no option,' Franco said.

As Franco brushed past Sara, his hand touched hers, Danny was sure of it.

'Ciao, bella,' Franco said softly.

Even he wouldn't have the audacity to steal her gold bracelet from there.

Danny felt flat. Sara hadn't moved aside. Was she flirting with him? Perhaps it was to get at Danny for being 'married to the job'. Maybe she was winding him up? If that was the goal, it had worked.

Sara went back to the house.

Danny wanted the last word and shouted over to Franco, 'She's not for touching.'

Franco froze with one leg in the car. Those teeth made a return as he said, 'I steal money, not wives.'

Danny hoped he hadn't sown a seed into the mind of that playboy.

He now felt empty inside and not because he'd skipped breakfast. He'd made an enemy but for what? He was no nearer to putting a block on whatever scam Franco and Rhys were up to.

Leave me no option, kept running over in Danny's mind. Franco didn't appear one for hollow threats.

His mouth felt dry and his head was banging again. The stress-hangover had been given a new lease of life.

It wasn't so much the threats, but the delivery that shook Danny up. Not once did Franco show even the slightest flicker of losing composure. No fury, or anger, or even slight annoyance bubbling behind that swarthy skin and brown eyes. It's as if this wasn't the first time he'd dealt with a threat to his way of life and probably wouldn't be the last.

Danny entered Samuel House via the heavy oak door at the front. It was the first thing that sold it for Sara, rather than a farm ripe for conversion further up the valley. It was an original feature of this 1870s cottage, so the agent reckoned, though they'd say anything to get it off their books. There wasn't much call for a smallholding with such hilly land and thirty stables up here. Training racehorses was about all Samuel House was fit for.

He recalled she'd pressed her face against the thick oak and said, 'Marry me.' Danny was more interested in the stable block.

Sara had barely noticed him enter the lounge. No change there, he thought.

Danny said, 'Show us your wrist.'

'Why?' she asked.

'Your bracelet.'

'Jesus, Danny.' Sara pulled on her sleeve. 'Okay?'

The bracelet was there, but where was the wedding ring?

'And before you ask,' she said, 'it was itchy. Washing up liquid was getting trapped and making my skin crack.'

'I wasn't going to,' Danny said.

'Good!' she cried. 'Now turn it up and watch.'

Danny saw she'd taken the effort to freeze the recording with him on the screen. 'Great.'

He cringed as he heard himself say, 'Wouldn't sell it for the world, no way. And it cost me nothing.'

'Why the hell did they have to show it?' He left to grab a beer.

That evening Sara was giving him the quiet treatment. He didn't even get a reason. She just turned the pages of her magazine loudly and avoided eye contact.

8.07 PM Danny put Jack to bed and made up a story about a horse enjoying a gallop across the valleys. It was more like sorting out in his mind the day's events.

10.23 PM. He retired to bed early. Sara said something though it filtered through the door as muffled noise. Probably telling him she was off to her parents again, or leaving a memo to get the weekly shop in the morning, he thought, as he turned on his side, hands clamped between thighs in the foetal position. He buried his face in the cool of the pillow.

Soon he was drifting in and out of light sleep for what seemed like hours but was probably just minutes.

Suddenly a noise rudely shook him from that comforting place. He bolted upright. His wide unblinking eyes shot to the door in the corner. Beyond, the hallway floorboards were moaning. Probably just the heavy breaths of an old house, he believed, or wanted to believe. It was blowing outside.

He then heard shuffling. The brass door handle began to rattle and then turn. Danny sat perfectly still, frozen.

He felt like he was back in the woods. Was this place haunted too?

Danny knew it best to stand from beneath the covers, at least give him options, but he just stared at that handle, waiting, hoping. It turned loudly again and this time the door was kicked open.

'Who's there?' boomed Danny with a manly baritone voice but he couldn't hide a vibrato. He had still to get over the last break-in.

Was this another dose of his own medicine spooned out since his wayward years as a kid? He understood karma, but hadn't he suffered enough.

Danny emptied his lungs. It was Jack in his Spiderman pyjamas, clutching his blankie. 'God, Jack, you scared me half to death, come here.'

He scuttled over and then burrowed like a mole under the covers. He was now sat on Sara's pillow. It was then the smell hit Danny. 'Oh. Jack,' he groaned and then swore under his breath. 'Not now.'

Jack's innocent eyes sparkled in the cold grey-blue from the moonlight threading a gap in the curtains. Danny was secretly overwhelmed with relief but didn't show it. He reckoned Jack would pick up on something was wrong. He smiled at how fear and paranoia had messed with the mind. Haunted? Ha!

'Show me how Spiderman beats the baddies?'

Jack turned and flicked his wrists. Danny made a swishy noise and added, 'That's it. He fires a web to catch them.' Jack joined his dad in laughter. 'Come on poopy galore, let's get you changed.'

'Me naughty,' Jack mumbled.

'Who told you that?'

'The man,' Jack said, tiny hands gripping his silky patchwork pacifier.

'Don't be silly, Jack. What man?'

Jack's thumb emerged from his mouth and he pointed a tiny finger to the corner of the room.

Danny squinted, not quite sure what he was looking at.

'Where is it?' a voice came from the darkness. Danny flinched and made an 'f' noise, as if there was no longer enough breath left to form a word. The voice was deep and rumbling, as if narrating a trailer for a blockbuster film, though there was venom behind these words. He sounded more like the devil. Confusion made Danny, for the briefest moment, think his time was up and the dark one had come to collect him for all the wrongs he had done.

There was no chance of escaping this if the intruder was intent on killing.

Danny shifted to shield Jack. That's all he could do. There was movement in the dark and Danny could make out an unidentifiable black area, as if the wall had been ripped apart.

Sitting down in the dark, it was hard for to determine the intruder's height or build. He'd know the police would ask, if he was still alive to call them.

'What?!'

'You know,' the voice replied slowly.

'But I don't. Is it money? We've got none.'

'The painting.'

Danny stopped himself from revealing its whereabouts under the sink. He didn't know what or who he was dealing with. If he cowed to this demand and handed over the three panels, what then? What next would he want? Danny would no longer hold the ace card. 'And if I don't?'

The black shape grew larger, 'Salamanca will be next.'

'Next?' Danny said. 'What have you done? Where's Sara?!'

'Where is it?'

Danny swore he saw a glint of metal. 'Go, I won't call the police.'

'Then tell me its secret!'

Jack was quietly whimpering now.

'What?' Danny asked. 'What secret?'

'You will regret this, Daniel.'

Why should he give it over? 'Or what?'

'I would sleep with your eyes open in future.'

When Danny heard a distant loud clatter, he immediately thought it was Sara. He glanced over at the window to see if the porch sensor had triggered but there wasn't a hint of light. When he looked back the black shape had gone.

Danny sat there. Had the intruder been scared off by the noise, or was he lurking somewhere in the dark?

After about a dozen heartbeats, or four seconds, he jumped up and fumbled with the curtains. He heard a low thud of the front door. Headlights then swept over the shale driveway but Danny couldn't see a number-plate. He blinked as if his stinging eyes were failing him. He couldn't make out a thing, unless they'd taped it over, or removed the plate lights.

He turned to see Jack with a beard of sheets bunched beneath his chin. Even in the cold light, Danny could see his son was shaking in silence.

'Wait here,' Danny said and made after the intruder. 'Daddy will be back with some sweeties.'

He flicked on the landing light. It was as if nothing had just happened. Perfectly still, almost serene.

He rushed down the stairs in his boxers and t-shirt, fuelled by anger rather than sense and reason. The hallway was dark and silent but it was the cold that first struck Danny. He tugged on the front door but it was locked from the outside. Yet from upstairs he had heard the dull thud of the door. He reckoned it must've been left open while the intruder crept around Samuel House. He went to pick up the coat stand which had presumably been blown or pushed over. Danny felt like thanking it, as the clatter had seemingly spooked the intruder.

He checked the ground floor windows and kitchen door, all shut and intact. The lounge light was on and made Danny squint. He felt a migraine coming on. Everything was a shock to the system at this hour. He saw cupboards were open and a few things were strewn about the place. He returned to the front door and peered out on to the driveway. The cold air spread goosebumps up his legs and he could now see his heavy breaths disappear into the night. No sign of the intruder though. Not even a sound, just the tribal drumbeat of his heart. It was a relief Sara's Renault had also gone, so she had been spared this ordeal and Jack was too young to remember it. Danny had noticed the solo visits to her parents were becoming as frequent as her mood swings.

Everything was as it should be. He held his head. Was he cracking up? Except he knew deep down this was only too real.

There was the painting, the ghostly image in the woods, and now this.

Before the heavy oak door shut, he tested the old cast-iron lock and latch. Although they were still working fine, Danny knew he would only feel happy once they'd been changed. About time, he thought, they were as old as the door. He noticed his hand tremble as he released the latch.

Danny now suspected the expert's valuation was wide of the mark. With Jack about, he didn't dare think what might have happened had the intruder been after something other than the painting.

It was hard not to make enemies in racing. With big money at stake tensions will flare. Danny had had more than his share of altercations both on and off the track. He recalled veteran jockey Ronny McBride smashing a golf club through the windscreen of Danny's first car, a 1.2 litre Fiesta. He wouldn't have minded so much but he was in the car at the time, trying to escape from Sandown's car park. All because Danny, an inexperienced apprentice at the time, had cut up the wily McBride as he went for a gap that wasn't there on the rails. Why McBride had a four-iron handy at the track that day, Danny still didn't know. It made him realise this intruder could be anyone of a growing list with motives.

Something like this also made him think why he had security cameras covering the twenty-eight boxes, yet there wasn't one to protect his own family. It was a wake-up call in every sense.

The words of the intruder again came back to him: 'I would sleep with your eyes open in future.' He couldn't do that but cameras were the next best thing.

Computer sensors on the monitors in the study could pick up on unusual movement in each stable and send a bleep to Danny's messenger, warn if a horse had got cast in its box or knocked a joint on the stable wall.

Moving a camera wouldn't prevent the intruder coming back but it would give Danny some time to barricade his family into one room.

He'd ring the security firm first thing and have the cameras in empty boxes twenty-nine and thirty repositioned in the hallway and looking over the driveway. It wasn't as if he was expecting a fresh injection of bloodstock any time soon. He felt ashamed he had provided more for the horses' safety than his family but that would change.

Danny finally decided to call the police. The two constables ran through some 'routine questions' and dusted for prints on the front and bedroom door handles.

By mid-morning, he'd also shown the security technician out. Satisfied by the picture quality of the refitted cameras, he returned to the kitchen for a Diet Coke and a very plain ham sandwich.

On the pine table, he'd set out the three panels side by side in the order with which they were originally intended. He sat and stared at them. He wanted to take a closer look at what had compelled the intruder to hunt him down just hours after the recording of the TV show went out to the nation. He then got to his feet, hoping a different angle would help him. He didn't want to give the painting an airing too often, so saved an image with his camera phone.

He'd hoped the TV plug would attract new owners to the yard not burglars. He secretly wished he'd left the queue before being picked him out.

In the left panel there were just two horses with jockeys standing up in their stirrups, as if to portray that they'd already given up the ghost and were easing down. The bulk of the field were in full flight on the middle panel. Their spindly legs outstretched with the jockeys' whirling whips held aloft. The right panel was spoiled by a patch of board where presumably the winner had once been.

The intruder was after its secret, not the painting itself. He took a step back, like the original artist would have in the 1920s. Perhaps only then would he get some perspective on the scene, rather than scouring the finer details, or the brushwork. He hoped the hidden meaning, if there was one, would jump out at him though he wasn't confident. All he saw was a tatty and crudely painted picture that wouldn't stop him at a car boot sale.

Afternoon came and the shudder of the kitchen door sticking in the summer heat made Danny flinch. Rhys briefly moon-walked on the boot scraper and then stepped inside. 'Did the police come?'

'What?' Danny asked.

'The break in.'

'How the hell did you know?' Danny asked. 'Let me guess: Twitter, or was it Facebook this time?'

'Kelly told me, he'd got in your bedroom. Must've freaked you out, would do me. He needs locking up.'

It's the last time he confided in his head-lass, Danny thought. He then recalled giving Rhys a skeleton key to Samuel House for emergencies or for opening up when Danny was otherwise detained. Was the prime suspect stood before him? Perhaps that's why it was spoken through a voice changer. He wouldn't? No. What would be the point in threatening his boss?

Danny hid those suspicions for now. It was pointless rubbing Rhys up the wrong way anymore. He just wanted to keep his jockey sweet while he worked out what the hell he was up to.

Right now he could seemingly do no right with his wife or stable jockey. With anarchy in the ranks, he knew the yard would continue a downward spiral.

Rhys asked again, 'Police been knocking yet?'

Danny answered, 'They came first thing. Usual questions: was the intruder armed? Was there anything taken? Was there a threat or use of violence? Any evidence of forced entry? It was a 'no' to everything. So they're not hopeful of catching him. For the first time I agree with them.'

'I've got to meet Kelly, will be late as it is,' Rhys said, and left.

Danny bagged up the triptych and went to the study to listen to some Florence and the Machine on his iPod while swotting up on Salamanca's looming comeback race.

CHAPTER 8

A ROUND TRIP of three hundred and thirty miles reminded Danny why Market Rasen wasn't a regular haunt.

He was there to ride in the Summer Plate which always took place on the third Saturday each July. At two miles and six furlongs, the feature race was over two laps of Lincolnshire's only racecourse, serving up a sufficient test of stamina and was an ideal prep race for Salamanca's Czech bid. Having never actually ridden there, Danny was relying on the course map pinned up in the weighing room.

The worst of the thunderstorm had blown over, leaving polite rain with a freshening breeze across the track.

Danny went to sign in his only runner at the kiosk window beneath a sign that read: Declaration and Medical Record Books.

He had planned to mark time with a soft drink in the owners' and trainers' bar opposite the Tote betting office but he didn't make it that far. Just minutes before they went to post for the Summer Hurdle – another prestigious race for the time of year – Danny stopped as if shot.

Not far from the weighing room, Rhys was shouting at his agent Lance Taylor, who was giving as good as he got.

At first Danny had thought they were just messing around, as it looked more like an outdoor am-dram production, arms flailing and voices up. Then moving closer, he saw that the emotions on their faces were as raw as they were real. If the fight was fake Rhys had a viable second career as an actor.

'What contract?!' Rhys said. Lance then pulled a folded document from his jacket. 'Not worth the paper it's written on.'

'That's it then?' Lance fumed. 'Five years twisting arms to get you rides and I'm getting the elbow! Good luck to the next mug that represents you. Fucking waster.'

They were now attracting the course reporters and racing journalists like flies to shit.

Rhys replied, 'And I'll be claiming prize-money owed me.'

'I'll see you in court, *mate*!' Lance shouted and then ripped up the document.

Bloody hell, Rhys, Danny thought. This looked like career suicide.

Top jockeys can afford to make their own way, courted by equally high profile trainers and cherry-picking those rides offered. Rhys was not a top jockey.

Danny wanted to get between them, like a boxing ref, before they found themselves in tomorrow's paper, but thankfully the worst was over. Lance had now pushed aside the quote-hungry press and was soon lost in the crowd. Danny also suppressed the urge to have it out with Rhys, for now. Instead he went to the Tote screens and waited patiently.

As they circled down at the two-and-a-quarter miles starting post for the Summer Hurdle, the racing channel flashed up the final betting show. Rhys' ride Bake Jake Cake trained by Bill Watchman had been the subject of a monster gamble, backed off the boards from 4/1 to 7/4 as if it was buying money.

'It's gone post time, shouldn't be long now,' blared from the TV speakers. 'Making a good line and they're off.'

After the Turnabout gamble, Danny eyed Rhys' every move in the saddle. He'd watched enough of Rhys down the years to mimic his action, riding with a short rein, extra low in the saddle and quick flicks with the whip. Rhys' technique was more stylish than most, resembling a Flat jockey, and a recent flurry of winners showed this. If Rhys was faking it or holding back in some way, Danny would know. Was he giving Franco inside info from Watchman's yard too?

73

He saw Rhys push Bake Jake Cake into an early advantage. Despite a few sketchy jumps, he was already turning the screw out in front. Rhys clearly meant business, no risk of a false early gallop and therefore potentially a false result. He clearly knew his horse was the best on this day and was keen to show it.

As with Turnabout, Rhys barely had to show up. It soon developed into an armchair ride with the horse surging clear from halfway to post a bloodless success, one that left the opposition standing and somewhat embarrassed. The handicapper would also be left red-faced by this mauling as he framed the weights each runner was set to carry with the aim for all of them to finish in a dead-heat crossing the finish line. However this contest could have been called off before the turn for home. The money was once again right and Danny suspected much of it was Franco's.

Danny looked on at a safe distance as he saw Franco approach Rhys, who was en route to the weighing room. Franco stood close by as Rhys shook a pen and then signed a racecard. Why the hell would Franco want an autograph?

They were now masked behind a handful of race-fans also looking to get things signed. Rhys was clearly mending any damage to his public image from the earlier spat with his agent and had now taken refuge in the clerk of the scales' office.

Danny hung fire but when Rhys failed to emerge from the weighing room, he decided to make a move. He quietly entered the men's jockeys' changing room. He noticed the valet had hung Salamanca's colours on a peg nearby. He'd soon be in them as the big race was next up but he couldn't let this stew any longer. His eyes were drawn to the far corner.

'–and she was just the cleaner!' Rhys bellowed, holding court over a gaggle of jockeys, as if nothing had just happened. With no other rides, Rhys' work was done. Off were his winning silks, now in shirt and tie, with shiny jacket slung casually over one shoulder.

Danny held back in the shadows but the jockey of the moment had already clocked him.

When the chorus of laughter had died, Rhys asked, 'Mickey, you good for a lift to Ludlow next week.'

A fresh-faced apprentice jockey, girlishly thin with a voice to match, replied, 'Sure, give us a call, mate.'

'Gotta love you and leave you all,' Rhys added. 'Boss is looking daggers.'

With the lynchpin gone, the group quietly dispersed.

'Why the face?' Rhys asked. 'Not jealous I'm successfully playing away.'

'Don't care how many outside rides you win on,' Danny said. 'But I am concerned by how and why.'

'You've lost me,' Rhys said.

'Don't take me for a fool,' Danny barked.

'Chill, boss. Freaking out will only give you ulcers.'

'I witness first hand a thirty-K bet on my Turnabout, who you steer home to win. Fair enough, but when that same punter is seen talking to you at the gates of Samuel House, and then asking for your bloody autograph on track, don't you see how that might look to the public?' Danny waited for an answer. 'Stop me *freaking out*. Say something.' He hadn't known Rhys this quiet. 'I'm guessing he's not an informant, as you're closest to the horses' mouths. So, who is he – your placer?'

Rhys pursed his thin lips, as if choosing his words. 'It'll never get out, so what does it matter to the public, none of their business.'

'So you admit you're–' Danny was suddenly aware of the valet looking over. He turned the volume down when adding, 'I'm not one of those pie-eyed jockeys that look up to you, laugh at your wisecracks.' He noticed Rhys' slight shoulders drop. 'Follow me, someplace quieter.'

Danny led Rhys to a shady path at the back of the weighing room. 'Now tell me what the hell happened out there.'

'I've had enough of my agent,' Rhys said. 'Big deal.'

'You're not bothered about it then.'

'Not as much as *you* it seems.'

'Haven't you learnt anything?!' Danny asked. 'I'm a tadpole in the training ranks. You won't survive without topping up on outside rides.'

Rhys looked away dismissively. He clearly didn't want to hear this truth as it hurt.

Danny added, 'Great, so that's it then.'

'I'll find rides myself, can't be that hard. I'm a "name" in the game and I'm on fire, they'll form an orderly queue.'

'Trainers also know your failings, your attitude. For Christ's sake, until you've been hanging around this Franco crook, you were on the cold list for months. Now you're magically on board more steering jobs than a driving instructor.'

The bell rang out for riders in the Summer Plate to mount.

'Oh, go fuck yourself,' Rhys said, and palmed Danny's chest away. He began to walk.

'Who's supported you down these years, kept the faith when you couldn't buy a winner – muggins here! I never expected a thank you, but didn't bank on a "go fuck yourself" either.' He grabbed Rhys by the shirt collar. Apparently Rhys now found the brickwork more interesting.

Danny smelt grilled steak carried on a breeze and then noticed they'd been spotted by a kitchen chef having a quick fag not far away. He eased his grip. Rhys began to leave silently. Danny followed.

Franco's words came flooding back, 'I have more influence over Rhys' career than anyone.'

Danny said, 'It's Franco, isn't it?'

Rhys stopped briefly, as if struck by a stun gun. Danny was testing the water. He had nothing concrete on the gambler but Rhys' reaction told him enough. At least Rhys now knew Danny was on his case.

Danny spun Rhys round and grabbed his thin arm tightly, enough to bruise. 'I'm not finished.'

Rhys reacted by raising his clenched fist. Instinct led Danny's arm to block it just an inch from his right eye. He now had a close-up of Rhys' Mazda car key, protruding between fingers. There was a stalemate for a few rapid heartbeats.

'But I am with you,' Rhys hissed. 'My retainer ends next month and all this makes going freelance tempting. Remember there's no longer an agent pushing me into a full-time gig at yours, just so he can take his ten per cent for writing up a single contract.'

'Get that away from me,' Danny said. When Rhys failed to pull the key away from his eyeball, Danny slowly lifted his hand and did it for him. 'Gouging my eye out won't help either of us.'

'It'd stop you spying on me.'

'I'm looking out for you, always have.'

'I'm old enough to look out for myself.'

'But not wise enough,' Danny said. 'You and Franco are fleecing punters, destroying racing.'

'Doubt there's many long faces in the betting ring, Bake Jake Cake was backed at all rates, even told the owners to have a few quid on, didn't go too bullish mind, just a nod and a wink,' Rhys said.

'This is a game to you,' Danny snapped. 'It's not a victimless crime, what about the connections and punters of those in behind?'

'If we're sharp enough to get away with it,' Rhys said, 'that's their loss.'

'So you admit fixing races.'

'Get off my case,' Rhys said. 'You go whistle-blowing to the BHA and Samuel House will be on the market before you can say snitch. Mud sticks in this game and an investigation will have your yard on the front pages for all the wrong reasons.'

Back to the wall, it looked like Rhys had resorted to playing his trump card but the words sounded awkward from his mouth. It was too well-prepared, like an over-rehearsed actor. Was Rhys being a mouthpiece for Franco?

'At least tell us how you're doing it.'

'So you can get in on the act?' Rhys said. 'No thanks. Now, if you've finished, don't you have a horse in the next?'

Danny knew he had minutes to spare and said, 'It can wait.'

Rhys looked at Danny as if he were a traffic warden slapping on a fine and then snarled, 'Jesus, don't you ever give up. Could have you arrested, or sectioned like Sara.'

Danny composed himself at the waspish remark; better to retaliate with his brain than a fist. 'You can rip into me all day long, but don't you *dare* attack my family!'

Rhys shook his head dismissively though Danny could see a shred to guilt in those almond eyes, as if they both knew he'd overstepped the mark.

It was more in Danny's interest to finish on speaking terms. He added, 'Perhaps I am being too harsh. Guess it's the pressure of riding Salamanca, looks like he's favourite, all eyes on me.'

'Dance like there's no one watching,' Rhys said and then left for the car park.

Danny went to get into costume himself. He buttoned up and smoothed out his brown and green silks. He then picked up his number one cloth and foam-cushioned persuader. He felt shaky. Whether it was the altercation or the fact it was show time, he didn't know. He didn't just want this prize-money, he needed it. The credit crunch had strangled his disposable income and no new owners were on the horizon.

Salamanca shouldered top weight in this handicap as he boasted the best form. Danny had often heard the old racing adage 'weight stops train' but they hadn't reckoned on a tank.

Danny rested his number cloth on the clerk of the scale's desk and stepped back on the electronic steel plate, cradling a saddle packed with lead.

The clerk looked up at the digital screen flashing red twelve stone, zero pounds and nodded. Danny knew if he weighed in over a pound light or two pounds over, unless there were exceptional circumstances like the loss of bodily fluids after a marathon race on a sweltering day, or significant kickback on sand or mud clinging to the silks, the clerk would lodge an objection. It rarely happened, with most objections called for jockeys finishing in minor placings and forgetting to weigh in at all. It was set in stone to ensure the integrity of the sport, so that all runners carried the correct weight. If Danny didn't, he would likely be thrown out.

'On your way,' the clerk said.

Danny left for the parade ring knowing his stable jockey was a cheat and found it hard to get in the zone. A huge crowd in their light and airy t-shirts, shorts, shades and summery skirts, gathered around the parade ring. Many held racecards and newspapers as they studied the runners slowly circling on an asphalt path. One by one they were led by their grooms onto the track.

Going down to the start, Salamanca stayed calm yet alert. Some white sweat had lathered his strong neck, beneath the saddle and between his hind legs but no more than to be expected on such a muggy day. He was now glad they'd pushed for that extra mile on those rare sunny days in the valleys.

Alongside a signpost marked 2m6f110yds, Danny had Salamanca turning circles, among thirteen others. He pushed everything else to the back of his mind. It was nearly race time and he had a job to do.

He knew this was no cakewalk. Giving weight to Class One rivals in this Listed handicap was a proper examination and Danny hoped, rather than expected, they'd pass with honours.

He pulled up his tinted goggles. He then stretched his arms and lungs one last time.

'Final turn, jockeys,' the starter shouted from his rostrum. 'Walk in.'

He urged Salamanca towards the elastic tape. This was it.

CHAPTER 9

SUNDAY JULY 21ST. The office curtains were drawn. When something nipped at the back of his throat, Danny feared the onset of a cold or, as he liked to call it, man-flu. He hoped his defences would fight it off before then.

His finger hovered over the play button. Face inches from the LCD screen, he sat perfectly still.

The early stages of the Summer Plate were about settling in and finding a decent rhythm, clean jumps with a metronomic regularity. Throughout the first lap and a bit, he recalled Salamanca had indeed produced a string of clever, clinical leaps which were now his trademark. At that stage, Danny could kiss him. However Danny knew he could only learn from the mistakes and held down fast forward until the depleted field of runners headed out on their second and final circuit. Soon he was sucked into the action, as if a hand had yanked him through the TV screen. It all came flooding back.

The racecourse commentator took it up. 'It's Robin Redbreast with a clear lead as they go out into the country once again.'

Momentum pulled the leaders wide off the turn on this oval track. There he remembered sensing his chance and made a sharp yank right on the reins in a high-tariff manoeuvre to bag the inside rail. He soon found a dream passage, darting into a length lead as the rest forfeited ground. But he'd cut up French jockey Jean Ricou, who'd made the trip over especially for this big prize. Danny didn't care; it was unlikely they would clash swords again.

Danny smiled as he watched Salamanca soar over the next three fences. He felt a spike of adrenalin and was rocking gently in synch with every stride. When his memory bank emptied, he stopped mirroring his ride on screen. Suddenly aware of his cluttered surroundings, he pressed pause. He then swallowed and blinked his eyes into focus. With face even closer to the action, he forced himself to punch 'play' again. Win or lose, he hated taking apart previous rides. The past is the past, his mum always said. *Here goes nothing.*

By the time he'd jumped the second last fence, Danny held a tight rein and an unassailable twelve-length lead. He watched the approach to the final fence in slow-mo. Three … two … one. He'd produced his chaser perfectly at the five-foot six inches of birch, so what the hell went wrong he asked himself?

Inside the rails a course photographer came into shot, steadying a massive zoom lens. If Danny saw it, then perhaps Salamanca had too. He found it inconceivable that just a few frames on of this recording they would part company. Inexplicably the horse failed to raise a leg and left a Salamanca shape in the forgiving birch. Danny reeled in The Tank. He relived the moment and recalled thinking they'd enough strength and energy to find a leg the other side. He was wrong.

He felt his heart drop a little as he saw himself ejected from his crumpling mount. It was now about survival and damage limitation.

Reluctantly flicking the horror film on frame by frame, he watched himself curl into a ball mid-flight and bounce off the ground. It's as if he was witnessing someone else, an out of body experience, yet seeing the impact made his right arm now twitch with pain.

He grimaced as he imagined what might have been. He'd stolen defeat from the jaws of victory.

As the camera homed in on the newly promoted leaders, Danny was soon lost from shot, lying prostrate in the grass. It all came back to him, face buried in a carpet of thick grass, blades tickling his nose and chin. He remembered thinking at least he wasn't paralysed all over.

Everything hung for what felt like minutes but must've been seconds. If it wasn't for blades of grass swaying this way and that, Danny swore time had stopped. That's when he saw the brown flash of Salamanca slide to a stop nearby. He had heard a loud pop and, against instinct, hoped it came from him and not the horse. He could easily get a replacement rider but there was no replacing Salamanca. Then, as though shellshock had lifted, an almighty pain pulsed all over his right shoulder. It was almost too painful to be a break. Ironically, it was bouncing off the firm ground that probably helped him escape with skeleton intact. He then remembered the commentator from a tower somewhere in the stands tapering off his call with only the stragglers left to complete the course.

Before the medics had chance to put on a foam neck-brace, Danny moved his head enough to see Salamanca had gone. The fact there were no green screens being hastily erected had more impact than any morphine injection. Looking back, he was thankful Salamanca had taken an offshoot to the stabling area, rather than bolt out on another lap.

In his office, adjusting the sling, he sucked in air through gritted teeth.

Staring at the screen, he recalled the silhouette of a racecourse doctor looming over him, blocking out the white light. He reckoned it was merely a sprain. Precautionary x-rays taken that evening at a local General Hospital proved the doctor right. It was a relief to see neither jockey nor horse were to blame.

He didn't need to read the internet racing forums for a few days. He could already envisage the predictable tirade of abuse aimed at the untimely fall of the warm favourite with the likes of 'get a bloody pro jockey on Salamanca next time,' or 'just done my bollocks on this clueless part-timer,' or 'he's got the touch of a trampoline that one.' Kicking a man when he's down was all part of the game, he thought.

Danny stopped the recording and scooped up his bleeping mobile. It was a text from Rhys. *Fall not your fault. Salamanca trended for a bit on twitter. Every cloud!*

Was he being genuine or taking the proverbial? That was the problem with texts and emails. Danny suspected the latter.

Danny's fingertips touched his stinging neck, fingertips now glistening. Just a weeping graze, he thought, relieved it wasn't anything more permanent.

It was the growing pile of windowed envelopes on his desk that really hurt him. Some were open to reveal final payment reminders for unsettled bills, while others he couldn't face. He'd rather stick his head in the sand as there was no way he could find the money, not at short notice. And there was that red letter from the horse feed company for sixteen hundred pounds. His business overdraft was nudging nine thousand of a ten-grand limit last time he dared look.

Yesterday he'd had to ring Marcus Jones, who had three in his colours at the yard, to remind him again that last month's cheques had bounced. He was also going to threaten to sell the horses to cover costs but it came as no surprise he'd got no answer, even to the messages he'd left.

He glanced at the calendar on the desk. The cash flow drying up couldn't have come at a worse time as there was an important breeze-up sale at Chepstow. It focused his mind and efforts on getting well.

As he rested up and recuperated for the next few days, he delegated duties to Megan and Kelly, with Rhys and a few local apprentice jockeys working the lots in the morning. Snacks were most definitely out as he recovered to get back on Salamanca, whose confidence needed restoring if they were to be treated seriously in the Czech Republic.

CHAPTER 10

TUESDAY 30TH JULY.

Do this well, Danny hoped, and Prague here we come.

The smell of seaweed and ozone cleared Danny's nostrils as he reversed Salamanca from the horse box.

He tacked up and led Salamanca down the stone slipway. He threaded his charge between rock pools on the beach. He swung his arm like a windmill. The painkillers had kicked in.

The rippling wet sand was made silvery by the closed sky. Danny jumped on board and blew a calming breath.

As they effortlessly shifted up the gears, he afforded a glance down at Salamanca's powerful galloping physique reflecting back up at him. The squiggles in the sand made the moving image flicker like an old film. He could still make out that trademark raking stride glide over the forgiving surface, as graceful as a speed skater yet with the awesome power of a rugby prop forward. In Danny's eyes it was a perfect, majestic action though he couldn't say the same for his own. He studied the reflection in the sand and then crouched lower, ticking his elbows in to reduce drag and energy. His gloved hands gripped further up the reins.

Adrenaline now pumped his veins and tiny hairs on the back of his neck and arms stand to attention.

The hooves slapped the sand in turn, immense rump powering him on.

Danny glanced back at the sloppy sand and saw the wet prints slowly dissolve like a plane's vapour trail. Any doubts about the stretches of plough at Pardubice had also dissolved.

He looked up from the sand and saw a growing number on the pier ahead. They had stopped and appeared transfixed as the top-flight chaser strut his stuff along the water's edge.

He was now nearing a series of four wooden groynes rising up from the swelling sea. Dark and bloated with rot and slime, they were three beams high and just inches wide, between joists jutting like crooked teeth. No problem for Salamanca, whose range extended up to thirty feet.

Danny was tempted to give the onlookers a proper show but didn't want to risk Salamanca for the sake of impressing complete strangers. Knowing what his horse could do should have been enough. But he couldn't resist playing to the gallery like a rock star. He looked up again, closer this time. One of them wasn't a stranger. He recognised the black leather jacket of the man stood second from the left. It wasn't his clothes that stirred Danny's suspicions but the brown briefcase between his legs, resting on the wooden planks of the pier. It had to be Franco in his bookie's attire though Danny didn't want it to be true. Was Franco lining up his next big bet?

Perhaps he was going to place the contents of the briefcase on an ante-post wager with a bookie that had priced up a betting market for the Pardubicka.

How could he possibly know about this morning workout? It wasn't flagged up in the trade or local press. Had he been followed here? It's not as if he could confront Franco. There were no laws against stalking unless there was evidence of impending violence. Anyway, he couldn't even prove this guy was following him. It was a popular beach in the mornings. Many came here to fill their lungs with bracing sea air to put them right for the day.

As he turned Salamanca on the wet sand, his thoughts ran through who he'd told about the gallop. Rhys. That's all. No one else in the yard was there to tell. It only took one mole to shake the foundations of Samuel House. He needed words with his stable jockey before more sensitive info leaked from the yard. The fact Rhys was feeding a high roller like Franco could be toxic in the hands of a hack from one of the trade papers.

Danny was looming in on the first of the four groynes. He'd proved Salamanca's ability to gallop sand but how would he jump out of it. There was little or no time to back out, even if he wanted. Stuttering now would be like being in two minds crossing a busy road. He knew sending out mixed messages to a horse hurtling towards a barrier would end in one result.

Three-two-one. Salamanca's coiled hindquarters pushed off the sand and knees bent and forelegs tucked up, they sailed over. The bracing salty air brushed his face. He felt at one with nature. If he didn't feel alive at that moment, he never would.

When he cleared the next groyne, Danny looked up. He could hear the onlookers cheering, except Franco. There must've been a dozen or so now. It urged him on to complete the four jumps. Each jump was more efficient and faster than the last. It was as if Salamanca's confidence grew with every leap, now pushing off and landing on the slop with the surefootedness of a mountain cat.

Perfect, Danny thought, as he pulled on the reins. The onlookers began to disperse, leaving just Franco.

Danny's was on tiptoes in the stirrup irons as he stood tall in the saddle. He held his gaze on Franco, let the stalker be in no doubt his card was marked. He then turned quietly and gave Salamanca a dip in the sea. He felt wading through salty water would help the chaser's legs. They were thicker than most but the burden of supporting a half-ton body four miles and dozens of jumps took its toll. Legs were the most common source of problems and no wonder many of the top chasers like Best Mate were wrapped in cotton wool, seen at the track just a few times each season. Workouts on Southport Beach never did triple Grand National hero Red Rum any harm in the lead up to the Aintree spectacle in the Seventies. He felt like hopping off and getting his own feet wet to soothe his battle wounds in the frothy water breaking over the shoreline.

Salamanca's big ears swivelled like satellite dishes as he splashed through the crashing waves. Who needs an all-weather gallop and swimming pool when there's this on his doorstep?

Danny led Salamanca up the stone ramp cut into the harbour wall and towelled him down by the van. He looked deep into Salamanca's eyes. He picked up the sense this positive experience would banish the memory of Market Rasen. His hand ran down Salamanca's face, whose black lips and bristly chin tickled as he snaffled at Danny's palm, made saltier by the sea spray. As his fleece felt heavier and darker now, he regretted not choosing waterproofs.

They then made a swift exit, just in case the coastguards wanted a not-so-friendly word, or Franco came over for an even closer examination. He wanted to arrive at the Chepstow breeze-ups that afternoon in plenty of time before the first lot went under the hammer. He had circled three on the pre-sale catalogue list as potential worthy additions to the Samuel House string but finding owners to part with their hard-earned would prove trickier.

CHAPTER 11

DANNY ARRIVED at Chepstow in plenty of time.

He had planned on keeping a low profile towards the rear of the salesroom. Even back there, he soon found himself cornered by a suited man. He could place him at a few of these events but they had yet to speak, until now. He must've been edging fifty, the decades of pressured wheeling and dealing in bloodstock showed up on his fleshy face. Danny didn't know whether he was a consignor, or bloodstock agent, or seller and wasn't particularly keen to find out.

Before Danny could press his brochure to his chest, the man had pointed his biro at the first of Danny's circles and sighed.

Danny gave him a look but the man didn't take the hint. Seeing as he couldn't get away, he humoured the man, 'Slow is he?'

'Slow?' the man said. 'Couldn't get out of his own way that one.'

'That's no bad thing, I'm after a jumper, not a speedball,' Danny said.

'But he's got more flaws than a skyscraper,' the man said.

Danny fought off a grin. 'And lot eleven?'

'Saw him walking in the stables. No word of a lie, he plaits in front, almost crosses his legs. And I've seen him run, let's just say, he's got good herd instincts.'

'You mean he likes to follow rather than lead. Sorry, I'm terrible with names,' Danny said and offered a hand. 'It's?'

'Geoff Old.'

'You wouldn't be telling me all these nuggets as you're trying to flog the only other one I've marked in the catalogue,'

Danny enquired, pointing at lot fourteen, further down the glossy page, beside *Seller: G. Old.*

'What do you take me for?' Geoff said and then took a step back. He looked Danny over, as if it was he that was pulling a fast one.

'Not a fool,' Danny said. 'Clearly.'

'I see as I find.'

'Well I don't, particularly in these places,' Danny said. 'More smoke and mirrors than an Eighties disco. Trust no one … no offence.'

'Any chance you'd shift Salamanca now that he's past it?' Geoff asked.

'Past it?!' Danny snapped. He could say what he liked about me, Danny thought, but not Salamanca. 'He's eight!'

Danny theatrically put a line through lot fourteen, make sure Geoff knew about it.

The sale got underway. As he'd feared, it took just four telephone bids to pass the twenty grand ceiling set by one of Danny's owners on a tight budget. Having frequently burnt his fingers, Danny didn't join in the bidding war.

As the red electronic board had flickered to fifty-five thousand, a waiter blocked Danny's view. He adjusted his black bow-tie awkwardly and pulled his green waistcoat straight. 'Daniel Rawlings?'

Danny studied the young man and thought it best to neither confirm nor deny. 'What?'

'Sorry to intrude, sir, but there's a man asking for you in the bar.'

'Who?'

'I didn't catch his name, sir.'

Danny shook his head. 'What did he want?'

'You,' the waiter said. 'He gave me this.' He handed over what appeared to be a business card. 'Said to hand it over, if you needed convincing.'

Danny read the words penned on the back. It was either 'need answers?' or 'need answers!'

The waiter added, 'Please sir, it'll be worth it.'

'For you or for me. What'll he pay?'

'Twenty, if you go.'

Danny showed the waiter the card. 'Tell me is that a question or an exclamation mark there?'

'Does it make a difference?' the waiter asked dismissively.

'To you, I'm guessing it's twenty quid,' Danny said.

The waiter looked and then replied, 'A question mark.'

That chimed with Danny's suspicions. He would now go.

Probably smelling another juicy tip, the waiter became distracted by a fat bidder waving an empty champagne flute and left without apology.

The bar was buzzing as Danny entered without fanfare. There were plenty of 'faces' milling about. It would have been hard to find someone in this place, even if Danny knew who to look for.

He found a quiet spot at the bar and waited to be sought out.

'Can I get you one?' a man's voice came from his right. Danny faced that way and was met by a man sitting bolt upright on one of the barstools. His slim frame fitted a tailored suit that had never seen a peg in its life. He nursed a glass tumbler of yellow liquid, glistening under the halogen spots and chrome of the bar. He appeared to be the wrong side of forty though that was possibly the drink, or the harsh downlighting. His emerald eyes looked Danny up and down.

'Do I know you?' Danny asked. *Trust no one.*

'Not yet.'

'Haven't got time for this,' Danny said, keen to get going before rush hour and road works made the M4 a car park.

'Barman!' the man beckoned.

Danny was tempted by a free drink and some answers. 'Go on, swift one, about time Rhys took the wheel.'

The man asked, 'Rhys Morgan?'

'You're a racing man then.'

90

'Dabble, now and again.'

'Are you a buyer, seller or watcher?'

'Would like to say I'm a rich buyer, but afraid I'm not here for the horses.'

'What then?'

'I'm here to see you.'

Danny showed the calling card. 'You've got the answers then.'

'Depends on the questions.' The man eyed Danny's reflection in the mirror behind a line of spirit bottles.

'Let's start with your name?'

'Ralph,' he said and turned to face Danny. 'I'm guessing they'll get tougher.'

'Why are you here?'

'I read of this inaugural sale in the *Racing Post* and bet you'd be here. Looks like I won.'

'Now you're worrying me,' Danny said. Wasn't one stalker enough? 'Why do they want the triptych?'

Ralph arched his eyebrows.

'Had a visitor during the night,' Danny added. 'Up at Samuel House.'

'Oh yes, send my regards to the Samuel Estate?'

Danny's mind ticked over. 'Who are you really?'

'Ralph,' he repeated. 'Ralph Samuel.'

Ralph Samuel.

'You lied about your name,' Danny said.

'I never lied, just economical with the truth. I've long since dropped that family name.'

'Ashamed of it?'

'It was once one of the most respected names, not only in their parish but the whole of South Wales.'

'But not anymore?' Danny enquired.

Ralph's silence spoke volumes.

'What's this really about?'

'I'm after something of yours, before it falls into the wrong hands.'

'It's Rawlings on the deeds with Land Registry.'

'Relax, Danny, nothing so grand.'

Danny added, 'And my name's above the door.'

'What door?' Ralph asked, as if Danny was the one making no sense.

'Of Samuel House.'

Ralph laughed and then waved the tumbler at the barman. 'Another.' He then turned on his stool to face Danny. 'Samuel House doesn't exist.'

'I think he's had enough,' Danny said to the barman.

'It's only his third, sir,' the barman assured.

'That tiny cottage you call Samuel House,' Ralph said. 'Well, here's the scoop, it isn't. It was the groundsman's keep and your stables housed Philip's hunters and pointers.'

'I've had enough of this,' Danny said and stood. He feared this a descendent who'd hit hard times and was after reclaiming his land by some ancient or obscure law?

'Do you really think that three-bed cottage was the beating heart of the whole estate?'

Danny wondered why he had hung fire to listen to this crap. Five minutes of his life he would never get back. Then a thought made him drop onto another stool. 'It wasn't a war room.'

Ralph made a face and said, 'And you accuse me of being drunk.'

'I think Salamanca stumbled upon the base of Samuel House.' Danny wet his lips with the whisky. 'It looks down to the main road.'

'Except the road wasn't there,' Ralph said. 'Merely a track back then.'

'Always wondered why they'd built my house lower down when there were views like that just a few furlongs away.'

'The *real* Samuel House was never used as a war room or shelter, though, as with many stately homes, it was a makeshift hospital for American serviceman in the Second World War. Not long after, it was razed to the ground.'

'During the Blitz?'

'The Blitz was in the cities. Rather it went the way of other country manors, upkeep costs became too great. But it was out of the Samuels' hands by then. The colossal gambling debts racked up by Philip saw to that. Have to pop down one time, still have distant relations there.'

'And you came all this way to tell me this.'

'I'm thinking of owning a horse one day if ever get the money together. It's not cheap.'

'Tell me about it,' Danny sighed.

'Always had this dream of snapping up some top chaser and riding a big race winner, lap up the adulation, prove them all wrong.'

'You were a jockey?' Danny asked, now trying to place his face.

'My grandfather Philip was.'

'The gambler?'

Ralph nodded. 'Convinced the apple never falls far from the tree, I tried my hand but it seems this apple was rotten.'

'Did you actually get to ride?'

'In the loosest sense,' Ralph said. 'Horseman would be truer, failed at that too.' He smacked the tumbler down so hard the barman filling optics looked over. 'What about your stable star Salamanca?'

'He's not for sale if that's what you're getting at.'

Ralph smiled. 'Couldn't afford him even if I was.'

'Shouldn't say this,' Danny said, 'but wouldn't buy to race in the UK, it's just too hotly contested for the prize-money offered, compared to parts of Europe and the States and it looks to be only going one way from here. Often have to finish second in a race just to cover travelling costs these days.'

'Aren't you shooting yourself in the foot saying that?'

'You're not a buyer,' Danny said. 'The shrewdest are farming the big prizes overseas. That's why I'm off to the Czech Republic, got Salamanca entered up for the Velka Pardubicka, winner of that takes home one hundred and seventy grand. Worth the trip if you've got a classy stayer that jumps.'

'I'll keep my eye out,' Ralph said. 'Velka Pardubicka?'

'On the second Sunday every October.'

'A man can dream.'

'So I'm guessing you weren't born with a silver spoon in your mouth.'

'Philip probably lost those as well,' Ralph said.

'At least you can joke about it,' Danny said.

'Do you see me laughing? At no point has my life been easy, let alone privileged. And I'm not talking money.'

'Don't reckon I'm the one you should be talking to about that,' Danny said and then returned to his whisky.

He felt his mobile vibrate. He quickly checked the text. It was Megan asking, 'Where the delivery of feed had been dropped?'

He feared they'd frozen his account until the sixteen hundred pounds was paid. He told her to use reserves in the feed room, kept in case they'd become snowed in.

'Sorry about that.' When returned the phone in his jacket pocket, his fingertip caught a sharp point of the medal. 'More answers needed.' He removed it, along with the stopwatch. 'Did Philip fight in the wars?'

Ralph nearly spat out the whisky in his mouth. 'Nearest he came to going through the wars was being dealt a shocking hand at those poker nights. He'd entertain other landed gentry in the smoking room of Samuel House. The gambling had long-since spiralled out of control when one drunken night he blew his worldly goods on the turn of a card, beaten by a pair of Jacks.'

Danny swallowed loudly. He thought *he'd* caught the betting bug bad. 'I found this near the foundations of *the* Samuel House.' He handed over the medal.

Ralph studied it. 'Must have been dropped that night.'

94

'What night?'

'When The Whistler blew no more.'

'Eh?' Was this spy talk? He then recalled the photo on the wall at Rhymney Miners' Club.

'His unbeaten wonder-mare, well she was unbeaten until the big match up.'

'She won the Cardiff Open Steeplechase in thirty-six,' Danny said confidently.

'Something of an anorak are we?'

Danny shrugged.

'What about the H.M. on the back of the watch?'

As soon as Ralph saw the neat engraving, he waved the timepiece at Danny. 'Where did you find this?'

'Up in the woods.'

'On the estate?'

Danny was suddenly aware of every word he spoke. 'Yes.'

'That makes me believe it was Herbie's.'

'Another Samuel.'

'It's H.M.,' Ralph replied curtly, as if to say keep up with the gallop. 'Herbie Morgan, the head groundsman.'

Danny recalled the same initials were on the back of the triptych but he held that back for now. 'Philip clearly had enough left to pay his staff well.'

'It must've been a gift.'

'They were close then?'

'They must have been,' Ralph said. 'Understand, this was well before my time, and I'm only going by hearsay. He worked under Philip for the best part of twenty years.'

'Did he lose a triptych in the bet?' Danny asked.

'What?'

'A three-panel painting.'

'I know what it is, but why do you ask?'

'I found it,' Danny said. 'Behind a vanity mirror.'

'You will be popular,' Ralph said.

'Who with?' Danny asked; the recent night-time invasion still painfully fresh. 'Who's after it?'

'Take your pick,' Ralph said. 'Seven million tune into that show.'

'But it's worthless, the expert said so.'

'The physical painting might be.'

'But there's a secret,' Danny asked.

'A secret that's worth more than you could ever imagine.'

'Shame I got rid then,' Danny bluffed.

Ralph stared intensely into Danny's blue eyes, as if he was the one searching out the truth. 'You did well. That bloody painting will ruin you, like it had the Samuels.' Was he also bluffing? 'My father used to tell me of its legend. Growing up in Samuel House, he used to recall it hung in the dining room. Ever since Philip was gifted the triptych by a rival racehorse owner, the Samuels' fate was sealed.'

Perhaps that had something to do with the secret behind it, Danny thought. 'Why would he think a painting could wreck his life?'

'He believed it was cursed,' Ralph said.

'Because it came from a rival.'

'Rivalries didn't come much bigger, just flick through the record books. They exchanged many titanic duels with their horses but with the help of The Whistler, Philip held the upper hand. That was until the painting was carried into Samuel House.'

'Who was the rival owner?'

'Michael Johns.'

Danny suddenly wanted to know more about Ralph, if that really was his name. He had some information to chew on but had it come from a trusted source?

'I now know more about Philip than you.'

'What else is there to tell?'

'Anything,' Danny said.

'I was orphaned at fourteen.'

'I'm sorry,' Danny said.

'I'm not,' Ralph replied and groaned.

Danny felt it best to change tack. 'Where did Philip and Michael race their horses, Chepstow?'

Ralph smiled. 'Wouldn't be seen dead here, apparently used to call it the devil's arse.'

'Bit harsh,' Danny said. 'Always enjoyed it.'

'Back then it was the new boy, opening in 1926, and would've been an unwelcome competitor. Don't forget, Philip had, shall we say, vested interests elsewhere.' Danny sent a quizzical look. 'Ely Racecourse, once Wales' premier track. Indeed, among the best in Britain so I'm told. Philip – I've long since stopped calling him grandpa – always said he'd bet the family silver Ely would still be thriving long after Chepstow closed its gates for the last time. Just about sums up his betting prowess. Thieving shit. How did my father put it? He was "a workshy waster, a dandy with no redeeming features", yes, that was it.' Ralph's eyes grew cold as he talked of his ancestors. 'It was all about outdoing the other in shows of wealth. He even had a gold tooth, just to get one over the Johns. A gold fucking tooth, while the rest of the family struggled by. Complete waster.'

'Maybe your father was wrong.'

'He said I'd never amount to much, was right about that, so must be a good judge of character. Funny how things worked out in the end, given he'd blown the family fortune, my inheritance, to a gambling habit that turned into an obsession. I would say an illness but by all accounts Philip would've done it out of spite anyway.'

'Lost everything?'

'Including Philip, vanished one night and never came back. Lord Lucan has nothing on him.'

'Ashamed to admit,' Danny said, 'didn't know Cardiff had a racing history. The media doesn't help. Welsh sports pages are mostly rugby and football, particularly since the Swans went up, racing doesn't get a look in.'

'And it's some history at that, all the way back to the mid-seventeen-hundreds on the Great Heath, which stretched almost as far as the two parishes making up Cardiff at the time,' Ralph said.

'How is that linked to this?' Danny asked, as he showed Ralph the photo he'd taken of the triptych on the kitchen table.

Ralph eyes lit up as he grabbed the phone. 'An elite group of sporting and hunting families like the Williamses, Lindsays, Copes, Homfrays and of course the Samuels combined forces and the Cardiff Racing Club was born,' Ralph said. 'Collectively they owned much of the land that Cardiff stood upon. Remember the city is only just gone two hundred years old. The youngest in Europe.'

'And that was worth a lot back then?' Danny asked incredulously.

'At the time, Cardiff was also the biggest port in the world. It's still the fastest growing capital in Europe,' Ralph said and gave a knowing look.

'So what are you doing getting drunk in a bar at Chepstow on a rainy Tuesday,' Danny said, 'and not soaking up the sun on a yacht in St Tropez?'

'They sold much of it off to the shipyard owners who then built houses upon houses to cram in the migrant workers in what turned into Tiger Bay.'

'That doesn't explain why you're not rolling in it. What went wrong?' Danny asked.

'Understand a lot went right before the tide turned.'

'They must've been some publicists this Cardiff Racing Club, Simon Cowells of their day.'

'They didn't need to be,' Ralph said. 'The once-famous 1897 clash between the mighty Cloister and Grand National hero Father O'Flynn fired the public's imagination and helped promote Ely as a top venue, much to the delight of Philip. They let the horses do the talking. Just a few years later, forty thousand were cramming the stands. Anyone who was anyone would be drawn to that magical place. You name it, star jockeys like Bruce Hobbs, Fulke

Walwyn, Fred Rimell, and horses like Kirkland and Brown Jack. Yet this probably means nothing to you though you've probably walked its turf.'

'Where was it?'

'It stood where Trelai Park is now.'

'So what happened?'

'Philip Samuel happened.' Ralph opened his throat and slugged back a large measure. 'Grandfather, except he wasn't so grand.' He burped silently into his mouth and then hummed contently, as if the alcohol was kicking in. 'He bet like a man, a bloody foolish one at that.'

'And you still can't let it go,' Danny said. He could see Philip's behaviour was slowly eating away at his grandson Ralph, even after all these years. From what he'd heard, Danny guessed Philip wouldn't be turning in his grave, wherever that may be.

'It will ruin you too,' Ralph said. 'Don't let it.'

Danny left Chepstow harbouring mixed feelings. As his calling card had suggested, Ralph came up with answers, just not *the* one Danny sought. Why were they after the triptych? What else was hidden by Herbie at the former groundsman's cottage Danny called home? He now felt the urge to finally venture up to the attic.

CHAPTER 12

DANNY WOKE smothering with a cold. He'd longed for a full night's deep sleep but had just stared up at the ceiling, swallowing with a dry mouth and gravelly throat until he felt sick and kept burping.

With no distractions, his fears also came out to play. His thoughts and outlooks on life quickly became as cold and dark as the night sky outside. He kept turning over, contorted face buried in the warm pillow. At his lowest point, when he found himself worrying about whether a speed camera had flashed him or the car behind the day before, he forced himself to take a reality check and get a grip.

When the alarm bleeped, he dragged himself up from the pillow but then felt his heavy head banging away. He quickly switched the clock to 'ten-minute snooze' mode and fell back in the hope of doing just that. Waking Sara wasn't among his worries; she was still in the spare room, or perhaps she was back at her precious parents. Recently she'd spent more time there than with her husband.

Showered and dressed, he play-slapped his face, as if putting on aftershave. It didn't help.

Rhys was in the kitchen.

Danny said, 'Morning.'

Rhys flicked on the coffee percolator but his lips were pressed in a thin horizontal line.

Danny mirrored the silent treatment and went over to the window. He popped an aspirin.

Megan was busying herself picking up empty bags of feed and piling them up by the tack room. They'd honoured the latest delivery order but Danny suspected that would be the last time, unless he could get another increase on his overdraft. Of all the staff, she was the first to arrive and the last to leave. Whether that enthusiasm would fade with time and fatigue he wouldn't yet know, but early signs were good. He just wished her energy first thing would rub off on him.

He noticed Kelly pace into view. Looking at her face, she might as well have been wearing war paint.

Danny didn't want or need to witness the sparks fly, so turned to Rhys, who was also making a face. He wasn't going to bring up the race fixing or Franco, they were barely speaking as it was.

'Crashed and burned did we?' Danny asked.

'Wha-'

'You look like I feel,' Danny said. 'Who was it? Megan?'

'Wouldn't touch her with yours,' Rhys snapped, now at the table with a mug.

Danny leant forward and pressed a palm on Rhys' brow, lined like a rack of lamb.

'Leave off,' Rhys growled and pushed him away.

'Just checking for a fever,' Danny said. 'New pretty blonde on the scene, you're normally in there like a shot.'

'She's got a partner, heard her on the phone. Besides I'm already seeing someone. And no, you don't know her.'

'It's Kelly, isn't it?' Danny said, trying to cue some friendly banter, but he could feel things had changed between them.

Rhys said, 'Think whatever you like.'

'Then are you stressed or ill?'

'I'm fit and well, why shouldn't I be?' Rhys snapped. He ran a hand through those thick blond curls of his and could no longer hold eye contact. 'Ridden enough winners for you lately, haven't I?'

Perhaps money worries were making Rhys sick and moody. Danny knew enough about that. 'If you ever need a lend?'

'I get by,' Rhys replied.

It wasn't defensive body language that made Rhys fold his arms, Danny suspected, but more to cover the sparkly gold Rolex on his wrist.

'So if it's not stress, illness, women or money, tell me why you keep puking your guts up.' Rhys sipped his steaming coffee and then grimaced. 'Is it Franco? Is he putting you under pressure? This is a friend talking now, not your boss.'

'Friends know when to stop talking.'

'It started when he first appeared on the scene.'

'Franco is nothing to me.'

Rhys was now studying the patterns of steam.

'It's just, until I'd met Franco, I thought *you* were the definition of vanity,' Danny said and sat opposite. 'You certainly wouldn't stay like a rake for the fun of it. Are you a flipper?'

'Christ, I'm a jump jockey that's nine stone wet through. Only need to make nine-ten to make minimum weight, minus the tack and silks. Why the hell would I need to be a flipper?'

'Well, what then?!' Danny asked and fist came down on the table. Some of Rhys' coffee spilt over. 'If you're in denial, how can I help sort this all before it hits the fan?'

'Simple, don't help.'

'You seem to forget I was there at Market Rasen that day, thought pantomime season had started early,' Danny said. 'I hope you've patched things up with Lance.'

'Like I said at the time, I just fancied a change, that okay?!'

'Lance knows, doesn't he?' Danny said.

'No, he doesn't.'

'So there *is* something you're hiding.'

'Why the sudden interest in me, nosing about when it's not wanted? You get where dirt can't.'

'Can you blame me? I pay your retainer, don't forget.'

'Not for much longer. My contract runs out in November, and was worried about breaking it to you, but that seems easier now.'

Danny shook his head. 'Think before you say any more, Rhys.'

'I won't be renewing it.'

'Oh, this just gets better,' Danny said, still shaking his head. 'Always reckoned you had blond moments, but this? Not only are you dumping Lance – your golden goose for outside rides – you want to quit your day job here. You must be thicker than your hair. Or have you come into money?'

Danny could hear what sounded like cats fighting in the courtyard.

It wouldn't have been distracting but for the fact there wasn't a stable cat. Danny returned to the window and swore under his breath.

Kelly had a fistful of Megan's blond ringlets and had her bent double screaming wildly. 'We're not finished, Rhys, stay there.' He poked his head from the kitchen door and shouted, 'Megan, in my office now!' Danny clocked Kelly smirking. 'I'll see you after.'

Christ! I'd have less hassle running Jack's nursery group, Danny fumed.

Megan was now stood in front of the sink. She looked like she was about to face the firing squad with Danny soon to level his rifle.

'Care to explain what's going on?' Danny said. There was the tick of the kitchen clock. 'Any time you like.'

Rhys sniggered as if he'd escaped the worst.

'Megan, I saw your face when you got this job and I don't think you realise how close you are to losing it.'

'It's not me, it's that bossy cow.'

'Enough of the bitching, Megan!' Danny shouted. 'If we're going to make a success of this, do you really think squabbling over whose turn it is to do feed or muck out helps!'

Her shoulders had dropped and her blue eyes sought the slate floor tiles. She looked crestfallen.

He hated this part of the job and was glad when Kelly poked her head around the kitchen door. They could share the blame.

103

'Get in here, both of you need to hear this. If we get through this, it'll be down to hard graft and that means working together. Imagine if a prospective owner had turned up to check if the "friendly, welcoming atmosphere" I've plastered over the website was true. Just what kind of image are you going for? Your screams will upset the younger horses. They could probably hear you both in Cardiff.' Kelly and Megan swapped mournful glances. 'Kelly, I've given you a more senior role, grow up. Give orders but respect Megan's opinions. If there are any disagreements come to me. Agree?'

Megan protested, 'But Kelly told Rhys–'

'Remember!' Kelly snapped and glared.

'But this is important,' Megan pleaded. 'The yard's in trouble.'

'What?' Danny asked Megan. 'What did she say?'

'Nothing.'

'If there's something you're hiding…'

Kelly explained, 'Megan had been flirting with Rhys and I told him watch his back.'

'Is that right, Megan?'

Without looking up, she nodded.

'Just keep your mind on the job and not that–' Danny managed to stop himself before letting rip on his stable jockey. He didn't want to join in the bitching. 'And that goes for you, Kelly, too.'

'You can't do that, I'm seeing Rhys.'

'But not on my watch, I don't pay you to go necking behind the stables.'

'But I'm working my arse off out there,' Kelly said. 'And she said the other day–'

'I don't give a flying fuck who said what, just sort it out quickly, or we'll all be out of a job.' Danny sighed. 'Don't need this, really I don't.'

'Are we done then?' Kelly asked.

'I feel like a headmaster, you know why?'

Kelly replied, 'We're acting like kids, I know, it won't happen again.'

'Megan?' Danny asked.

'It won't happen again,' Megan said.

'Right, get back to work, both of you.'

None of that added up, Danny thought, but he was too tired and stressed to give it any more energy.

Rhys had remained seated, smirking over a *Racing Post*.

Danny asked, 'Planning your next coup, are we?'

Rhys closed the paper. 'Whatever pleases you, I'm done.'

'I'm not,' Danny replied, voice larger.

Rhys stood and headed for the kitchen door. Danny rushed over and blocked his way.

'I'll go out the front way, then,' Rhys said, 'unless you want to be done for false imprisonment.'

'The net's closing, Rhys, just know that. Lance knew what you're up to and now I do. The more mouths you need silencing, the less control you'll have and the greater risks you'll need to take, just to cover your arses.'

'You wouldn't dare blow the whistle. Remember, mud sticks,' Rhys said.

'Keep clinging to that hope – no one will squeal as it's in everyone's interest to keep things under wraps.'

'No hope involved,' Rhys said, smiling.

'There's something I've held back to protect you. Samuel House is going under fast, and when the inevitable eviction letter from the building society hits the mat, it won't make a blind bit of difference to me whether your corruption makes the headlines.'

Rhys left silently. Danny heard the door slam. He entered the hallway and saw the door swinging open. Rhys hadn't hung around long enough to lift the latch and the door had bounced back off the door frame. He looked out and saw Rhys climbing into the driver's seat of a white Jaguar XK Coupe.

'Jesus,' Danny whispered. Franco was generous with his cuts, Danny reckoned, must be worth sixty grand minimum. No wonder Rhys was easing off the rides, it looked like he was already well placed to retire comfortably. Would be interesting to see what the tax man had to say about this. He wasn't going to grass on his own jockey, not yet. Rhys wasn't the only one who needed a trump card.

Danny felt a wave of tiredness wash over him. It was his first proper day off in weeks. It's as if he simply hadn't the time to be exhausted until now.

3.00 PM. He was lying on the settee slowly losing the plot of some made-for-TV thriller. He couldn't hold up his heavy eyelids any longer. Drifting off felt like bliss.

He was woken by fits of giggles. Danny opened his eyes slightly. Megan was on the carpet, back to Danny and playing with Jack. She was quietly singing 'Mary, Mary, Quite Contrary'. Danny lay there silently listening to her soft, rich voice. What was it about the lyrical Welsh lilt, he wondered, as he saw her end the rhyme by tickling Jack's tummy which set him off again. Danny smiled. He hadn't heard Jack laugh like that in ages.

'Again, again!' he shouted. Megan whispered, 'Quiet mind, Dan–' As she turned to check the sofa, she stopped.

'Don't mind me,' Danny said in an octave-lower just-woken-up voice.

'We tried to keep it down,' she said. 'How long have you been awake?'

'Seconds.' Danny then noticed the shawl over him.

'I felt gutted, that I'd let you down,' Megan said. 'It's just those two are thick as thieves. They're plotting something and they threatened me not to breathe a word. I'm worried for the yard, and you.'

'I've got my eye on them, don't you worry,' Danny said.

With Sara off the scene, Megan was increasingly stepping in to save the day. He wasn't sure how he'd have coped without her. Jack would be calling her Mummy before long.

'Daddy!' Jack shouted excitedly, as if now broken from Megan's enchanting spell. He only wished Sara would be like this with their son.

'I'll get some tea on,' she said. 'This little tinker's been fed. I gave him a cookie as a treat, hope you don't mind.'

'What time is it then?' he croaked, rubbing his eyes.

'Six-thirty,' Megan said.

'God, what happened,' he said, pulling himself from the impression he'd made in the warm sofa.

'You must've needed it,' Megan said. 'Play with your Lego men, Jack, I'll put Daddy's steak under the grill.'

'Megan, if this is to make up for earlier, you really don't need to.'

'It's not. I want to, just stay there and play with Jack. He's done a drawing of you.'

Jack ran over, clutching a crumpled A4 sheet showing numerous seemingly random shapes and lines in green and purple crayon. Danny studied it and smiled. 'Oh, wow.'

'Other way up, silly,' Megan said and left for the kitchen.

Danny laughed.

The medium-rare eight ounce rump was done to perfection and was so tender it melted on his tongue. It was topped with a pepper sauce. 'Where did you learn this?'

'Self-taught, my last boyfriend could barely work the toaster.'

'You're not together,' Danny said and then finished off the wine. 'Sorry, didn't mean to pry.'

She smiled. It's then he noticed she was wearing lipstick. 'No, I'm free as a bird.'

'Not for long, I'm sure,' Danny said. 'And thanks again, you needn't have bothered. I'll pop something extra in your next pay.'

'I'm not doing this for money,' she said.

'I know,' Danny said. 'It's just I don't know how else to thank you.'

Megan breathed in and opened her mouth but nothing came out. Danny began stacking plates in the dishwasher. 'Mind, can't afford too many of those, Salamanca's legs will be bowing next time I'm up.'

When he looked up, she'd grabbed her coat. Danny noticed her soft cheeks were as pink as her lips. 'Nothing I said?'

'I've got to go. I'll see you first thing.'

'Yeah, you okay?'

'I'll see you.'

'Yeah, see you,' Danny called after her and was left to wonder whether he'd ever understand women.

He put Jack to bed with another read of *The Gruffalo*. Killing the light, he looked back on his son, now fast asleep clutching his little blanket under his duvet. Danny hoped Jack would grow up to be as proud of him as he was of his own father. Being on the verge of losing his wife and business, he was only glad Jack was too young to remember any of this. He thought about ringing Sara to see when she'd come back. For the first time in their marriage, he could honestly say he wasn't counting the days.

The sleep had helped and he now felt ready to climb the stepladder on the landing. He pushed the loft door up, until it flipped over, leaving a black void. Bits of grit fell in his eyes. He blinked and then climbed another three steps. Enough light escaped the landing for Danny to make out rows of thick wooden beams and a lonely light bulb, naked and suspended from a wire. The air was dry.

Deeper in, he could piece together some square shapes. They were crates and boxes piled high and collecting dust. One had a cargo stamp with a palm tree logo looming over the number 1928. Surely they hadn't been here since Herbie's time here, he thought, didn't they have house clearings or jumble sales back then?

He pushed himself up and then stepped carefully over the beams and joists, trying to ignore the big gaps in the insulation. He simply couldn't afford to repair them right now.

There were no lids on the boxes just a thick and furry coat of dust. Looks like past owners hadn't ventured up here. His former boss Roger Crane wouldn't have fitted through that trapdoor.

He wiped the top layer and then blew a grey cloud into the air. He coughed. This wasn't going to do his throat any good. The box was crammed full of stuff. Danny tried a lucky dip. He wiped again. It was a paper pamphlet.

Danny turned it to face the dim light from the landing below. It was an old racecard. The names and numbers were like a second language to him. He could make out the runners' weights and form figures, all blocky as if they'd been typed out. He flicked through the six races. Some of the borders, alongside the names of trainers and jockeys, had been signed. There were inky squiggles next to names like Sir Gordon Richards and Fred Winter. At the top someone had taken the trouble to ink the time the race took to complete: six minutes and thirty-one seconds.

Obviously a racing enthusiast, Danny reckoned, a historian wouldn't go to the bother. He looked at the date, November 14th, 1936.

There was Ely Racecourse in bold font on the front page. Ralph wasn't so drunk after all.

He delved deeper into the box and began to pull out trophies, framed photos, batches of racecards, racecourse badges, both cardboard and metal. He then untied and unfolded what looked like a map. It was the plans of Ely Racecourse.

Danny picked up one of the many monochrome photos. It was similar to that in Rhymney Miners' Club. Danny found himself trembling ever so slightly. He slowly lowered himself on one of the beams, now surrounded by racing memorabilia. To Danny this was like discovering the city of Atlantis. Even in dusky light, barely a candle's worth, Danny's wide eyes sparkled. It was like a racing man's survival kit. He'd even come across binoculars, brass with leather grips and tagged with a nest of cardboard racing badges for the Premier Enclosures at courses as far afield as Ayr and Brighton. Beneath an engraving Le Jockey Club Paris 1895 near the left lens of the bins, there was a silver insignia – P.S. *Philip Samuel*. Ralph wasn't exaggerating; Philip liked his racing. Yet it was in Herbie's attic. Was he storing this prized haul for when his master returned?

Danny bundled up a selection of the find and returned to the kitchen. His eyes pored over the photos. The sight of women turning out in their Twenties get-up, looking like flappers with their slim dresses, straight waists, hemlines above the knee and cloche hats that gripped their boyish hair, short and flat, styled with that Betty Boop wavy finger pattern. They stood like fashion models, toying with cigarette holders, their fur-collared coats from a bygone era when wearing dead animals would get stares of admiration rather than disdain. Some cocked one leg off to the side, as if about to back kick their way into a Charleston once the camera bulb flashed. They locked arms with men posing in their neatly cut suits with hair smarmed back with Brylcreem and wearing ties and boaters. Looked like a Hollywood film, rather than the ghost of a Cardiff racetrack.

Danny knew it wasn't the fashion that got him fired up, after all that came and went, but the fact he held in his palm a snapshot of a forgotten yet rich past in the sport he loved.

This was a different era in racing's history though the similarities to today's scene were as stark as the contrasts. Back then legends really were legends, when hype was constricted to word of mouth or newspaper print. There were no viral videos or marketers stoking the hype machine. Their greatness was achieved through their actions and achievements. Danny's fingers ran over the glass on one of the race photos. Most looked in their twenties here but they'd all be dead by now, Danny thought with some degree of melancholy.

He couldn't identify them, even if the photo had been sharper, but these were responsible for laying the foundations of the modern-day sport. That image came alive in Danny's mind's eye like a film, another world, a fantasy world. Danny wanted to be whisked back when times were simpler, no distractions like computers, mobiles, internet and hundreds of TV channels, many showing crap around the clock, all scrambling his mind. It was all

110

about the racing back then, where the skills of horsemanship counted more than the over-analysed art of race-riding, when honour and prestige meant more than prize-money, when they wished each other good luck and let the best man win. When sponsors and TV rights and drugs and whip bans and political wrangling between racings factions didn't overshadow what the sport was about. It simply boiled down to the best jockey and horse won. He pictured them fearlessly attacking the fences, with only their woollen silks to soften a fall; there were no back and body protectors then.

He lost track of time as he immersed himself in this treasure trove.

Danny believed if he could achieve a fraction of what these racing legends had in his lifetime, he'd be choked with pride and hopefully little Jack would feel the same one day.

It was all here, as Ralph had said. Aside from the racecards and badges, there was a photo album and even a rusty horse shoe with The Whistler scratched into the metal. Danny held it up and read out loud, 'The Whistler.' His thoughts spun back to the photo nailed to the wall in Rhymney Miners' Club. He made a mental check. No, he wasn't mistaken. In his hand, he held the shoe once worn by the winner of the 1936 Cardiff Open Steeplechase. This was like a Beatles fan stumbling across a pair of Lennon's specs.

Danny knew this group of courageous and ambitious horse-folk made jumps racing, engraving the sport on the hearts of the British and Irish public. From that day forth, its future was secure, unlike that of Ely Racecourse itself. The stands in some of the photos were a sea of people. He wondered what had become of it. He felt it a travesty that this track, along with the racing and local community it served, had long since died and left the public eye. Even Danny hadn't come across it and his life revolved around racing.

He remembered once seeing old pictures of Rhymney's grand ballroom, packed with dancers and sumptuously decorated, now

111

boarded up, awaiting demolition. Time changes everything and not always for the better.

Danny wasn't ashamed to admit, his heart now ached with pride. He was touched by what he'd found. Whether it was the emotions he'd pent up since Sara's absence but he felt a tear tickle his cheek. He quickly wiped it dry with a sleeve and said, 'Bloody dust.'

When he picked up another framed photo, it wasn't the picture that caught his eye. Lying beneath it was a small green book, scuffed at the edges with a threadbare spine. Danny carefully opened it. Inked on the inside of the front cover was the name: HERBIE MORGAN.

Danny leafed through the tiny pages, torn in places and covered in fox spots and mould. Danny could make out, scribbled in doctor's hand, lots of dates, together with notes about weather conditions and ground conditions, ranging from heavy during the depths of winter right up to firm in the spring. Was Herbie the clerk of the course too? He was certainly had a close connection with the track. Herbie Morgan. H.M.

He typed the name into Google on his smartphone. Nothing relevant came back though. After all these years, that came as no surprise.

As he continued to rifle through the pile of attic photos, he came across a family snap. The father's eyes were pale, bordering on albino, and the young child was made to look a few years older than he was. It was a formal photo and all three wore solemn clothes and expressions. There was foxing on the cardboard border surrounding the printed words: The Morgan Family - Herbert, Lucinda and Walter. '37.

Danny wanted more and removed the photo from the glass and cardboard frame. On the back was pencilled 'Paid c/o Philip Samuel.'

Perhaps Philip wasn't such a waster as Ralph had made out. At least he looked out for the estate's groundsman.

112

Something flimsy fell to the floor silently. Danny leant down and unfolded it. It was a grainy newspaper clipping. There was a photo with the tagline: 'Presentation of *Gunning For Glory*. Pictured: Sir Michael Johns (left) and Mr Philip Samuel (right).'

However the copy beneath, if there was any, had been crudely cut off.

The photo showed two suited men. Initially, however, Danny was drawn to the painting stood on a tablecloth between them. There were three panels of a racing scene. Danny was convinced it was the triptych now under his sink. So the picture had a name then, Danny thought. Philip was probably in his late thirties but, like many in these photos, appeared middle-aged. But perhaps late thirties was regarded as middle-aged back then, Danny thought. He stood with a regimental bearing, shoulders back and chest out, like a strutting peacock. He was the recipient of the painting from his rival owner. Had Philip's horse won the race and Johns was the sponsor?

They were both looking down the lens, serious faces and hands lost in pockets of their tweet jackets. Johns' jowly face was covered by a candyfloss beard and 'his' hair was suspiciously off centre and neat. This appeared like a show of solidarity between the big guns at Ely. But their expressions and demeanour suggested it was just that – a show. There was no love lost between these two, Danny reckoned, but he wanted more.

Walter must be Herbert's son. He quickly ran through the dates and reckoned he'd be in his eighties now. Danny wanted to meet him before the intruder carried out his threats.

He searched for Walter online. He found a contact number for a Walter Morgan, who, up until two years ago was C Team captain of Ely Crown Green Bowling Club. Danny reckoned at that time of life, he was more likely to move on from this earth than move house. He called the number.

CHAPTER 13

HERBIE MORGAN was dead.

Danny was sure of that. Living in his thirties during the Thirties would now make him Wales' oldest living man. And Herbie didn't look a picture of health back then.

Danny pulled on the handbrake and left the car on Greencroft Avenue; a safe distance to be conspicuous but near enough to make a quick getaway.

He'd remembered playing frisbee here as a kid. Once he came down with his dad and a Chinese dragon kite he'd unwrapped that birthday morning. He looked on in awe as the long red and green tail swished and swirled in the blue sky as he turned the wooden handgrips until a gust fired it into the unforgiving ground. The kite wasn't the only thing to return home in bits as his parents simply couldn't afford to replace it, not with the soaring mortgage rates.

Now he was stepping through the iron gates of Trelai Park with a new understanding and appreciation of its rich and colourful past. It was where Ralph had claimed a good portion of Ely Racetrack once stood. Treading the same hallowed turf once shared by the thundering hooves of the best steeplechasers on the planet was a humbling, almost spiritual, experience for Danny.

Looking over at kids playing on the expanse of green, these days it seemed they played tag rugby and cricket. Hyena laughs and excitable shouts were carried over on a freshening breeze.

He ran a hand over his brow and then pinched his orange Reebok t-shirt away from his chest. He didn't mind it warm but this was ridiculous. He was relieved to spot a man reclining on one of many broken wooden benches, as he said he would be in their phone call. He was beside a yapping Jack Russell, hopping mad and gagging as he strained at the leash.

Nearing, he heard a click of claws on the pathway. Now both of them appeared to view Danny with suspicion. His pinched nose and small eyes certainly resembled those of Herbie in the family photo: like father, like son. It had to be Walter, Danny reckoned.

'Down, Gus!' the man croaked. His bald crown reflected the sun's rays and wispy white strands at the back were surfing the warm air. The old man adjusted black-rimmed Seventies glasses, though Danny suspected he wasn't going for the retro look. He wore a rumpled mud-brown sweater over beige shirt and a stretched elastic waistband supported grey slacks. Danny sat the other end of the bench, give them some space. He was glad he did.

Gus was all eyes and teeth as he took a running jump at Danny, who instinctively leant back over the arm of the bench. Gus' slobbering jaw was snapping away, but was yanked short, just a foot from Danny's crotch, by a lead that was tied to the other bench arm.

'He's playing.' It looked like an effort for the man as he turned. 'I think he's taken a shine to you.'

Wouldn't want to get on his wrong side, Danny thought.

Waiting for Gus to settle, Danny sat silently, eyes screwed up, warm sunlight stroking his face. He watched the kids in Ferrari-red Welsh rugby shirts tossing the egg-shaped ball and fumbling catches some sixty yards away. Two of them were now bent double in fits pointing as their pal had hit the deck.

'There are other benches,' the man said. His voice rattled, as if heard through old loudspeakers.

'But you're on this one,' Danny said.

'I'm waiting for someone, you see. Do I know you?'

'No, but I know you, Mr Morgan.'

'Daniel Rawlings?'

'Yes.'

'That's queer.'

115

'What is Walter?'

'I had you as older,' Walter said.

'I got into racing early, still learning the ropes as a trainer.'

'I know.'

'You still follow the sport then.'

'When my father first dragged me along to the races here, I was just glad of an afternoon out of the house and to spend time with my father. He was a workaholic. Soon it was the horses I was tagging along for.'

'Your house,' Danny said, 'That was Samuel House?'

'But it's now home to you,' Walter said. 'Holds many memories that place.'

'Your father was head groundsman there,' Danny said.

'Where?'

'At the estate,' Danny said, slightly perplexed.

'And the racetrack.'

Looks like Herbie was made to work for that painting and stopwatch, Danny thought. 'Shame it's long gone.'

'It's more than a shame, lad,' Walter said. 'A shame is when you miss the bus or catch a cold. This was a travesty. Once the old racecourse up at the heath closed, the way was open for a new track. When the Cardiff Racing Club was born they had the money and faces to get the ball rolling.'

'Like the Samuels,' Danny said.

'This place was rocking with the top chasers in the country, proper stars mind,' Walter said. 'And that attracted the top riders. Never forget Sir Gordon Richards galloping by, it was like he was floating, could almost reach out and touch his woollen colours. Thrilling it was, even at my tender age, I knew I was witnessing something. Can still hear the rumble of hooves as they galloped by, still swear the ground shook under my tiny feet. Used to hear the riders' helmets too, clattering the low branches down the back straight as they searched for a faster strip of ground sheltered from the rain. Where would that be now, over there I guess.' He raised an arm towards a clump of oaks far away.

116

Walter, who perhaps from loneliness, appeared to relish this chance to relive and share his memories.

'Racing was big back then, like football is now. These were household names. They say the shilling gate broke from the crowds pouring in one year, turnouts some of today's fancy football clubs would envy. You can imagine the crackle of anticipation here. We all lived for race-days at Ely. Once, when my dad Herbie was ruing his luck, he made me pick one out. So I did, Cabin Boy in the Cardiff Open Steeplechase, liked the name, see. Up against the mighty Golden Miller, who was a superstar, won a hatful of Gold Cups and a Grand National.'

'I've heard of him.'

'But I bet they didn't tell you he couldn't win the big one at Ely, just went to show that race's standing back then. Anyhow, my pick only went and beat The Miller; got an ice cream as a reward and could stay up late. Never forget my excitement watching the rails bookie count out the pound notes on my father's palm. The bookie was also beaming under that trilby, probably knew he'd get it back soon enough. I knew I'd done good though, made Herbie proud and that made me proud.' He smiled. 'Still, none of this would mean a thing to a youngster like you.'

Danny wondered when he'd last been called a youngster. Would've been an insult back in his teens, fearing the shame of being turned away from pubs and clubs, but now it was a compliment.

'Go on,' Danny said.

'Herbie used to skive off with the other Irish kids in Grangetown. They used to save up the pennies by working at what used to be the brick works over there, near Ely quarry; we're going way back now. And you can guess where the hard-earned silver would end up on race days, in the bookies' satchels. He told me they were known as the brick yard pupils. When he took over as the groundsman, he'd let me run loose on the track some days, it was like an adventure playground to a kid, loved wetting my feet in the ditch of the water jump. Herbie would whack me for climbing on any of the fences, mind.' Walter laughed again. 'Never told him I once left the crusts of my final jam sandwich on the landing side of the third last fence, thinking the horses would be tired and hungry by then. I'd often see them kiss the ground after a bad jump, got me jealous as I thought they were nibbling other treats left there, see. Must only have been seven or eight, funny the things you remember.'

'Where would those fences be now?'

'They built a pub where the water jump used to be, the ex-jockeys could wet their lips instead of their feet there. The drinking hole was named after the legendary Anthony brothers, The Anthonys. They both swept the boards as jockeys and trainers, remarkable family. Getting a pub in your name was like a knighthood in these parts back then.'

'Might go there for a pint later,' Danny said, eager to find other Ely racegoers.

'You'll do well to get served.'

'Busy is it?'

'It's under that supermarket over there.'

Danny looked across at the glimpses of a low-level roof hidden beyond the tree-line. He'd popped in there a few times to get cheap booze when the local off-licence was shut. Little did he know at the time, he was walking over the graveyard of this once-great racetrack.

'And the third-last fence, oh I don't know.' Walter said, stroking his prickly chin. 'Looking at the oaks over there, it probably wouldn't be far away from the changing rooms, they replaced the Nissen huts.'

'And where would we be sitting here?'

'Let's see, if the trees lined the back-straight, we're in the third row of the middle stand.' His chuckle turned into a wheeze. He removed a ventilator spray and puffed twice. As Walter painted with words, Danny's fertile imagination filled in the picture.

'There was more than one stand?' Danny asked.

'A whole string of them. Massive they were. Mind, everything seemed massive at that age.'

'And they managed to fill them?' Danny said. 'I mean, with all the big English tracks.'

'Decent prize-money was put up and they flocked to see the stars,' Walter said, 'The Cardiff Open was once worth more to the winner than the Cheltenham Gold Cup. Nothing talks louder than money. They even held the Welsh National here, before Chepstow was a mere twinkle in the developer's eye.'

'When did it close?'

Walter came straight out with, 'April, 1939.'

'Damn sight sharper than me.'

'No trouble recalling years back, it's what I did this morning that gets me stumped.'

Danny smiled.

'The fact I had a shilling on the final winner there, ridden by Lester Piggott's father Keith, Dunbarney was the horse, yes … always recall my winners, precious few to remember, see.'

'What the hell went wrong?'

'Grandstand went up in smoke in '37. That proved the final nail in the coffin, racetrack closed not long after, two years or so.'

'An accident?'

'No,' Walter said.

'Who did it?'

'Officially the finger of blame pointed at a jockey called Charlie Moore.'

'Was he found guilty?'

'The court did in his absence.'

'Did a runner?'

'He was in the stands at the time.'

'Suicide?'

'They blamed a faulty lock, health and safety didn't exist back then. They say petrol was found all over the stewards' room. But that's all very old news now, buried with the track. Few people know of Ely's rich racing past, unless they're an old codger like me, or I tell them.'

'What then?' Danny asked. 'It was turned into this?'

'Laid dormant for years first, while they worked out what to do with it. For me though, all I recall was coming down here. It seemed like hot summers and white winters back then. Chat in the sun how we'd change the world and tease the young 'uns that Martians had come to get them.'

'Eh?'

'With the war looming, Air Ministry assumed control of some of the racecourse land to defend Cardiff and oh boy, they meant business all right, anti-aircraft guns and a rocket battery. A Paras demo team used to leap from balloons, big and silver they were, some sight in them days, mind,' Walter said. Again a smile played on his thin lips. 'Looked like nothing of this world, an alien mother-ship, the little tykes would start crying they did, give them an inch and they'd run a mile.'

Walter's gnarled and blotchy fingers wrapped around Gus' tiny skull, pressing down those pricked dog ears. It seemed to calm the terrier, whose popping eyes were blinkered on his master, tail wagging and pink tongue licking the air as a fresh breeze picked up again. Danny let the silence linger. It was the oldest trick in the book to get more info, play on the human's natural need to fill silences.

Walter added, 'By the early Fifties, they'd sorted the legal stuff and worked out what to do with it. I remember following its progress closely in the papers and on the wireless, hoping they'd change their minds, but the council went ahead and turned it into this. The track was Herbie's life you see, I was just glad he wasn't around to see it go. All of this was celebrated as … now what did they call it? Cardiff's largest recreational centre, yes, made headlines it did. Depressing read for me.'

'Strange, it doesn't look big enough for a track.'

'The rest of the racecourse was given up for housing over there, should be thankful for small mercies they kept this green, as it would've been like black gold to developers. Mind, they dug up some of it in the Sixties sometime, searching for a Roman villa, of all things.'

Buzzing like gnats, a couple of teenagers were slaloming motocross bikes between park benches and orange cones left after morning football practice.

Walter pointed his wedding finger. There was no ring. 'At least kids are still making the best of it. Remember us lads went off making rafts to go on the River Taff, up near Monkey Rocks. And when it rained we'd shelter in the woods, take turns on the rope-swings.' Danny let Walter continue to revel in his comforting past. 'We'd often sit up by the railway embankment. Remember hiding in a ditch once, air raid it was, when the battery opened fire. Never shook so much since, even when saying my wedding vows.'

'And it was the fire that did for the track.'

'I later read somewhere they were struggling by then. Competition from Chepstow and there wasn't as much money to go around in the Great Depression before the war. What turned out to be the final Cardiff Open Steeplechase attracted just three runners, which wasn't a draw for punters. So that was it, they closed the gates and walked away.'

'I just can't believe they just gave up.'

'Use your eyes, son,' Walter said. 'Only horses you'll see running here is the odd harness racing meet. Mind, even those attract big crowds. Should still be racing here if you ask me, put Ely back on the sporting map.'

'You never know,' Danny said.

'Not with Chepstow and now Ffos Las on the scene, doubt they'll grant any more tracks in Wales, not in my lifetime.'

Danny was convinced the triptych and Ely racecourse were linked in some way. He removed the newspaper clipping. 'Does this ring a bell?'

Walter fumbled in his cardigan and produced a magnifying glass which failed to instil much confidence in Danny. 'What is it?'

'A triptych,' Danny said.

'Oh, my goodness.'

'You recognise it?' Danny asked.

'Recognise it?' Walter wiped the magnifier with a hanky. 'I was there.'

'In the photo?'

'Wouldn't be allowed, this was a show for the hacks. Let it be known there was no ill feeling.'

Danny recalled the names pencilled on the back. 'Between Philip Samuel and Michael Johns.'

'Ely's head honchos. Any bad air between them was supposed to have blown away at that prize giving.'

'Was it?'

'They hadn't become rich by being nice. That smile of Johns is as real as his hair. Competition between them remained fierce until the bitter end and it *was* bitter.'

'Had Philip won the race?'

'I remember that day as my dad took me to the posh end to see his master, Philip, being presented with the painting from Michael, who was on the board of a company that stepped in when the sponsor dropped out at the eleventh hour. Only discovered that years later,' Walter said. 'At the time, I simply wondered why Mr Samuel wasn't upset seeing his present was broken in three pieces and what Michael kept in his big bushy beard. Aunt Marylyn always told me I was an odd child.'

'From that, Philip looks quite short.'

'He used to ride,' Walter said. 'I dare say he was a good bit taller stood on his wallet. Used to roll up in his fancy Daimler but he wouldn't be grinning in this photo if he knew what lay ahead. The win this day in thirty-six was his last day in the sun as an owner, amazing downturn in luck. Even his prized mare The Whistler let him down.'

122

'Do you believe the painting was cursed?' Danny asked.

'Who told you that?'

'Can't remember,' Danny lied.

'Let's just say Philip liked to blame everyone and everything but himself. My father got much of the brunt of it, poor sod. Rarely saw Philip out of this Cardiff Racing Club blazer pinned with a member's badge. My dad liked to collect the badges thrown away or lost by racegoers. He said they'd be worth something one day. Philip's one was metal, it shined in the sun.'

Danny recalled the collection in the attic crate and he then removed the stopwatch from his jeans pocket. He handed it over.

As Walter turned it over and saw the H.M. on the back, he took a sharp intake of breath.

'You okay, want to move into the shade over there.'

Walter began to rock himself up.

Danny firmly held him down by the arm.

'Where did you get that?' Walter asked, seemingly now as keen as Danny for answers.

'On the estate,' Danny said.

'That's because it was my father's. It was a gift from Philip for all the years' loyal service, or as my father liked to call it hard labour. He used to time the races at Ely with this thing.'

Danny recalled the six minutes thirty-one seconds inked at the top of the Cardiff Open racecard.

'Not much for all those years, given he was a rich boss,' Danny said.

Walter said, 'And there was that painting, remember it hanging on our landing where you now live. It was the first thing I'd see leaving my bedroom to get ready for school.'

'Another gift?'

'Hardly, Philip was richer than he was generous. He wanted rid, once he'd convinced himself it had been cursed by Michael, who had cleaned up in the coming seasons.'

'May I keep this?' Walter said. 'It's my one and only link with my childhood, would mean a lot to me in my final years.'

Danny nodded. 'Was Herbie ashamed of the gifts?'

'Why would you say that?'

'I found one hidden behind a mirror and another in the woods.'

'That I can't say, you see he didn't talk much about anything other than work and rest of the time wasn't to be disturbed listening to the wireless in a walnut cabinet in the corner, another hand-me-down from the big house. From what little I can remember, this is sixty years ago we're talking.'

'Over seventy,' Danny said.

'Is it? Suppose it is. My, the years are just flying by, you lose track.'

'Didn't sound much fun.'

'Herbie wasn't a monster you understand,' Walter added, 'my favourite son, he'd joke. I was his only son, you see. If he had a flaw, it was that he just lived for his work, family was nothing but a distraction. Remember my mum always telling of his dreams of retiring to some exotic island with golden sands and crystal waters but she suspected he'd be miserable away from the estate and racetrack. It was just a pipe dream. I used to believe that's the reason for him vanishing, and he'd be there with Philip supping fancy cocktails, though it would make me sad, thinking he'd deserted me when I needed him most.'

'So he did have plans for the future,' Danny said. 'I'm finding out the hard way that this painting is worth more than it looks, perhaps it was his retirement fund.'

'He didn't top himself,' Walter said. 'He had too much to leave behind.'

'But he did leave, didn't he?'

'One night I do remember shuffling off to relieve my bladder. When I stopped and peered through a crack in my door. I blinked from the bright yellow light on my face. I heard noises. It was the floorboards. Perhaps that's what woke me. I remember watching my father and Philip Samuel, both dressed head to foot in dark clothes. Even then, I thought that odd, but just accepted it, you do

124

at that age. They were carrying heavy hessian bags, they were moving slowly along the landing. Neither said anything. Then I suddenly backed into the dark, my dad had seen me. My stomach tightened. That feeling has stayed with me. I thought I'd feel the sole of his boot. But he just said the oddest thing to me. He looked over one shoulder, as if to see if Philip was eavesdropping and whispered, 'Listen, son, if something goes wrong tonight, please remember this: the winner is where our fortune lies. 1936. Please, can you remember that? The winner is where our fortune lies.' I nodded but more for his approval than to say I understood. Then there was another glance over his shoulder, back down the hallway where Philip was gathering up the sacks, hunting rifle slung over one shoulder and gripping a shovel. Dad then shook my arm, his grip hurt. It was as if he was trying to physically shake this moment into my mind. Well, it worked.'

'Did you see them leave that night?'

'Philip called over, 'No more goodbyes, let's get moving,' or something to that effect. Herbie left with, 'Good boy, now go back to bed.' The whole thing unsettled me. It was like a weird dream. When I woke up a few hours later my pyjamas felt warm and wet. I'd been too afraid to get to the door. Felt so ashamed at the time.'

'You did well to remember that word for word, after all these years.'

'It's because they were the last words he ever spoke to me.'

'The winner is where our fortune lies,' Danny said distantly. 'Stating the obvious, isn't it? Why would he say that?'

'You think I haven't asked myself that?' Walter said. 'He clearly feared this was his farewell speech, so why not tell me that he loved me, or to take care of mum.'

'Perhaps he felt these words were more important.'

'What's more important than love?'

'For Philip it sounds like wealth and status,' Danny said. 'And your dad was probably following orders to avoid getting fired. That was definitely the last time.'

125

'It was the last time we spoke,' Walter said. 'Not the last time I saw him.'

'He came back?'

'To Samuel House, not to me,' Walter said. 'I couldn't get much sleep that night. Those words kept turning over in my head. I lay looking out the bedside window upslope to the ridge.' Danny guessed this was where Jack now slept. 'The low sun was burning off the morning mist and I could make out two figures, men wearing black, pacing, they were.'

'Are you sure it was them?'

'Certain.'

'It's just, over time your imagination may fill in gaps–'

'It was them!'

'Were they carrying anything?'

'Not anymore.'

'Do you think they were heading up to the old Samuel House?'

'Very little else lay beyond that ridge. Wherever it was, neither came back. Just gone, swallowed up by the mist.'

'Are you sure?'

Walter nodded. 'I'd have waved goodbye if I'd known.'

'No wonder they made up ghost stories about the estate.'

'I don't believe they died that night.'

'Don't believe, or don't want to believe?'

'I'm not kidding myself, if that's what you're implying,' Walter said. 'Sometimes I wish they had died that night, better than my dad thinking that little of me to just silently vanish. However much trouble he was in, he only had one son. Me. Wouldn't it console me more to think he didn't come back because he simply didn't have a choice? That he'd been killed. People say you'll get over it, time's a healer but they don't tell you it can shape the rest of your life, change you forever. If I'm being honest, don't think I've ever got over that time. It was the not knowing, the feeling of abandonment, I felt pain, proper physical pain here.' Walter's hand clawed at his chest. 'I was convinced it was my fault. Mum certainly never got over it.'

'Who led who?'

Walter made a face. 'Philip was leading, as I recall. He was lord of the manor you understand but my father was close behind. And there's something else that's just come back to me.'

'What?'

'I thought it odd them being in such a hurry, the day had barely begun. Reminded me when my dad used to march me upstairs when I'd spilt my milk or taken a sneaky look through his racing memorabilia. He'd locked them away in a cupboard full of *his* things but I knew where the key was, on top of the Welsh dresser.'

'I've come across some of it,' Danny said, recalling the attic find. 'Racecards and photos.'

'And much more besides, even had a few horse shoes,' Walter recalled, 'Herbie made sure he'd pick them up if they'd been re-shod at the start or lost one during the race.'

Danny recalled The Whistler's shoe in the crate.

'Philip lost the estate to a pair of jacks, didn't he?'

'And can you guess who held those jacks?'

Danny replied, 'Michael Johns?'

Walter nodded.

'It seems their competitive streak didn't end with racing.'

'Is that what made Philip do a disappearing act?'

'I recall we remained on the estate for a good few months after it made headlines.'

'He'd refused to pay out?'

'I don't know, lad,' Walter said. 'I suspect he'd hung about in the hope his mare The Whistler would win the '37 Cardiff Steeplechase to buy him some time. That shared the day both my father and Philip vanished.'

'And did she?'

'With Michael Johns' unbeaten Shadow Master in the line-up, Philip must've known the writing was on the wall. It was billed by Ely officials as the showdown of showdowns but with five to jump you could see it was a one-horse race. No surprise my father never kept the photo of Michael Johns collecting the trophy. Poor Philip. Kick a man when he's down, couldn't have happened to a nicer fella.'

Danny suspected Walter's tongue was lodged firmly in his cheek. He clearly couldn't forgive gambler Philip Samuel for somehow dragging Herbie down with him.

He'd gambled away the fortune and respect on a whim, for the buzz, Danny reasoned. If he had it all, why risk it all?

Had Philip killed Herbie as he knew too much?

Or did Michael bet Philip Samuel his life as a double or quits. It sounded like they were sworn enemies and either Philip had been murdered or disappeared before Michael had collected on his bet. Was he that much of a tyrant?

'Other than me,' Danny said. 'Have you ever told anyone about that night?' Walter took his glasses off and pinched the bridge of his nose. 'This is really important.'

'Mother,' Walter said. 'My small shoulders couldn't bear such a burden. I'll never forget the look in her eyes. I never saw that painting or my father again. Neither of us ever even talked of it again.'

'Anyone else?'

'No.'

'She believed in the curse.'

'Why?' Walter asked.

'Why else would she hide it behind the vanity mirror?'

'I don't follow.'

'If you're certain the painting was hanging in the hallway that night and Herbie never came back, it had to be her, unless she had lodgers or was seeing someone. Perhaps he'd left because she was having an affair. Would explain why she kept quiet about the reason for his sudden disappearing act, you'd be too young to understand.'

'Take that back, young man!' Walter fumed. 'She was faithful to my father until the day she died.'

'When was that?'

'1986,' Walter said. 'My biggest regret was that she went to the grave not knowing what really happened to Herbie.'

'Did she try to clean the painting?'

There was another pause. It was as if they were conversing by satellite link. 'I can't say.'

'Can't or won't?'

'As you say, it's seventy years ago, lad.'

'Think,' Danny said. 'It's important.'

Walter shook his head. 'I don't recall.'

'Being a handyman, Herbie would have things like solvents and paint-strippers lying about.'

'I doubt she'd ever clean it up,' Walter said. 'She hated the triptych, blamed it for my father's disappearance you see. And who can blame her? It destroyed the Samuel Estate like a cancer. And not long after they had been gifted it, Herbie was gone.'

'Then why didn't she just burn it?' Danny asked.

'How could she? It was a gift for my father. He'd worked his fingers to the bone for that. I used to secretly watch her stare vacantly from the lounge window up-valley to the ridge, waiting, perhaps convinced her husband would come back into her arms, so how could she just get rid of it, give up on their memories and all hope. I guess it was like parents of missing children, leaving bedrooms untouched.'

With that in mind, Danny felt it odd she felt the need to wipe out one of the runners.

'I want you to meet someone,' Walter said and pulled a pocketbook from his trousers. It was a 1996 Raymond Barton Betting Diary.

'They dish them out free every year you know,' Danny said.

'I know. But since my dearest Martha passed on, I use it for phone numbers not a diary,' he said, 'and most of those need crossing off, either lost touch with them or they've passed on.

Don't grow old, kid.' He thumbed the pages until stopping at F. He then tore the page off.

'Won't you need this?' Danny asked, waving the page.

'No.'

'Who's Fred?'

'An old friend,' Walter said. 'A very old friend, Fred Myrtle. We first met when I asked him to sign a racecard, then got talking, you see. He knew my father, Herbie. I still check up on him, sometimes take fruit round, not as often as I should but he's got a nurse. Stubborn sod he is. Still refuses to go into a home. He says they'll have to carry him there kicking and screaming. I've still got the autograph somewhere.'

'God, how old is he then?'

'There's a birthday card from the Queen on the hearth. First thing he'll mention, bless him. And probably the last as well, memory not that great, see.'

Danny didn't reply. He'd become distracted by three men on the pathway, growing larger. Perhaps they'd pass on by. But something about them didn't add up, dressed all in black, their faces were hidden by dark shades and baseball caps, though thankfully they weren't brandishing bats. Two of them had the stocky, broad-shouldered build of a thirty-something, though they dressed more like teenage goths.

'What is it lad?' Walter asked.

'I'm not sure,' Danny said, voice tapering off.

'Oh dear lord!' They'd clearly now walked into Walter's range. 'They've come!'

'They? Who are *they*? Tell me quick.'

'Go lad, you might be spared.'

'Did you call them?' Danny asked, voice sparked by anger. Was Walter one of them? Had he fallen into a trap? But if it was – why would Walter urge Danny to flee? What he saw in Walter's grey eyes was the kind of fear that couldn't be faked.

'Daniel, listen! This is a great opportunity, far greater than you ever imagine. Find what my mother couldn't. Now go, please, I can deal with this. They want me, I'm last in the line.'

'Last in the line?' Danny asked.

'I am the last one,' Walter said and handed the stopwatch back.

'Last what?'

Danny turned again and found himself staring down a pistol.

CHAPTER 14

BEHIND THE HUMAN SHIELD of two hired heavies, the gunman stood silently.

Being stark daylight, Danny was convinced it must be a toy or a replica. He glanced at Walter, whose jaw was shaking. When he looked back, a loud crack, like an old car misfiring, made him flinch. The bang was soon lost in the open spaces. He felt nothing. Was he in shock? No. That changed when he checked on Walter again.

A single bullet had ripped into Walter's saggy chest and a wet claret shape grew down his pullover. Walter's fragile and limp body slowly slipped off the bench, like one of Dali's melting clocks, moaning as he went. The glasses fell off as he lay to rest on the path, slackened face. The moaning had stopped. Danny's jaw tightened. He felt feverish. Then one of the henchmen stamped on Walter's head, as if to rub it in. 'Enough!' the gunman said.

Like an assassin, the man still held the gun confidently and with a cool detachment, as if this wasn't the first time and wouldn't be the last.

Gus was now licking his master, occasionally growling and glancing up at the killer.

'Now I have your undivided attention,' the man said with the poise and control of a hitman. But something told Danny this was no professional job. Surely the first two don'ts in a killer's handbook were: avoid daylight and avoid public places. For their sakes, he hoped the biker boys had fled.

Danny made rapid, almost involuntary, nods as tension overloaded his neck muscles.

'Good,' the gunman added. He glanced at the left heavy. 'Dump that in the ditch. Give the foxes a treat.'

The hulking frame of the man in a black shirt tugged on matching leather gloves. He picked up Walter by his bloody pullover and dragged him like a heavy bin bag to a broken hedge behind the bench. He heaved and let the limp body roll down a bank. There was a faint splash.

'No!' Danny cried. 'Fucking animals!'

'We'll take you someplace quieter,' the gunman replied. 'You think you're sweating now, we haven't started.'

'For Christ sake, he was a harmless old man,' Danny cried and glanced back at a row of houses hidden by trees and bushes, beyond the ditch. 'Someone will have heard. The police are coming.'

'Youths are letting off firecrackers all the time. And he was in the way,' the gunman said. 'The last in the line.'

Had Walter carried a wire?

'I'll find the painting for you,' Danny said, hoping to buy some time.

'It's not the painting we want, but the secret it holds.'

The right heavy pulled Danny up and then grabbed his arm, twisting from behind, leaving him immobile and wincing in a back arm lock.

Danny glanced over at the kids. They were looking back. His gaze then fixed back on the killer. The gun had gone, clearly aware they now had an audience.

As his arm was forced higher up his back, Danny expected to hear a clean snap. It was like his schooldays all over again. His dad's words came to him: 'Strike where it hurts son, then run.'

Survival instinct had helped Danny fight the bullies off but they were less than half the size and weight of the thug he was pinned to. The other heavy was on lookout and mercifully kept his distance.

Danny relaxed his locked arm and then widened his stance to the width of a shoulder and a half. This lowered his centre of gravity to help balance. He was right footed in kickabouts, so shifted his weight to the left leg, farthest from the heavy. In one swift motion, he bent down from the waist, pulled in his toes, gritted his teeth and pointed the heel. A quick look at goal and he kicked back like a mule, the rear thrust sent his trainer's heel buried in the attacker's soft groin. It was now the attacker bent double, loosening his grip enough for Danny to break free. The gunman lunged forward. Danny raised his right knee and, while rotating his body on the bent supporting left leg, he kicked out with the heel pointing sideways, stamping a dusty tread mark on the gunman's chest. The impact sent the attacker back.

'That's from Walter,' Danny growled.

The other heavy now came for him. But Danny had already taken his dad's advice and ran faster than he ever thought he could. With every footfall, he expected to be struck down; a clinical bullet in the back and that was that. Never see Jack and Sara again, or Megan, or the horses. The yard would soon be sold off and, not long after, all he'd strived to build up would be gone, like he'd never existed.

He closed in on one of the three scrambler motocross bikes on stands. His hours biking over the local slag heaps on his granddad's 125cc Yamaha were flooding back. He could hear heavy feet pound the firm ground some distance behind. Why had they spared him and not Walter?

Clearly not last in the line, Danny thought, whatever that meant.

The gunman had a clear shot. Danny had even run in a straight line. Was it because he'd headed towards the kids, or was he worth more alive?

He leapt on to the leather saddle and stamped on the stand, firing the ignition. He turned the throttle on the handlebar. The warm motor growled.

He revved up and sped away, leaving a dust cloud behind. He anxiously glanced over a shoulder and could see the henchman close in on one of the other bikes. The kids had backed away, probably silenced by shock.

He turned and sped for the embankment, hoping it was steep enough to slow the pursuer who was anchored by an extra six stone of muscle and fat. Danny had found another way to turn his size into an advantage.

Hearing Walter call this the railway embankment, Danny had a good idea what lay beyond. He hovered over the saddle, allowing him more leg room to shift his weight forward to prevent it flipping back. He pulled on the handlebar and the front wheel came off the ground. He turned the throttle full on and shifted down the gears. He met the foot of the slope at full speed and hoped momentum would carry them up and over. As they made the ascent, the motor whined like a chainsaw under his ten stone. He was thankful Salamanca possessed the class to lump bigger weights.

Just before cresting the rise, he pulled on the brake and spun to look back down, see if the other bike had buckled under the henchman's heft. He'd already ditched the bike and was clambering up in pursuit on heavy feet.

Danny turned and looked down the other side of the ridge. He spotted a tear in the chicken-wire fence guarding the track, probably made by kids on a dare. He knew it was a way out. Another quick glance back and he could see the henchman halfway up the slope, breathing heavy, his reddening face still shaded by a baseball cap and sunglasses.

Danny sat back in the saddle and delicately turned the throttle. He couldn't help but skid this way and that as he slalomed a steep dirt track to the bottom, losing traction on the powdery surface. He was helped by a balance finely tuned from years of being perched on horses careering towards fences. He assessed the gap, just big enough for Danny and his bike. The wire was warped and buckled as if blown apart by an explosion. He ducked theatrically as he squeezed under the sharp barbs of the ripped mesh to avoid tearing strips in his scalp.

The henchman slid and tumbled down the slope. Danny stood up and looked both ways along the railway track, still straddling the purring bike. The henchman was now trying to make the hole big enough to slip through.

Not keen to hang fire, Danny sat low on the leather saddle and skidded away, firing a fountain of crushed stone the way of his pursuer. He bunny-hopped onto the track, which he knew would lead him into Cardiff Central. He knew a train could come from either direction and his arms were tensed to react.

'They were right, you're fucking mental,' cried after him. He looked back and saw a pistol trained on him.

There was a teeth-chattering rumble, like a tribal drumbeat, as the wheels ran over the wooden sleepers of the track. He looked back again. The henchman was limping back up the embankment, still dusting himself down as he climbed. Danny could hear and feel the rumble increase, it was like an earthquake. But Cardiff wasn't on a fault-line. Feeling he'd lost them for the time being, he was about to stop and turn back. When a two-carriage passenger train appeared from the bend, his arms and legs felt like they'd been anaesthetised. He was desperate not to ditch the bike, least of all to risk derailing the oncoming train possibly full of people. Instead he turned the throttle.

Danny could now see the contorted features of the driver and his free arm waving. He kept his head down, sure that this would go on some report and when they'd discover the body of Walter lying in the ditch, he'd then be prime suspect.

The screech of brakes was hurting his eardrums as he sped head on. Now fast enough to clear the metal track, he edged closer to the left steel rail and sat back in the saddle to shift the centre of gravity on to the rear wheel. Arms and legs slightly bent, he gripped the bike tightly with his hands and thighs as he pulled a wheelie. With all remaining strength, he'd jumped over the rail and having steered sharply was soon separated from the bike. He felt the push of warm air from the blurry train rushing by. Salamanca's fall in the Summer Plate came as flashbacks as he rolled to land softly in a pillow of long grass growing around the base of the fencing the other side. He lay there until the sky stopped spinning and heart felt like it had returned from his neck to his chest. He could still hear the train's brakes. It now was out of sight but not out of mind. He had to get away before he felt the wrath of the driver and blast of sirens.

He wanted to Ctrl-Alt-Del a backlog of thoughts. What are the risks in returning the bike? Those kids would already have called the police. Perhaps he could somehow talk his way out of this, explain that he was merely a witness. Apart from the gang, perhaps no one had got a good look at his face. The kids were too engrossed in tag rugby to spot Danny until he was away and gone with the bike. Maybe they'd give a description of the pursuer instead. The train driver would've been more concerned with the brakes. He decided to clear the scene and hope they had nothing on him. And too right, Danny thought, he'd done nothing wrong intentionally. The only guilt he felt was the fact he'd unwittingly put Walter in the firing line.

He pulled himself from the tangle of long grass and lifted himself over the fencing. He sprinted down a path and over waste ground. Entering a housing estate, he looked down to see what state his clothes were in. He brushed away grass and dust from his jeans and t-shirt. He could see the supermarket where Walter had told him the water jump had once been. Considering the track was failing, he could see why they sold the land.

By the time he'd reached Grangetown and then the River Taff, his face had dried and his pulse had settled. Wanting to be placed in the city centre, he strolled nonchalantly under as many cameras as possible. When the adrenalin had also run dry, he felt a hollow emptiness inside, one of remorse and some guilt. Although they'd only briefly met, Danny felt grateful to have known Walter, however fleetingly, and he wasn't sure he'd ever fully get over what he'd witnessed in the park.

Why the hell didn't they finish both of them off? They had ample opportunity, Danny was a sitting duck on that bench.

137

Although the secret he was supposed to know had put him in danger, he suspected it saved him this time. But his only link with that long-forgotten time had gone in the curl of a trigger finger.

Danny removed the piece of paper ripped from Walter's bookies' diary. Fred Myrtle. He doubted the centenarian would remember anything useful, if anything at all, but more concerning was the possibility *they* would also follow him to his Ely address. He wasn't as convinced as Walter that he should visit a man on borrowed time; he'd already lived through the winter of his life and was on to spring second time around. The stress may prove too much.

CHAPTER 15

EVEN AT THE YARD, Danny needed to escape.

Sara was no longer receptive. He felt like a stranger in his own home.

That sickly image of Walter slipping off the bench to rest in a growing pool of his own blood kept replaying in his mind, again and again.

It was far too early for a finger of whisky and Salamanca had already blown hard from a circuit of the estate at first light, so he once again sought solace in retired grey Silver Belle roughed out in the lower field. The veteran mare was a pet, friend and therapist all wrapped into one. He found her nipping contently at the grass. When she heard the crackle of feed from a tilted bag squeezed under Danny's arm into her metal food trough, she instinctively walked over. She was a shadow of her racing days but there was still plenty of life behind those ebony eyes. He pinched her grey ears as she devoured the grain and seeds.

'You'll be a teenager next year, girl.'

Despite money being a constant worry, he'd rather starve than cut back on Silver Belle's keep. She had enabled him to find the deposit on this place. Although her career was cruelly cut short after knocking a joint, she owed him nothing more than to suffer his rants and sob stories. He came here to clear his head. It saved money on hiring a shrink. She never used to walk away, even when Danny was boring himself.

'Sara's getting worse,' Danny said. 'Hope it's just a dip, as it won't be long before I'll crack.'

Silver Belle's mottled grey head, grown whiter with age, briefly emerged from the trough, probably to get some air.

Danny leant forward and rested his forearms and chin on the top rung of the fence. 'I dunno, Silvy, these are strange days indeed. I told you about that bloody painting last time. I laughed about Ralph saying it was cursed, I'm not laughing anymore. Don't go straying up near those woods. If you ask me, something terrible, unspeakable happened in them, years back. And what about this – Cardiff had a bloody racetrack and not one of the gaff tracks out in the sticks, it was the business, you'd have loved it. What I'd give for the same now! Imagine it, Silvy, owners would come flocking to have horses based a few miles from Ely races, would save on the crippling travel costs if nothing else.'

The mare lifted her head again. Danny continued, 'There's fresh water to wash it down. Lucky you, I've been on pasta bake meals for one this past week, if I see another bloody rigatoni…' Danny's fingers drummed the bar of the fence. 'Megan's been great mind, an absolute angel, this place would've gone under if I hadn't taken the risk on her. Hell, I'd have gone under. And she's only nineteen, but she's matured so much in the months she's been here. She's sure to make some man very lucky one day. Let's hope it turns out better than my marriage, eh, Silvy.'

Danny fished in his pocket and showed her the medal he'd found. She snaffled and slavered over the metal but soon lost interest, preferring to satisfy her belly.

'Turns out I'm not exactly lord of the manor, too. Samuel House is no more. I'll take you up there soon, all that's left is a great stone thing.' Danny looked over his shoulder. 'And I'm being hunted. Well, they're not after me, but the triptych. Don't know what the fuss is about, wouldn't hang the bloody thing in the barn, even if it *is* a racing scene. And what the hell was the secret Philip tried to bury?' Danny bolted upright. That's it! He recalled Walter seeing Philip carrying a rifle and a shovel that night. 'The bastard only went and buried it. Whatever the hell *it* is!' Absently he ran a hand down Silver Belle's face. 'Serial killers stick to their home patch, something about familiarity with their own surroundings, right, Silvy? And if he'd buried

140

something, he'd more likely know the lie of this land than any other.'

Given where he'd unearthed the war medal, the foundations of the old Samuel House was as good a place to start than any. Perhaps there would be a cluster of shallow burials. Was that the secret – a stash of war memorabilia?

Danny couldn't rest and said goodbye.

He rolled back the steel doors of the barn behind the stable block. Inside was piled high with all imaginings of heavy machinery gathering dust and rust, scrap wood and metal, black sheeting used to cover the landing and take-off sides of the practice fences during winter and pesticide containers, kept away from bags of feed. Messier than my digs at Lambourn, Danny thought.

The smell of oil caught the back of his throat as he grabbed a pickaxe and a spade resting against a grass cutter.

He paced upslope, tool in each hand. He then stood atop the ridge and drank in the splendour of the panoramic views. His breath was taken away by a freshening gust, as pure as mineral water, and the twisting U-shaped valley below, a sumptuous emerald carpet lit up by the morning sun, bruised by the shadows of clouds scudding across the open sky. He swore he'd never get tired of that sight. How green was *my* valley?

He panned from the brown brushstroke of Samuel House Mark II, across to the woodlands, then a meandering brook the other side of the ridge and to the valleys beyond.

Danny cranked up the weighty pickaxe behind his head and, winging from the shoulder, came down hard, a jolting ping of iron on stone. The judder shook his bones and made his fingers tingle, like a static shock. For a few breaths, his arms and fingers then felt numb, as if he'd got white finger syndrome, like his father had suffered, yet never got the chance to claim for, after years drilling down the pit.

Staring down at the pinpricks he'd made in the stone slab, he suspected he'd done himself more damage. He swung again and again. He leant back, hands pressing the small of his back. If Philip Samuel had buried it here, he was welcome to it.

Danny was about to come down hard again when mid-swing he saw a figure appear over the ridge. He mentally sighed. He'd told Megan to only get him if it was serious. She cut quite a sight, braless under the yard's t-shirt. Her tousled hair also bounced as she ran. But he couldn't make out why she was running, cheeks flushed as she slowed some fifty paces away. She cupped her hands and shouted, 'It's Sara.' Her shrill voice ripped the hillside.

'Oh, what now?' Danny muttered and then shouted back, 'Coming.'

'She's … it's hard to say, acting odd?'

Danny felt like saying, 'And?'

He dropped the pickaxe and, seeing Megan begin to run back to Samuel House without waiting for him, he also quickened. What could be so urgent?

When he'd caught Megan up, she added, 'She's in the kitchen.'

Danny slammed the kitchen door. First he saw a galaxy of white pills on the table and then Sara with head buried in her hands.

A million questions seemed to flood Danny's mind but they all pared down to, 'What?'

Sara looked up. Her eyeliner had run in charcoal lines.

'Tell me this was some accident, or a cry for help,' Danny said as he swept the pills from the table into his palms.

She shook her head.

'No?' Danny fumed. 'You selfish bitch! Leave Jack motherless, was that the plan? If you're that fucking miserable here, just leave. There's the door. I can survive. My god, I'll positively thrive without you eating away at me but don't you *dare* choose this – the easy way out.'

'I wouldn't!' she blurted, as if Danny had shocked her from whatever place she was. 'I'd never want that.'

'I'll call a doctor.'

'Don't!'

'What do you want then?

'Time,' she said, 'and space.'

'I can't move out,' he said, 'I wouldn't just be quitting my home if I did.'

'I'll go,' she responded calmly, almost as if premeditated. That wasn't a decision to be taken lightly, Danny reckoned, not on the spur of the moment. Had it had long been in her thoughts and wishes?

'Where?'

'Anywhere but here. My parents probably, though you won't know. I don't want you calling, visiting, texting, nothing. Clear?'

'This seems a bit–' Danny said. 'Is it being stuck up here, trapped in these walls with only a toddler to chat to? Because, like I've always said, I'm willing to move back to Cardiff, if that's what has made you like this. I know you barely get a chance to meet your friends and go out. And I'm always on the go, either in the yard or at a track.' She didn't reply, not even a twitch. 'Well?'

'Work with me not against me,' Sara pleaded.

'That's rich coming from you.'

'Let's not start again.'

'Why were you crying?' Danny asked. 'Are you sad for our marriage or is it self-pity?'

She stormed from the room and less than a minute later, he heard the front door and then an engine rev away.

He couldn't help feeling that was the sound of his marriage fading. Suddenly the house felt a degree cooler and quieter. Something occurred to him as he sat there stewing in silence. He bounded up the stairs and burst into the master bedroom. He checked the cupboards. Some of her dresses and best tops had gone – the fancy ones she'd worn to Royal Ascot on a hen party once – but she'd left her jeans and pyjamas and tracksuit pants. He looked out on to the drive her Renault was still there, so was his Golf. Was she off on holiday? He rang Valley Cabs – the firm they always called on nights out before Jack arrived – and asked as a 'concerned relative' whether a taxi had turned up at Samuel House. There wasn't even a booking.

She'd left her purse and, more significantly, her debit and credit cards. Everything would be on her parents, he guessed.

He returned downstairs and had that finger of whisky he said he wouldn't. It soon turned into a hand's worth. Megan poked her head around the door.

'What?' Danny snapped.

Megan opened her mouth but nothing came out.

'Why did you leave her with these?'

'She pushed me away.'

Danny asked, 'She didn't hurt you?'

'It's okay, not the first time it's happened, lived in Merthyr for a decade.'

'Really sorry, Megan, don't know what she's playing at,' Danny said. 'You don't need this.'

'Neither do you,' Megan replied. 'Seriously, forget it. I'm more concerned about her. I had come down to say Jack's in his room, playing. Made sure he didn't see or hear a thing.'

'Thanks,' Danny said and shut his eyes. 'What have I done?'

'You haven't done anything,' Megan said.

'Shouldn't I be saying that?' Danny said. 'I shouldn't have snapped at you. You were the only rational person around I could have a go at.' Some colour returned to her soft cheeks. 'Go home, Megan, I'll sort it. You've already gone beyond the call of duty for one day. Just promise me one thing.'

'What?'

'Pretend this never happened,' Danny said. 'Don't think I'd cope if this got out.'

Head still down, he hadn't noticed her approach. She rested her hand on his shoulder, already tight from swinging the pickaxe 'I wouldn't dream of it. Are you sure? I can stay if that's what you want.'

'Go,' Danny said. 'And thanks.'

'Hope–' she then stopped, as if her internal editor kicked in.

Danny nodded. 'I know.'

He hadn't realised just how bad things had got. The whisky had kicked in. He felt drowsy. Perhaps an afternoon nap might make things look better. When he saw 'Two Can Play your Game' daubed in red lipstick on the mirror of the bathroom cabinet, he knew sleep was no longer an option.

He returned to the kitchen and stabbed the wrapping of a microwavable chicken tikka masala found at the back of the freezer. The diet would have to wait. He sat and flicked between the two channels dedicated to horse racing.

But for all the male pride and bachelor comforts in the world, the home suddenly felt more like a house, an empty, lifeless, soulless place. Danny hoped the break would help find the old Sara – the one he married. He put his knife and fork down. Suddenly his appetite for food and racing had gone, he listened to the silence until he could take no more.

He flicked on Sara's Adele CD in the Blu-ray machine. He couldn't listen to happy music right now. But when that voice came from the speakers, singing about loss and heartbreak, it proved too much. He didn't want to sulk around the house when jobs needed doing. There was a part of him that was relieved. Sara could recuperate. He'd fill the freezer with her favourite dessert, strawberry ripple, and help Jack make a Welcome Home banner for her return, make her know how Danny felt about her, in the best way he could find. He felt awkward, cringeworthy, showing his emotions in front of others, even Sara. Perhaps she was right, he was emotionally crippled and would prefer to say anything that really mattered through a ventriloquist's dummy, as if some level of detachment would make it easier. A psychiatrist's fantasy, he'd once called him. He'd responded with, 'I'm a bloke, what do you expect?'

Although he had no plans for becoming a new man, whatever that meant, he was determined to change and try not to store up his problems and feelings.

145

Late afternoon, Danny was returning from collecting the pickaxe from the other side of the ridge when he saw a stranger appear from the kitchen door. It was as if Danny's eyes were telling him one thing and his brain another. It took a while for them to agree. The stranger was Rhys. A brutal crop had left his blond surfer's hair as short as greengrocer's grass.

'Christ, Rhys, barber lost money on one of yours did he?'

'Barber? What is this, *Life On Mars*?' Rhys asked. 'It's a hair stylist these days, grandpa. Any case, it's what I asked for: new look, streamlined, sleek,' he added, running a hand over his scalp.

'Grandpa?!' Danny said.' I'm the third youngest trainer in the country.'

'What Wales?'

'You've only got a decade on me.'

'And always will.'

'Suppose it cuts down on air drag,' Danny said and smiled. 'And you needed that cushion stuffing.'

Rhys snapped, 'Had enough grief in the weighing room. It's no shorter than yours.'

'Probably lost half a pound too,' Danny said. 'I guess that's why you rarely see a jockey with a beard. Mind, most probably can't grow one.' Rhys looked away.

It's then Danny was struck by a thought. 'You're not being sick because of a reason but for a reason.'

'What reason?'

'You've not been sick and lost your hair because you're ill or stressed and have no choice, it's your choice all right.'

'Doesn't matter how light I am, still have to carry the allotted weight in the racecard or I'll get chucked out by the stewards. Nice try Danny, but time to move on quietly.'

'Like Lance, I now know.'

'Lance knew nothing, that's why I sacked him; I've got more contacts than him. Enough about business – how's the marriage?'

Danny studied Rhys. Was that a cruel dig or genuine concern? He said flatly, 'Fine.'

146

Having changed the subject like that, Danny suspected Rhys had picked up some of Franco's diversionary tactics. *Diversionary tactics!* That's why Franco was at the track.

When he first burst on the scene as a tender yet talented teen, Rhys had brushed off the pats on the back and taken the plaudits as the current 'bright young thing' with humility. Yet it never occurred to him that there was always the next bright young thing ready to take his place. The hype machine never stalls. And now, six stuttering campaigns down the line, Rhys' frustrations were manifesting themselves in mood swings, lack of interest and, most worrying of all for Danny at least, cheating on an unimaginable scale, lured by the instant and plentiful rewards of the dark side in their sport.

Now he was not so bright or young anymore and, crucially, still to realise that potential.

Rhys had fallen from grace. This rising star had faded and was now among the scores of journeyman jockeys scratching around to eke out a living. Danny knew money was tight for them; he was one once. There was a time when Danny had felt a fraud for bagging a retainer like Rhys for his small valleys yard but that guilt had long gone.

Rhys turned and headed towards the stables.

'It's Franco,' Danny said, following. 'He made you shave it off.'

'Why the hell would he?'

Danny pursed his lips.

Rhys slid the bolt from Turnabouts door and entered. 'I don't take orders.'

'You make an exception for that lowlife.'

'He's done all right for himself,' Rhys said. 'Thriving business, you ought to ask for advice.'

'Turds always rise to the top,' Danny said.

'Don't go all preachy on me, got a thing about high horses haven't you,' Rhys raged. 'If we're starting, you're no Mother Teresa. Just remember one thing – if you ever feel the urge to ease

147

your conscience.' He emerged from checking Turnabout and shut the stable door. 'You'd better keep these bolted.'

'Get out of my sight,' Danny said.

'For good,' Rhys said and grinned, seemingly content he'd got the final word.

Danny hated confrontation and had been left feeling unsettled. An uncomfortable sense that something was so wrong, it would never right itself.

Again he felt the need to drop in on a trusted confidante. It was a balmy summer evening for a change as he spotted Silver Belle lying on her side in the lower field, basking in the sunlight. Danny filled the trough hooked to the fence and then, with his fleece sleeve, buffed the plaque showing her name and roll of honour alongside. He then left her in peace. Unburdening his worries could wait for another day.

He returned to the stables and did a quick headcount before entering the kitchen of Samuel House to a waft of sweet-smelling bacon sizzling away on the hob of the bottle green Aga.

'You've got the day off,' Danny said.

'And I couldn't enjoy it knowing you were in such a state,' Megan said. 'Thought you needed a treat.'

'It's not right you spending so much time at the yard,' Danny said. 'Haven't you got friends to see, Facebook pages to update?'

Megan pressed the bacon against the pan. 'I'm not a kid.'

'That's not what I meant,' Danny said. 'Just think you should be seeing people more your own age.'

'I like it here,' Megan said. 'Danny?'

'I can't do pay rises.'

'It's not that,' Megan said, still busying herself with the fry-up. 'What it is … you know I said about my parents and well, how it's getting me down, well I've had an idea, that is, if you agree-'

She turned to see Danny scribbling on a yellow post-it note. He slapped it on the fridge door. He then studied the note. 'Sorry, what were you saying?'

148

There was the sizzle of bacon and then she replied, 'Doesn't matter, nothing important. Milk reminder is it?'

Danny read the note: 'the winner is where our fortune lies.' What the hell did Herbie mean by that? Stating the bleeding obvious if you ask me, he thought.

Megan dabbed the bacon with kitchen roll and said, 'Could be the motto of the yard.'

'It has to be more,' Danny explained. 'Those were the last words from a father to son. Just seems too obvious, it's hardly going to be the horse finishing ninth is where our fortune lies.' Given the much smaller horse population, he bet they didn't have many double-figure fields back then anyhow. There were only eight in the painting and the winner was rubbed out. His thoughts began to fragment and dart in different directions. 'That's it!'

'What?' Megan said. 'Your bacon's butty's going to get cold.'

'Herbie wasn't glancing at Ralph on the landing when he said those words.'

'You've lost me.'

'It was the painting,' Danny said, already removing the boards from under the sink. 'Hung on the landing.'

'Can't this wait, Danny?' Megan said and picked up the plate. 'You'll get dust on these.'

Danny was now rooting in the crate he'd taken down from the attic. He kept removing racecards and dropping them to slap the tiles, until he found the one printed in 1936. He checked the number of runners for that year's renewal of the Cardiff Open Steeplechase. His excitement grew when he saw eight had lined up. On the racecard, beside the race, there was a list of previous winners, including jockeys and trainers and, most importantly, the number of runners. He could see over the last ten years, 1936 was the only year with eight runners. On the racecard for the '36 renewal, Herbie had even gone to the trouble of inking each runner's finishing position next to its name.

'Is this what you do for entertainment when I go home?' she asked.

Danny briefly looked up. 'What?'

She was now chewing on the butty. 'Shame to waste it.' Her shoulders briefly touched her blonde curls.

'Be my guest,' Danny said distantly. 'Have we got any vinegar?'

'I don't know, it's your kitchen. Vinegar? Each to their own I guess.'

'Not on that,' Danny said, pointing at her plate. He rooted in the cupboards until he found an old Sarson's bottle. Danny ignored the right panel alone as all that remained of the lead pairing of horse and jockey was a square of board.

Instead he wetted some kitchen roll with the vinegar and began to dab the thick and cracked oil paint depicting silks worn by the other seven jockeys. He went through the runners starting with the two stragglers on the left panel and jotted down the colours on another post-it. The runner in eighth and last wore a yellow body, red cap. The seventh was dark blue with white sash. He went through the others. He then compared them with the colour descriptions printed in the racecard. One by one, he could put a line through the matching descriptions of the silks. When he'd gone through all seven runners on the painting, he checked what colours the leader on the right panel had worn. Green and yellow hoops. Sammy's Date. He went to check for the '38 racecard. In the list of previous winners, it wasn't Sammy's Date that won but The Whistler. Michael Johns had presented Philip Samuel with a gift showing a race which his wonder-mare had won. That made sense, if it was a peace offering.

Danny stood back and saw Megan grinning. 'What have I done now?'

Megan replied, 'I love the way you scrunch up your nose and run your hand over your head when you're thinking.' She then mimicked him.

150

The silk colours in the painting and the racecard had matched but the finishing order didn't. He went back to the jockey in eighth on the painting in vivid red and yellow. On the racecard, Herbie had noted: *third - finished well.* He checked the fourth in the painting. It went on to finish last in the race. Herbie noted: *eighth – weakened late on.* He recalled Ralph telling him 1936 was the last big race The Whistler had won for his grandfather. Her colours were brown with a blue cap. In the painting, she was racing in fifth. Herbie said: 'Quickened to get up.' Her jockey had clearly bided his time on the first circuit with a view to challenging late on.

'This could be massive, Megan,' Danny explained. He felt he could trust her like no one else in the yard, even Sara. 'Herbie's wife came close to finding the secret held by the triptych.'

'Where did she go wrong?'

'She was on the right track as she'd wiped out what she thought was the winner – Sammy's Date. Here in the lead,' Danny said, he pointed at the right panel. 'But these horses were passing the finish line for the first time. There was another lap to go, so this wasn't the finishing order of the race.'

'Why does that matter?' she said, plopping the dish to soak in the sink bowl.

'They weren't after the painting.' His fingers skated over the rippled and cracked surface of the thick oils. 'But the secrets that lay beneath.'

'Who are they?' Megan asked.

'I need to get some solvent from the barn.'

'You're not making any sense, Danny.'

'The secret they're willing to kill for lies beneath that paint. Herbie's wife got the wrong horse. No wonder she was met by blank board,' Danny said. 'It's this one she should've gone for.' His finger pressed against the jockey in brown and blue, positioned a few strides after the fence. 'The Whistler. Philip Samuel's mare won it. No surprise Johns commissioned a

151

painting where his horse was still ahead of Samuel's winner. Competitive to the bitter end, Walter had said.'

'But what do you hope to find behind The Whistler?'

'I don't know.' Danny recalled the final words of Herbie to his son Walter that fateful night. 'But I'm sure as hell going to find out.'

He came back from the barn with a glass bottle of solvent in his hand.

He began to rub at the paint, tentatively at first, like on a scratch card, afraid to destroy the potential fortune beneath. He massaged in a circular motion, frequently topping up on solvent. Soon the turps had gone to work and he found the paint peeling off in chunks, until he'd reached the tanned underlying hue of the wooden board. He felt like he'd struck oil, as he softly wiped away the primer and stared wide-eyed at the panel. He ran another hand over his scalp.

'What is it Danny?'

'Nothing.'

'Don't be like that. I might be able to help.'

'No, there's nothing - just wood, brown fucking wood.'

He turned it over and checked the back. Perhaps it was like the paper revealing a new pin number, only visible shining light through the reverse. Still nothing. 'Can't believe it.' He kept going back to inspect the panel. Perhaps it was a decoy to put Michael Johns off the scent. He didn't know what to think now. None of it made any sense.

That night, Danny felt like an early night and accepted Megan's offer to sleep over to help with Jack and the horses first thing. He got the spare room ready.

When first light came, Danny felt refreshed by an uninterrupted night. He led one of the young hurdlers Miss Cue to the schooling ring. When he crested the rise he stood by the pen of wood chippings containing poles stacked on tyres. He glanced down at Silver Belle, it turned into a stare. He tied Miss Cue's reins to the white railing of the schooling ring and ran to the lower field but it wasn't only gravity pulling him down that slope. His grey mare was still lying prostrate on the ground, precisely where he'd left her last evening. 'No, please no!'

Danny's heart thumped his ribs as he cleared the fence with daylight to spare. The food trough was still full. She would've finished that off by now, Danny feared. It was the first time in his life he wished the grey veteran was ill, the lesser of two evils.

Danny slowed. He didn't want to face it. Her black eyes were open, yet dull and lifeless. He tried to lift up her head but her neck was stiff. 'No,' he whined and began to rock slowly. When he knew nothing could be done, he sat there silently stroking her mottled neck though knowing she now felt nothing. 'Not now, old girl. Why now?'

He wasn't aware how long he'd been there but it was enough for Megan to miss him. 'Danny, what's happened?'

Danny blinked his wet eyes and turned to see Megan stood by the food trough, holding Jack's hand. 'Take Jack up,' Danny croaked. 'I won't be long.'

The intruder's word echoed inside his head, 'Salamanca will be next.'

Danny stood and speed dialled his vet, Jim Targett.

CHAPTER 16

DANNY WAS AWOKEN by Jack chattering to himself in his cot in the corner. The room was dark. Just when he was dropping off again the bedside phone chimed. Danny picked it up, rubbing his eyes.

'I've done the autopsy on Silver Belle'. It was Jim.

'What time is?' Danny asked with a predawn grunt.

'Seven-twenty, thought you'd be up.'

'Sure those curtains were made for the Blitz.' Danny knew something was up and was merely stalling the bad news. His vet wouldn't have called, particularly at this hour, unless he'd found something.

'More significantly, I have the toxicology report here.'

'Go on,' Danny said, not really wanting him to go on.

'It wasn't a bout of colic as we had first suspected, seeing as she'd been sick,' Jim said enthusiastically, living his job. 'But blood tests reveal poison, five times the lethal level.'

The intruder was now Danny's prime suspect but he needed more. 'Was it something she ate, plants or weeds or even her feed?'

'Anything is potentially toxic if the dose is high enough. Yet poisoning in horses is thankfully uncommon, Danny,' Jim said. 'But when it occurs, it can have devastating and profound consequences, as we've seen here. It wasn't anything natural.'

'What then?' Danny said and then swallowed, now sat up.

'Have you put any rodenticide about the place?'

'It's a staple,' Danny said.

'But is it safely locked away?'

'It's in the barn somewhere,' Danny said. 'Well away from the horses, if that's what you're thinking, including Silver Belle down in the lower field. And yeah, there's a lock.'

'Please check if it's still *somewhere* in the barn, and get back to me urgently.' Jim's tone had gone from friendly to serious.

'I'm careful, if that's what you're having a pop at.'

'No one is having a pop at anyone. I just have to find out what happened, so I can complete the findings in my report, you understand. I'll get back to you.'

He knew any sniff of malpractice or cruelty to horses would tar the reputation of Samuel House for years to come and rightly so. Many of the owners treat their horses like pets, and he'd soon have plenty of boxes to fill if this got out.

Danny pressed the phone off, and wrestled a t-shirt and sweatpants on. He got the key from the kitchen but needn't have bothered. He could see the barn door was swinging loose on the morning breeze. He quickly checked on Salamanca, who was stood calmly in box one.

The barn lock had been broken. Danny peered in. There were an assortment of products for killing fungi, insects, slugs and snails, even birds. But there was a gap where the can of rat poison had been. He kicked the grass cutter. Knowing the damage these pesticides could do in the wrong hands, he'd fastidiously kept them safely locked up. He was being set up. Franco had become conspicuous by his absence.

Had he come here to threaten Danny, spotted easy target Silver Belle together with the plaque listing her achievements and saw a shortcut to hurt her proud owner? Using stuff from the yard made it look like an inside job. He then recalled Rhys' advice to keep the horses bolted up. Danny knew Rhys wasn't a horseman in the truest sense. Horses were his vehicle to make money, nothing more. Like a taxi driver and his cab. Even if Rhys was following orders, would he stoop that low?

CHAPTER 17

WITH THE ORANGE GLOW of summer fading fast, Danny grew to notice and appreciate the positive impact Megan was having, not only on the horses in the stable block but also on Jack in Samuel House. So much so, the sleepovers in the guest room became ever more frequent in lieu of looking after Jack when Danny couldn't afford to divide his attention from saving the business.

Increasingly she'd felt the walls closing in on her at home, so he suggested it was only sensible for her to move in. Her parents helped her pack and waved her off. She also helped keep his mind off his broken marriage and the death of Silver Belle.

You never truly know someone until you live with them. He knew Megan was cute and bright as a button and was a hard worker. But he didn't know she was obsessed with dancing. That was the first thing he'd discovered, helping her carry in a guest room's worth of dance dresses, both Latin and ballroom, that needed storing somewhere. He held up a frilly pink frock and said, 'I'll keep this in my closet, shall I?'

'You into that sort of thing,' she smiled. 'Horses for courses I guess.'

'Funny,' Danny said. 'Well?'

'Good,' she said. 'As long as I've got permission to go into your room, there's midweek practice in the evenings. It's a good laugh. Some of us go to the pub after. You could join us, if you like.'

'The amount you work, you can come and go as you please. You've got the keys to Samuel House,' Danny said. He picked up another frilly number, daffodil yellow this one. 'You're no novice then.'

'Third in Glamorgan Seniors' Championship in group Latin and second in ballroom, aced my cha-cha,' she said.

'Don't tell me there are trophies as well.'

'I've left them with my Mam and Dad,' she said. 'Don't panic, there'll be room to breathe. I might have to train you up as it happens, just in case my partner twists an ankle. You can be my super sub.'

Danny gave her a look. 'The last time I hit the floor was the first dance of my wedding.'

Megan looked away, as if to say, 'awkward.'

'Scariest part of the day for me,' Danny added. He recalled sobering up with eighty eyes staring at them, isolated and spotlighted in the middle of the floor. Rhythm suddenly became a foreign language. It was the part of the day he'd dreaded, along with the speeches.

He carried on relieving his Golf of her stuff. 'But I'll warn you, we're running low on fake tan and sequins.'

Megan laughed and play-punched Danny's arm. 'It's not like that anymore.'

Initially he wasn't sure it would work but those doubts soon faded quicker than the evening light. They made a brilliant team and couldn't believe he'd even bothered trialling her. Most significantly there was no longer the tension for Jack to pick up on. Even Sara seemed a lot more contented, almost happy when occasionally making the effort to come back 'just to see Jack'. She didn't seem bothered to learn Megan was a live-in worker.

He asked when she'd be ready to come back but she never answered.

Jack also seemed more than content with the new arrangement, lapping up the love and affection he craved, not only from Danny but also Megan.

Danny could see the stable-lass blossom before his eyes. Sometimes he couldn't help thinking how much better his life

157

would've turned out if he'd met someone kind, considerate and loving like her before he'd got back with Sara years ago. When he caught the scent of Megan's perfume, left after her showering each morning, it gave him a kick, like an injection of caffeine, as if it was some kind of trigger. Ever since she'd moved in, he could suddenly face the days, even relish them. His religious mother always banged on about 'everything happens for a reason.' He always thought that was said to help people cope with bad situations, like the slow breakdown of a marriage. But maybe she was right; he wouldn't have Jack without Sara.

He found himself with the triptych back on the table. He was fascinated yet infuriated by it in equal parts. He tried shutting his eyes. Perhaps if he listened to his internal thoughts, blocking out all other distractions, the answers would come. They didn't. He had to find out its secret before he was paid another visit and, with Jack, Salamanca and Megan on site, he feared that day. As those after it grew impatient, he felt the stakes would now be raised.

Perhaps the numbers on each of the saddlecloths meant something, Danny thought, more out of desperation than confidence. Could it be a code?

He'd already worked out which number was on which runner and jotted them down in the order the horses appeared in the triptych: one, seven, three, five, four, eight, two and six. He picked up his mobile and then dialled in that series of numbers. He wasn't surprise when a woman's voice came back down the line, 'The number you have dialled has not been recognised, please hang up and try again.'

He rested the phone on the kitchen table and went to the van to fetch the A-Z of the British Isles. He thumbed the pages. It soon occurred to him the coordinates contained letters as well. In any case, Cardiff's landscape and landmarks would have changed out of all recognition over the eighty years since this was painted. Just need to look at Trelai Park to see that, he thought, it didn't even exist when Ely racetrack was open back in the Thirties.

This was hopeless, he reckoned, and went to load the three runners entered up for races at a minor Ludlow meeting. Kelly called in sick again, along with Rhys. He suspected it was no coincidence. So Megan filled in at the last moment.

Danny couldn't get Walter's final words out of his head: 'They've come for me.' He feared he'd be saying the same any time soon.

CHAPTER 18

SITTING LIKE A CHRYSALIS in a sleeping bag, Danny drifting in and out of a light sleep in front of the TV screen in his office. When his eyes were open, they wouldn't leave screens one and twenty-nine, showing Salamanca's box and the driveway respectively. Every half-hour or so, he'd wake with a fright. He was always the same whenever away from his own bed, like the alien environment of a hotel room.

When his bladder could hold out no longer, he unzipped from the warmth of the cocoon. Not to wake anyone, he instinctively pissed on the ceramic sides of the bowl. Only then did he realise Sara and Jack were at her parents for a few days. He agreed to give Megan a break. She had looked tired in recent days. He didn't want her to think she was being used. She hadn't said anything but she wouldn't anyway. He respected her more than she did herself.

Standing wearily under the lovely hot shower, he tried to convince himself the triptych wasn't cursed. But with Sara gone, Silver Belle dead, Rhys on the make, Franco prowling and final demands outnumbering winners, he wasn't doing a good job of it. Perhaps Ralph was right: 'That bloody painting will ruin you, like it had the Samuels.'

He pressed his wrinkly palms and fingertips against the shiny white tiles and saw the ghost of a haunted face staring back. He then screwed his eyes up and let the steaming water flow over the contours of his face. It tickled and soothed before finding its way to the shower tray. Whether this was an attempt to cleanse himsel of his troubles, he couldn't say, but for the most blissful of moments, he felt protected, safe in a womb-like stasis. He knew i couldn't last but still wanted to put off the inevitable. *Just five more seconds.*

He then turned the gushing showerhead on the tiled wall to keep the air and his feet warm as he grabbed the towel slung over the shower door. He towelled down.

When quickly feeling his balls for a lump, he froze, unable to move, as if dropped into an icy lake. All of the worries in Danny's world had been pushed aside by the bathroom door or, more like, the fist that was banging the other side.

This time Danny was quicker to realise he was home alone. His damp legs felt heavy.

The knock came again. The handle turned.

Danny scanned the room. His toothbrush was the sharpest thing there. He couldn't remember locking the door, but surely that was something he'd do without thinking.

The door remained shut. He breathed out.

Again the handle rattled.

Perhaps they'd go away. Give up.

Quickly as the saliva was drained from his mouth, his face became coated in fresh and instant sweat.

He stepped silently from the shower unit and pushed opened the frosted bathroom window, peering out on to the driveway below. A rush of morning air felt cold to his naked body. He could only see his Golf. No visitors. No intruders.

He waited in silence for what seemed like an hour though was probably just twenty minutes. He hadn't heard anything since the rattle. No creaks, or bangs, or whispers from the hallway, no engine's revving away.

He started to question whether that had just happened, or was he slowly losing it. He stared in the mirror and, spotting fine lines around his eyes, messaged in some of Sara's moisturiser. More to take his mind of things than vanity, he reasoned.

He hadn't seen or heard from Stony for a while and wanted to catch up.

Raymond Barton's 1.23 PM.

Danny said, 'Thought I'd find you here.'

Stony swivelled on the bookies' stool and, having seen Danny's face, removed reading glasses. 'What is it?'

'Oh nothing.'

'Something's up,' Stony said, 'say.'

'Gonna sound a bit of a lush, a soppy git,' Danny said, 'but it's Silver Belle. She's ... well, she's gone.'

'Dead?' Stony had now folded a copy of *The Sun*. 'When?'

'Not long ago.'

Stony sighed. 'Sorry pal, really I am. Know how much she meant to you.'

'Didn't think it would affect me this bad, part and parcel of the job, you know. But with Silvy dying, well, a part of me has too. She gave me my big break and what really hurts, she didn't get the retirement she deserved.'

'Quantity maybe, but not quality,' Stony reasoned. 'You couldn't have done any more.'

'It's just, if you looked into those sharp eyes of hers, I swear you could see her heart. She'd become more than just a pet and stable hack. She was part of the family. Jack adored her, what am I gonna tell him?'

'He won't understand, lad. Just tell him she's happily playing in another field someplace.'

'I know what you're really thinking,' Danny said. 'Shit happens, deal with it.'

Stony grabbed Danny's arm. 'You need to be strong, for the rest of your family and the yard. Never mind thick skin, you need armour plating to stay sane in your game but isn't that the case with everything? Isn't life about loss?'

'The times she'd put up with me rambling on about grumpy owners, soaring bills, unlucky losers. Those big ears of hers would lap it up and she wouldn't answer back, judge or walk away, perhaps in the hope of a mint, but still. She was intelligent, not like Salamanca bless him; he's got stronger muscles than his brain.'

'Just think of those times,' Stony said. 'And the races you won together. You couldn't have done any more, lad, so don't beat yourself up. Perhaps put a plaque on the fence where she used to wait for you.'

'Deserves more than a plaque but no chance I can afford a statue.'

'You'll think of something.'

'Guess so,' Danny said. 'You're wasted in here, ever thought about counselling.'

'Too expensive.'

'Not to take it but to dish it out.'

'I'll stick to the gee-gees, ta,' Stony said. 'Now, I feel there's a pint with my name on it.'

'Might join you in a bit. Think it'll pay for me to hang back here for a while.' He'd spotted Rhys and Franco chatting in the far corner.

Franco looked across and nodded. Danny mirrored the acknowledgement and was about to go over, make sure their next coup hadn't got Rawlings written by it. He had barely taken the first step when he felt something press the small of his back. 'You're leaving, now.' Danny pictured the pistol in his back. He didn't think they would do anything, not in the bookies but after Walter had been slain in the park, it appeared they were capable of anything. Had Franco nodded towards Danny or somewhere beyond?

Once stepping on to Greyfriars Road, Danny was ushered round the corner and several paces down a shady side alley. Danny's skull smacked the brickwork. He found himself pinned here. There were two of them, round heads and shoulders. They dwarfed Danny. He looked up at those impenetrable shades. 'Gunman got a day off.'

'Shut it!' the heavy hissed between the gaps in his gritted teeth. Danny felt the tickle of spittle on his cheek. Danny felt fleshy hands grip the leather of his collar. 'We've come to finish the job.' The smell of an old dog basket blew over him.

'I've got nothing.'

'Why don't ya grow a set?' the burly man growled. Danny felt a strong hand grab his crotch and groaned. 'Unlike those mangy geldings you train.'

'Checked for lumps this morning, thanks all the same.'

'We leave with nothing,' the man said. 'You will be dead within the week.'

Danny was now close enough to see the open pores and crow's feet of the heavy's face. He also noticed a white sliver of scar which ran from his fleshy cheekbone to the greying bristles of his jawline. Danny guessed he'd been emotionally scarred somewhere along the line too.

'Didn't you hear me,' Danny said. 'I've got nothing – no triptych, no secret.' He knew it wouldn't pay to put up a fight this time, not with this knuckle-scraping messenger. It would only serve to poke the hornet's nest. He had no idea how many others worked for his boss and wasn't in a hurry to find out. Glancing up, he'd discovered a safer way to wriggle out of this.

'We've got an audience.' He looked up again at a nest of CCTV cameras. 'Say hello to police HQ.' He'd spotted them having a drunken piss down here years ago.

'You'll think Walter got off lightly when I've finished with you. I'll fucking stripe ya to kingdom come, clear?' Danny felt the pressure on his balls ease. Even the attacker's parting play-slaps made Danny's flushed cheeks sting. 'Remember, a week.'

Danny made for the comparative haven of Barton's bookies. Franco and Rhys had gone. Franco was probably seeing what secrets his heavies had squeezed from Danny. They'd be disappointed.

'Thought you'd gone for a pint,' Danny asked Stony.

'It was like the *Marie Celeste* there. Even the barman was changing a barrel.'

Danny sighed and needed the sideboard as a support.

'You ill?' Stony asked.

'Why, do I look it?'

'A bit pasty like and you're shaking more than a first date.'

'Just been given a week to live.'

'Jesus.' Stony dropped the red disposable pen. 'This is a joke, right?'

Danny shook his head. It helped release some tension from his neck.

'Your doctor told you this?'

'Doubt he's a doctor,' Danny said. 'Two of them, got jumped in the alley. They're coming back for me.'

'They'll have to get past me first,' Stony said, 'dabbled in martial arts in my younger days, sure it's like riding a bike.'

'Riding a bike,' Danny said, 'is that one of your t'ai chi moves?'

'I'm serious.'

'Don't reckon throwing shapes like rolling the ball or painting the wall would send this lot packing.'

'Got a brown belt in karate as a junior,' Stony said.

'You'll have matching pants if you meet this mob. And you'd need the other hip doing,' Danny said. 'Thanks for the back-up, though.'

'Anytime,' Stony said. 'You know that.'

Danny delayed leaving. 'I may need a favour at some point.'

'Name it and I'm there.'

Back at Samuel House that evening, more to take his mind off everything, he watched endless clips showing past renewals of the Velka Pardubicka on the internet, meticulously counting paces

165

between the various obstacles, sometimes taking a step off each time to allow for Salamanca's raking stride.

He watched the jockeys and how they rode into each of the steeplechase fences, railed hedges, ditches, water features, stone walls, drops and embankments. It was a crash course and he knew it might not be enough to beat some vastly experienced jockeys who knew every blade of grass on their own patch. The Velka Pardubicka was the most searching test of jumping and stamina on mainland Europe, if not in the world. Danny regretted seeing the poor record of British and Irish raiders, unaccustomed to the parkland style of the Pardubice racetrack.

Danny looked over. Megan was standing in the doorway. She was dressed in a slinky black number. 'Off out?'

'Can you come to the lounge for a sec?'

Danny froze the clip mid-race and followed her.

He entered the lounge and noticed the glass coffee table had been dragged to a corner and the rug had been rolled up. She'd clearly added a log to the fire and stoked it. 'My partner, along with half the dance class, is down with the flu.'

Danny looked at the space she'd created and said, 'No way. I didn't promise anything.'

'Don't be scared. It's only me. I just want to see your moves.'

Danny dropped on the couch and said, 'That's my signature move, it's called the slouch.'

'On your feet, twinkle toes,' Megan said, pulling Danny up by the hand. Danny sighed. He felt his heart quicken. This was a fear he hadn't reckoned on facing tonight. She pulled him close. She positioned her feet offset from each other. 'This is so our feet can step between the others. Don't want you getting sore knees for Salamanca.'

'Step? You didn't say anything about any step.'

She appeared to have selective hearing and just extended his arm out, her left hand in his right, palm on palm in an upper-hand clasp. She pushed his fingers and thumb together. 'And *don't* point your fingers.'

166

'Of course not, that would be crazy.'

'Are you taking this seriously?' she asked. 'I'm the trainer now.'

Danny wouldn't let on but he was secretly enjoying this.

'Do the same with your right hand, cupped against my back. And my left hand and forearm rests here, like so.' She placed her hand near the seam of his t-shirt sleeve. Her hand came up and moved his head to look over her right shoulder. 'There's your head-placement done.' She looked him up and down. 'You have a good top-line.'

'Thanks, I think. Glad to discover I'm not a one-trick pony.'

'Now for the final connection, our bodies.' Danny swallowed. 'Ready? I won't bite.'

'Go on then.' For a moment, he was lost in her sky-blue eyes, lit by the crackling fire. Her waterfall of curls shone like spun gold. 'I'm doing this for Art, mind.'

Now her teeth were also lit by the fire. 'The right side of your front, connects with me likes so. And when the music starts, we don't want gapping.'

'Perish the thought,' Danny said.

'Serious face now and back straight as you can.'

They held the pose and Danny didn't want to release. It had been a long time since he felt the embrace of a woman.

'And that's more or less the classic ballroom hold,' she said. 'Not hard, was it?'

She took a step back and pressed the DVD remote. Some classical music came on. 'I'll keep it low, not to wake Jack.'

When they'd got back into hold, she added, 'Place your left foot over there.' Her hand touched his inner thigh. 'And your right there.' Danny moved. 'On the floor Danny, not my foot.'

He then overstepped, losing balance and stumbling forward, taking her with him, collapsing to the floor in a heap, a tangle of limbs. Danny laughed. For once this wasn't from nerves or politeness to placate an owner. He couldn't stop it.

167

She wiped a tear from her eye and caught her breath, 'Let's leave it there for lesson one.'

'What mark do I get?'

'Definite promise there, we'll make a dancer out of you yet.'

Danny had lived up to his own expectations but it came as a light relief from recent events. Their eyes met and her smile then went. He looked away. He suddenly couldn't think of what to say. He just got up. 'Think Jack needs a bath.'

She remained on the floor. 'He's changed and is out for the count. You know that.'

'Megan, you don't have to be doing all this, just for free board.'

'Don't have to, I want to, there's a big difference.'

He suspected she wanted to not only teach him to dance but also how to have fun again. He couldn't deny he was already looking forward to lesson two.

His mobile vibrated against his leg. He read the text sent from Ralph: 'Let's catch up! Say ten at Micky's Casino 2moro. OK?'

'What is it?' she asked, jumping up.

'Not sure, I'll have to find out.'

CHAPTER 19

DANNY WAS SITTING at the bar, glancing at his watch. These places didn't have clocks, make the customers to lose track of time. As he'd yet to order a refill, the barman was giving him the evil eye.

10.16 PM. Perhaps there'd been a crash on the M4, he thought.

Danny hated being late for things almost as much as he hated others being late. He flinched as a hand slid over his shoulder. Ralph came into view, 'Seems like you need another of those.'

'It's my round,' Danny said.

'Nonsense,' Ralph said, 'I suggested this, my treat.'

They moved to the gambling tables and sat at one of a dozen roulette wheels. Ralph had taken out what looked to be around a monkey's worth in chips. Danny watched Ralph stack up the ten blue chips, each worth fifty pounds. Drink was enough of a vice for one night, he thought. He knew as soon as he'd taste that betting rush again, he'd be hooked in the spin of the wheel.

Ralph said, 'Have the unwelcome visits stopped?'

'Got one the other day,' Danny said. 'Feared I wouldn't have any more kids, told them again I didn't have it. Seems they don't take no for an answer.'

Ralph dropped a blue chip on the red diamond of the playing matt. 'Test the water.'

As the silver ball flew around the polished mahogany, Danny asked, 'Did The Whistler outlive her master?'

Ralph waited for the ball to eventually drop. 'Red eleven.' He smiled. 'She vanished that very night. Locals in the village were said to have seen Philip ride off into the mist on his prize mare.'

The croupier pushed two chips over. The rest were funnelled noisily down a chute beneath his waistcoat.

'Reckon that's just a legend?'

'I wouldn't know for sure, it's all hearsay, happened before my time.'

Ralph now piled up four chips and pushed them on to red again.

'You don't like to hedge your bets,' Danny said.

'Life's about risks, you should know that more than most.'

'No more bets, please,' the croupier said and set the ball in motion again. 'Red nineteen.'

Ralph's stack was up to fifteen. 'Perhaps you getting rid of the triptych helped lift the Samuel curse.'

'That's the thing, I haven't,' Danny said. 'And I came close to discovering its secret.'

'Tell me,' Ralph said. 'What was Philip's plan?'

'Close I said,' Danny said. 'I was wrong.'

Ralph then waved a twenty at one of the waitresses wearing a low-cut blouse and high skirt which appeared to be proprietor Micky's uniform of preference. They weaved between the many gambling tables, balancing trays.

'Why don't you try the poker tables? Clearly got luck on your side.'

'I cannot bluff, my right eye twitches, it's a Samuel thing and probably what did for Philip in that fateful card game. Another?'

'I shouldn't,' Danny said. But he felt like shit and if he wasn't going to bet, he needed some form of fix. 'Just one more.'

The waitress came back with a tray, balancing two large whiskies.

Danny picked his up and said, 'Don't you want yours?'

'They're both for you.'

'Are you trying to get me drunk? You won't get anything out of me. I don't get loose lips when I'm pissed.'

Ralph smiled. 'In vino veritas.'

'What?'

'In wine there is truth.'

'Well, not from me there isn't,' Danny snapped.

'It's a night out, Danny, relax. When was the last time you let your hair down?'

Danny stared someplace beyond the green felt of the playing surface. He couldn't recall the last time he'd enjoyed a night out and it wasn't because the alcohol had now joined his bloodstream.

Ralph glanced at Danny and asked, 'What's worrying you?'

'Some fella called Franco, owns an ice cream parlour up in the valleys. Anything worth nicking and he's there, especially if he sniffs others are after it. Thinks he's an Italian stallion, too. Got a face you could punch.'

'Does he work alone?'

'There's a gang,' Danny said. 'They left a calling card.' He turned to show Ralph the brown-yellow smudge on his neck where he'd been pinned to the wall.

'Chin-chin,' Ralph said and sipped at the golden liquid.

Danny downed his and then grimaced. 'You're a bad influence, Ralph.'

'What are you worried about, that you'll say too much about Franco?'

'Already learnt that lesson,' Danny slurred. 'He is what he is.'

'And what's that?'

'A crook.'

'Any other recent new blood to the yard it might be?'

'Took a new kid on, Megan,' Danny said. 'But she's harmless, not so sure any more about Rhys and Kelly, both seem to be more interested in each other than the yard. Shame, had high hopes for them.'

The waitresses were now offering choice of salmon or cheese sandwiches on the house, though Danny knew customers would be paying for it by other means. The drinks also kept coming. When he struggled to say, 'Salamanca' he knew he'd had more than enough.

'Where are you off?' Ralph asked, glancing at his watch. 'The night is young.'

'The yard won't run itself.'

When he stepped out into the freshening night air, he was glad to see the sky was still black. He crouched to tie his laces and almost fell over. He hadn't realised how drunk he was.

He tried to walk a straight line back down Queen Street in search of the taxi rank when, passing a dark side-alley, he heard something.

'Daniel,' came from nowhere. 'We need to talk.'

Danny squinted into darkness. He edged to the mouth of the alley. 'What?' Nothing came back. Danny came closer. 'Who is it?'

'Daniel.'

'I'm Daniel,' Daniel slurred. This was getting really weird, he thought, and then laughed. His nose for danger had been blocked by the booze.

'Come here, closer.'

Danny did as he was told. An arm shot from the dark and yanked him from Queen Street. He was quietly dragged several yards in darkness.

'Your week is up,' the attacker growled and then hacked up a ball of phlegm which then ran down Danny's face.

Danny slurred, 'It's been two days since that hired help of yours put the heat on.'

'Arrivederci, Danny,' the attacker said coolly.

The booze and the dark meant Danny didn't see or react to a swift upper cut, but he certainly felt it, knuckles connecting sweetly with his jaw. Danny couldn't help but stagger back and, i it wasn't for the support of the cold brickwork, his legs would've buckled.

He saw double, then red. He suspected this slugger had a longer reach and pushed forward. A primal grunt came out as he grabbed the attacker and held him in a tight clinch to tie up his opponent's hands, stop any hooks coming his way.

In close, Danny's clenched fists fired in a string of body blows, again and again, over and over, like a piston, venting his fury with short, sharp jabs on this punch bag.

'Want some, do you?' Danny raged. A fist for Silver Belle, a knee in for Walter, an elbow for his marriage, another for the sleepless nights after the break-in; each blow striking the attacker's firm torso with venom. Even when there were no more groans, Danny couldn't stop. He felt a warm trickle over his sore knuckles. He wasn't sure whether it was his blood or the attacker's. He didn't tug off the balaclava, not wishing to see a human face, allow his conscience to pull any punches. This was a piece of meat.

Disappointingly he knew letting go would end it, as he suspected the attacker would flop to the ground, like a stuffed dummy. But he'd now run out of energy. When he let the attacker fall, he delivered a tired boot into the torso, and whispered, 'One for the road, Franco.'

But he felt no better, revenge wasn't sweet, just exhausting. As the red mist lifted, he now faced a sobering reality. *What have I done?*

He was breathing heavily. His heart drummed like a coke addict, yet he was fighting fit. Panic had taken over. He crouched over the body and pressed his palm against the chest of the attacker. It felt hard, as if already stiffening from rigor mortis. Can't feel a pulse, he thought, where's the bloody pulse? Not one heartbeat when he expected it to be firing like his own.

I was provoked, Danny reasoned, I didn't mean to kill him and it wasn't premeditated – six years max. Who planted the first punch? Who was it? Think, Danny, think! It was all a blur. He'd never spark a fight. It had to be this … body. Danny didn't want to talk, or even think, of the dead. But he'd made an almighty mess, and it needed cleaning up. He looked over at a builder's skip nearby, dimly lit by the glow of the fire exit for a first-floor Italian restaurant. It would have to do for now. Conceal the body and return before sun-up with a better idea. He recited the

173

wartime motto: Keep Calm and Carry On. Yet he was close to breaking down.

Danny suddenly rushed a hand to his mouth, mindful of the DNA about to spew over the crime scene. He wiped blood on his jacket and dragged the limp body of the man he'd floored to the skip.

From the flickering yellow embers of light from Queen Street, Danny made out a stack of wooden pallets. Despite the brain cramps, he reckoned the veg man and his van would search them out come first light. He'd use the rubble already in the skip to hide the body. Nobody would have any need for broken concrete. Perhaps they'd empty the skip and his problems would also go away. But that was a gamble and, unlike the adrenalin he'd relish from a punt on the horses, this was a bad rush; more a feeling of dread, with no anticipation or hope. There was nothing good going to come of this.

Body now under a thin layer of rubble, he made for the taxi rank but thought better of it. Instead, he began the long walk back to Rhymney. He thought he'd jog the flat bits and walk the hilly stretches over Caerphilly Mountain.

Passing a bus stop near the Student Union building on Park Place, Danny heard his name again. Should he stop or ignore it? 'Danny!'

He quickly turned and saw Ralph chasing after him. He was waving a wallet.

What does he want? He then realised the benefit of this potential alibi if Franco's death ever got to court. 'You dropped this, outside the casino.'

'Must've fallen out tying my laces,' Danny said and then couldn't stop a shiver. 'That's really good of you, Ralph.'

'You okay?' Ralph asked. Danny turned slightly and looked away. 'Is that blood on your face?'

'Oh nothing,' Danny said. He shifted his weight between feet. 'I fell, bloody laces.'

Please go home, he thought. He felt they both heard him swallow.

'Oh, right,' Ralph said. 'We must do this again sometime.'

'Yeah, perhaps,' Danny said and glanced at his watch.

Ralph appeared to pick up on the less than subtle signals. 'Well, good night, then. And don't take any grief off that Franco.'

Danny laughed nervously before continuing on the long trek home.

Two hours later he walked through the cool, dark hallway of Samuel House. He glanced at the mirror. His mouth felt like a sewer. He stuck his furry tongue out and inspected his pink eyes.

Even look like a murderer, he thought.

CHAPTER 20

THERE APPEARED to be no end to the night as Danny wrestled with the sheets and his conscience. It was half-three and dark. The crackly rain on the slate roof wasn't helping. Danny swore he'd turned over about fifty times and he'd almost run dry of nervous exhaustion. The guilt was too much. He felt like his head was going to burst.

Again he'd allowed his imaginings to run wild. He could see the blowflies now swarming over the body, alerting forensics in their crackly body suits, snapping latex gloves.

Yet it wasn't the potential repercussions making Danny squirm most, but the chilling fact he'd killed a man. And every fibre of his body knew that it wasn't self-defence, even if that was the plea he'd enter if they tracked him down. He may have been set upon and the first telling blows were planted by the masked man but he retaliated and kept going, long after the attacker had turned victim.

It was no good. He had to do something before the point of no return at sunrise. He thought about the best place to bury the body, somewhere more permanent than the skip. Suddenly he'd found the courage to beat his fear of those woods. If the clearing had been left untouched for seventy years, then there was a good chance he'd be dead before anyone discovered the body. He couldn't believe he was now thinking like a cold, calculated killer. He had to keep convincing himself that he was the one set upon and that the masked attacker had it coming, a case of provocation.

Danny couldn't risk a court deciding his fate, particularly given that his previous form as a housebreaker could now be taken into account. And he suspected a jury would see the thirteenth knee in the belly was going someway beyond self-defence.

If only he hadn't taken refuge in the casino, he thought, as he booted up and pulled down a ski hat. He checked the time. 3.46 AM. If he was going to do this, he needed to work quickly and decisively. Dithering would no doubt leave him beside the body red-handed in broad daylight.

He quietly fished for a torch from the Welsh dresser hogging the hallway and went to the barn for a spade.

He ran upslope. The exercise helped sharpen his mind and burn off some of the pent-up nervous energy.

As he paced deeper and deeper into the woods, Danny needed the torch. He pointed the beam at the jutting trunk he'd tied Salamanca to. He swallowed. He then turned the beam ahead. The light was absorbed by the densely packed trunks and overgrown weeds.

Danny followed the path of destruction he'd left from his last visit here. He couldn't quite believe he was doing this. It made him feel sick. His legs felt weak but they kept going. There was a job to do. He began to dig a hole in the clearing big enough to hold a body folded up.

It would be a shallow grave; there was no time for anything deeper. He glanced up. The stars were slowly dissolving into the navy sky.

He quickly retraced his path, ditched the spade and grabbed some loose tarpaulin in the barn. He rolled the black sheeting and fired up the Golf. He was no longer convinced he'd get there before the traders and shopkeepers arrived to unlock and set up. He now knew he should've collected the body first. What's wrong with me, he thought, think straight, man. He parked up safely away from the alley but not far enough to warrant a tense walk with a roll of plastic under one arm.

Suspecting he'd be tracked by the CCTV cameras looking over the main roads and Queen Street, he chose a more circuitous route. On the back of wheelie bins he leapt a series of walls, while hurriedly rushing across backyards, shop rears and loading bays. He now knew how Salamanca felt.

He dropped into the alley. A feeling of dread filled his body, returning to the murder scene while the emotions were still painfully raw.

He looked down the alley which separated a newsagent's and a baguette shop fronting onto Queen Street. He knew a fire exit for that restaurant on the ground floor would remain shut at this hour. He stared through the heavy gloom. All appeared quiet. Passing the mouth of the alley some thirty yards away, he saw the odd drunk staggering from an all-nighter at one of the clubs. Probably wouldn't notice a dead body if they fell over one.

He rushed forward and cleared the smaller rocks from the skip. He couldn't see any sign of the body, not even a foot sticking out.

Had the builders dumped more debris? He checked his wrist. 4.48 AM. No builder in the land would be up this early. He kept lifting more rubble. He'd left it here, he was certain. He then swung round, fearing a police cordon. Had they already removed the body and it was now a murder scene? There was nothing. No indication that the fight had even taken place. No blood on the paving or wall. Everything was shiny wet. Perhaps a shower had already washed the evidence away. All except what looked like a small piece of card on the floor.

Danny picked it up and turned it over. It was the passport photo of Megan. Must've have come out in the fight, Danny thought. He was now thankful he'd returned to the scene as this would've led police to Samuel House before the day was out. Her phone number pencilled on the back could still be made out. But he could less easily explain the absence of the body he'd flopped into the skip only hours earlier.

Like the haunting image in the woods, the intruder who came and went without a trace, the triptych and now this, Danny could no longer determine what was real. He recalled Megan saying,

'Pressure does funny things to the mind.' It seems like she was wise beyond her years.

'Do you need a hand there, mate?'

Danny's arse tightened.

Standing a dozen or so yards away was a scruffy man wearing an overall, a flannel shirt and jeans. He was struggling with a pallet of bananas.

Danny didn't know what to say.

'You looking for something?' the man added. 'Doubt you'll find anything in there.'

Danny found some words, 'Not anymore.'

The grocer said. 'I tried dumping some boxes the other day, builders went ballistic.'

'I'll buy a banana,' Danny said and offered the man a quid. His appetite was suddenly returning.

'On the house, kiddo,' the man said. 'Haven't opened the till. Just remember me next time you're passing.'

Danny didn't say the same back to him. The man disappeared through an open door in his veg van.

Danny smiled; suddenly the world didn't seem quite so bad.

CHAPTER 21

DANNY STILL HAD a fuzzy head as he sponged down
Salamanca, anything to forget the night before. Rule one: act like
normal to others, just in case the police came asking questions. He
was about to towel the gelding down when he sensed a presence
somewhere behind. He turned and was met by Franco, gone was
the moustache.

'Jesus, Franco,' Danny said and smiled, patting his chest.

'You look like you've seen a ghost.'

'Quite possibly,' Danny said. How the hell did he survive the
night? There was no pulse. For once he was glad to see that
swarthy Italian face. He was alive. Was he seeking revenge?
'Can't you whistle or wear cowbells?'

'You're funny,' Franco said but he didn't look amused.
'That's what I like about you.' Danny's sponge splashed into the
bucket. 'But I wouldn't like to be around you when the laughter
dies.'

'What's that supposed to mean?' Danny asked but got no
answer. 'Spare us the character assassination. Least I'm not
mugging everyone in sight, including punters.'

Franco came closer. 'Turnabout was a good thing, no law
against me making it pay.'

'It had a favourite's chance but it was no good thing. Yet that
didn't stop you putting thirty big ones down. And don't go
denying it, I was there.'

'Now that's a shame. You see, when I heard from my trusted
source that you were sticking this,' Franco said, fingertips
pinching Danny's nose, 'into places where it's not wanted, I

didn't believe it for one second, until now. Looks like I'll keep watching you.'

Trusted source? I'll kill Rhys, Danny thought, where the hell did his loyalties lie? Franco was obviously paying better.

'I'm not afraid to go to the BHA.'

'Where's your evidence?' Franco said. 'I've never been charged, or even arrested for theft or fixing races. You'll be laughed out of there.'

'You're good, I'll give you that, but one day the Franco Empire will come crashing down.'

'Daniel, are you threatening me?'

'If you like,' Danny said. He knew he'd already stepped over that line he'd been warned about by Mike at the Miners' Club and suspected it was now too late to retreat.

'Then you leave me no option,' Franco said. 'Il mio amico.'

'What?' Danny asked. 'What was that?'

Sara appeared on the scene.

Danny said, 'You normally call before turning up.'

'I live here, too,' she said.

Could've fooled me, Danny thought. 'I can't even be around either of you. And Franco, there's a camera in Salamanca's box, if you get any ideas.'

Franco smiled.

Fucker, Danny thought. He was mostly angry at himself, letting this creep get under his skin. He stormed into the kitchen, pulled the panels from the back of the sink cavity and ripped off the black plastic. He flung open the kitchen door. Franco was still there chatting with Sara.

'Here!' Danny said. 'Take the fucking thing.' He dropped the panels with a slap on the paving by Franco's leather shoes, spotless and fancy. 'And here's the secret, there is no fucking secret. So no more visits here, day or night. Arrive-fucking-derci.'

Danny stormed off. He heard Franco say, 'Why did you stay with him for so long?'

181

Danny looked back in anger but Franco was now busy lifting the panels.

Having defaced each of the runners, Danny was confident Franco wouldn't find anything, let alone a fortune.

Retreating to the quiet of his office, Danny couldn't stop his mobile from shaking as he dialled the number torn from Walter's diary. Fred Myrtle.

Friday 12.23 PM, October 12th.

Danny turned into Racecourse Drive and then into number twenty-three.

The finger-shake had returned as he thumbed the doorbell. His jacket was bloated with a selection of the Ely racecourse memorabilia from the crate.

He was about to turn when he heard the clink of the door chain. Slowly the door disappeared. He was faced by an old man, hunched over and attached to a machine on a stand and wheels. His skin was like crumpled tracing paper. He raised his head enough to check Danny over.

'Fred Myrtle.'

'Shoes off, please.' His voice was strained, almost as if it had been stretched, diluted by time. 'House rules, as my Molly used to say.'

While Fred struggled to wheel his bleeping contraption into the sitting room, Danny had time to read: *Celebrating the Golden Wedding Anniversary of Fred and Molly Myrtle.* It was beneath a large colour studio photo of the happy couple hung from the wall. He slipped off his shoes and threaded the safety chain on the door. He wanted a few minutes head start if someone had a key.

Danny wiped his brow. It was a mild day, yet it felt like the heating was on full. He suspected Fred wouldn't know where the dial was. The air was musty, almost cloying, and he wanted to open a window. The red floral carpet was fraying at the edges and almost felt alive with dust mites beneath his socks. It's as if he'd pressed blow instead of suck when last giving the vacuum cleaner a workout. The walls and Artex ceiling were a washy yellow, possibly from cigarette smoke. The only sound was the loud ticking of a wooden mantel clock, alongside two birthday cards showing the Queen, one wearing blue, the other yellow. There was an empty space in the corner where the walls were virgin white.

'Got yourself some fancy machinery there, Fred,' Danny said, tracking tubes from his cuffs up to an LCD screen on the stand now chair-side, glowing vital numbers and a heart line.

'Have to wheel the bloody thing everywhere,' Fred said and then coughed. 'Follows me like a bad smell.'

Danny wondered whether in the year 2080 he would be able to recall what he was getting up to now. He guessed not but perhaps that wouldn't be such a bad thing.

He couldn't help feeling honoured and somewhat humbled to be in the same room as a jockey from that golden era. Fred didn't really need to say anything; there was a presence about him. Just knowing this decrepit man had once done battle with the greats like Golden Miller and the twenty-six times champion jockey Sir Gordon Richards was enough.

A kind of reverential awe came over Danny, like when he looked up in Canterbury Cathedral on a school trip once. Knowing so much had gone on, mostly untold, in its rich and colourful past.

'Would you like a cuppa, lad?' Fred said, scratching his bulbous nose. His hand shook as much as his chin. 'Think there's biscuits too.' His voice was not only weak but also a few octaves higher than Danny, as if his larynx had wizened to the size of a young girl's.

'That would be lovely, I'm parched,' Danny said, and stood before Fred had chance to even think about rocking himself from that padded tall-back chair. 'Kitchen's through there?' Courtesy

183

had made Danny ask that rhetorical question. He could see the kettle from here.

Fred didn't respond anyhow, probably hadn't heard, milky eyes now staring ahead like a blind man. So Danny left. The kitchen clearly hadn't been touched since the Seventies. Danny went along opening the Formica cupboards. No sign of any teabags and Danny was living in Cardiff when those chocolate digestives were safe to eat.

He gave up and returned to the lounge. He was about to make his excuses, saying he'd changed his mind about being parched, when he realised Fred's concerns lay elsewhere, 'I don't want insurance, or windows.'

'No, Fred, I'm here to talk about the track, Ely racetrack, remember?' Danny spoke loudly and clearly as if talking to a child. He felt it might come across as patronising though he suspected it was the only way.

He hoped Fred's long-term memory was better than his short.

'That's where I met Molly,' Fred said, a spark made it through those milky eyes. 'She was a waitress in the restaurant there.' He paused for a breath after every sentence. 'I used to mix with owners after the races, and when I first set eyes upon her, I knew. Well, the rest is history, as they say. The restaurant went up in smoke, along with the rest of the stands, in thirty-seven. And Molly,' he looked down and stopped, as if seeking composure, 'she passed on, fourteen years ago yesterday. Lung cancer it was, poor thing hadn't a chance.' The spark had been put out.

'Bet they were good times to be around the track, champagne guzzling parties and the rest.'

'Oh, there was money flying about back then all right,' Fred said. 'Remember the white Rolls pulling up, unpacking their fancy picnic hampers. Still it's all just memories now, doubt any of it's on film, only the odd Pathé news reel. No such thing as racing on TV back then, very few houses had one. Used to like watching the racing when I retired, mind, is that big chap still on?' Fred said. 'Can't afford a licence now.'

'It's free for the elderly, my in-laws get it.'

'Oh, right,' Fred said and looked over at the empty space. 'Where the devil did I put that telly?'

'I'll drop by with a leaflet,' Danny said. He felt a responsibility. If he didn't care, seemingly no one else would.

Perhaps the new library would have some old clips of the track, he then thought. He removed the attic photo. 'Recognise this, Fred?'

Fred leant forward, eyes squinting through thick glass. 'What is it, lad?'

Danny opened his mouth to explain it was the triptych being presented, when Fred added, 'Is it a photo?'

'Don't worry,' Danny said and carefully put it away. 'Tell me, Fred, did you ever mingle with Michael Johns after the races?'

'Sir Michael,' Fred said and sighed. 'Would have been a fool not to.'

'Why?'

'He was leading owner at the track, year on year.'

'Are you certain?'

'Of course, he took over from Philip as the top dog there.'

'Philip Samuel.'

'Yes.'

'Was there a rivalry?'

'Fierce,' Fred said, still breathy. 'Mainly Philip's doing, jealous of Michael's success, see. Remember Michael trying to bury the hatchet many times but Philip was having none of it. He was a pig to ride for by all accounts, too.'

'I met your friend Walter.'

'Oh, dear old Wally,' Fred said. 'How is he?'

Hadn't Fred been told or had he just forgotten. He didn't have a TV and there were no newspapers lying around. Danny had managed to avoid all media, until Megan in all innocence read a local article saying a badly swollen body had been fished from the

185

ditch at Trelai Park. Gus had reportedly raised the alarm. He was found yapping away on the edge of the embankment.

Danny could grimace now but not when she was reading it. 'I haven't seen him in a while either, Fred. He told me he was last in the line.'

'Last in the line for what?' Fred asked.

'That's what I need to know. Was it his family line?'

'He always worried where his house and money would go when he died, had no family left, you see. I always said: you've got years left, look at me.'

Danny could see and hear Fred was breathing heavier now. A red triangle flashed on his screen. Going by road signs, he thought, that wasn't good. 'Do you want to take a break, Fred? Can come back tomorrow if this is too much?'

'No, lad,' Fred said. 'I want to–' He sucked through the long hairs sprouting from his nostrils, trying to fill up aged lungs. '– carry on. Takes years off me, this.'

'Was Walter in any trouble?'

That distant look returned.

'Look at me, no manners,' Fred said. 'Would you like a cuppa lad? Think there's biscuits too.'

Danny reckoned that was seven minutes since the last time. 'No, ta.'

There was a loud banging on the door. Danny reacted more than Fred. He turned. 'Were you expecting anyone Fred?'

'None that I remember,' Fred said. That didn't help Danny's nerves. 'Would you do the honours, lad? Bit tied up.' Danny glanced at the machine. He recalled what happened to the last elderly man he'd chatted to about Ely racetrack. If only Sara hadn't thrown that TV remote.

'Don't worry, lad,' Fred croaked. 'All my friends are long gone.'

That didn't help either.

'It might be Walter, mind.'

'I doubt it,' Danny said. 'Thanks Fred, you're a star.'

Stood in the hallway, he was about to slink off out the back way when he saw the outline of a large hairdo through the tinted glass of the front door. Perhaps she was collecting for something and would come back. A key turned, but the door caught on the chain. When a loud clatter bounced off the tiled floor, Danny noticed the letter-box flap open. 'You've left the latch on, Fred.'

The silhouette then disappeared as she bent double, eyes now peering in. Danny backed into the lounge.

'Who is it? Open up! Fred! I'm calling the police!' came the shrilly voice.

Danny thought about fleeing out the back door, but she'd probably seen enough to ID him in a parade. He took a deep breath and then slid the safety chain on the door.

He was met by a portly woman in a hugging blue uniform. She was panting. Late forties, creased face, shadowed by a towering beehive, like a nest of vipers. 'Excuse me! You are?' she asked, brushing Danny aside. He followed her into the lounge.

'Might ask you the same thing?'

She flashed some laminated ID card hung from her neck. 'I'm Mr Myrtle's carer.'

'Are you okay, Fred, my dear?'

'He's happy for me to be here,' Danny said.

'See this,' she barked, finger pressed beneath that red triangle on the screen. 'It sends a message to my beeper. Comes on when Fred here is suffering abnormal stress, or is unduly agitated. *Happy* did you say?'

'We were only chatting,' Danny said. 'Fred welcomed me in, didn't you.'

'No need for insurance or windows, not anymore,' Fred said.

'Think you'd better leave.'

'Just one more question, Fred, about Ely racetrack.'

'Go!' she barked. 'Or I'll call the police.'

'No!' Fred said and pawed at her arm. 'What is it, lad?'

'Do you remember seeing the thirty-six Cardiff Open?'

187

'Remember, I was in it, on Sammy's Date, real dog he was, pulling my hands off on the first circuit, was clear passing the finish line.'

'But you were caught by The Whistler.'

'I was clear at the finish line on the first circuit,' Fred said and smiled. 'Always sounds better if I leave that bit off. Was caught by most of the field.'

'Did Philip or Michael ever reveal any secrets about the track?'

'I just rode there, kept my nose clean,' Fred said. 'Move on, young man. Any secrets were buried with the track in thirty-nine.'

Those words made Danny's thoughts turn upside down. Perhaps it wasn't the actual painting but the setting: Ely Racetrack. *The track holds the secret.* The winner is where our fortune lies. Lying fourth at the time, eventual winner The Whistler was positioned in the middle of the triptych, a couple of strides after the final fence of the first circuit. He'd always suspected Philip would choose familiarity, but hadn't thought of the track. No wonder he roped in groundsman Herbie that night. He'd know every inch of lush turf on that racecourse.

Fred added, 'Sorry I can't tell you more.'

'It's more than enough, cheers.' Danny turned to leave. 'And if you really *cared* for Fred, apply for a free TV licence and sort the kitchen out. Poor sod deserves better.'

'How dare you!' she said.

Danny slammed the door and paced the path. Clearing the gate, he noticed a seated figure, little more than a shadow, behind the tinted glass of a silver Vauxhall Astra parked opposite. It wouldn't normally grab his attention but his senses were up.

Although Fred Myrtle spoke as if every word was gospel, Danny needed more. He'd already checked the web for articles in the Thirties taken from *The Sporting Life* and *Sporting Chronicle* but there didn't appear to be any archives for those extinct publications.

Danny headed down St David's Way to the New Central Library. Its triangular footprint formed the corner of The Hayes and Mill Street. As he looked up at the five floors of clear and coloured glass making up the exterior walls, Danny caught the glimpse of his ghostly reflection. He looked like a haunted soul.

He'd gone to the opening here a few years back, mainly to see the Manic Street Preachers play, but had yet to venture in, he was ashamed to admit. He got the attention of a librarian on the ground floor. He asked where was the 'machine that's like a projector that could scan over old newspapers.'

The fiftyish lady looked over her steel-rimmed spectacles. 'You mean the microfilm.'

Danny nodded.

'You're not a regular here are you, dear,' she said and smiled. 'It's all on computer databases now, public computers can be found on all floors except the ground. Our Capital Collection up on the fifth may be of interest, if it's the history of Cardiff you're after.'

'Cheers,' Danny said, making a mental note to come here more often. He'd always fallen back on the excuse: there weren't enough hours in the day and, in any case, Sara read enough for the pair of them. No wonder there was now a backlog of sporting autobiographies and racing history books he kept on meaning to check out.

The escalator carried him straight to the second floor and he then climbed stairs to the fifth. It was quiet. Many would be at work and students had clearly yet to find the work groove after their lengthy summer holidays.

Danny sat down in front of one of many computers and stared at the white screen. He filled the search box with: 'Ely Racecourse.'

The results from the internal database flashed up. There were local reports on the Cardiff Open win of Philip Samuel's mare The Whistler in 1936 and the subsequent reversal at the hands of

Michael Johns' star Shadow Master the following year. There was clearly nothing here at odds with Walter's recollections.

He clicked on a link containing an embedded MP3 file showing a forty-two second film reel made by British Pathé. He watched the film, all grey and flickering, and followed the commentator whose high-pitched cut-glass accent relayed the events of the day: 'Billed as the battle of the champions and even the battle of the sexes – this is the 1936 Cardiff Open Steeplechase.'

Danny was entranced by that tiny screen within a screen. He could make out the stands and fronted by a crowd packed so tightly it was almost like a dark seething mass. He caught the briefest glimpse of the clump of oaks in the triptych.

'Oh look!' the narrator enthused. 'Sammy's Date is keen out in front, he'll regret that late on! He's poached a clear lead under young jockey Fred Myrtle as they go out on the second circuit. But what's this?! Here comes Philip Samuel's unbeaten mare The Whistler. She produces a leap Pegasus would be proud of at her favourite final fence and blows the opposition away on the run-in to repeat her win in last year's race. Is there anything that can beat her?'

Funny looking back with hindsight, Danny thought, hard to believe she didn't win another race after this. He found himself smiling. The screen went black, so he played it again. This time he pause the film as the mare asserted on the landing side of the final fence. That's where the fortune lies, Danny reckoned.

He studied the grandstand on the right and the bushes on the inside of the track. Both were perfect markers for anyone burying at the time but they were long gone.

Danny knew it would be like finding a needle in a haystack. X marked the spot where The Whistler had just emerged from the shadow of the final fence. But where the hell was X?

He returned to the front page of the database and added 'fire charlie moore' to his search. Fewer relevant results came back. All were newspaper cuttings from the days and weeks after the main grandstand had gone up in smoke and with it, any hope of a revival in the racetrack.

It soon became clear the reports were painting the cremated jockey as the perpetrator of the fire – the villain of the piece who'd started the blaze with paraffin, only to be caught out by his own 'evil and reckless actions' and got his just deserts when trapped by the faulty lock to the stewards' room. They were all told with a matter of fact tone, as if to say justice had swiftly been done, may as well have said: 'Let the bastard burn.'

His poor family, Danny thought, not only had they lost him but were getting grief from the press too. And where was any mention of Philip Samuel in all this? He'd mysteriously vanished that night. He clearly had lots of friends in very high places and questions were never asked. Perhaps some of these friends or associates helped give him shelter and safety while he lay low and let the storm blow over. But why would Philip do all this? What on earth had gone on between the two powerful owners?

He typed in Trelai Park and clicked an ordnance survey map of the area. He first noticed the shaded clump of oaks and then the map scale at the bottom left. He zoomed in so far the lines, contours and features like churches and pubs became blocky. He then zoomed back out. That gave Danny an idea. Perhaps there was a way to find that needle.

He rushed to the newsagents just around the corner from the train station. He bought a pad of tracing paper and a black marker pen. He returned to the fifth floor. The computer's screensaver had kicked in but when he wiggled the mouse the online map of the park reappeared. He then removed the racecourse map from his jacket. Danny clicked on the ruler app on his smart phone and could see the scale on the layout of the racecourse illustration was six inches per mile.

Danny turned to the screen and zoomed in to the same scale. He tore a sheet of tracing paper from the pad and set about drawing over the map of the steeplechase course in the racecard with bold black ink. The felt tip followed the inner rail and then

191

the outer. He then set about drawing the lines across the track where the eight fences, including a water jump, would have been. He shaded in the clump of oaks – the one and only marker surviving to this day – beyond the outer rail but ignored the grandstand and other features that no longer existed. He then placed the tracing sheet over the bright screen.

He could see the librarian glance over from her station but remained seated. Danny shifted the paper so that the clump of oaks he'd sketched in overlapped the wooded area on the screen. The white light from the monitor made it easy to match them up. He now had a good idea where the racetrack was positioned in terms of today's landscape.

First thing he noticed was the water jump was indeed under the supermarket. Danny felt sorry for ever doubting Walter. He needed this printing off. It was an internal database that was read-only so he couldn't save the image. Instead he emailed the image to himself. He told the librarian it was a project on local history and she seemed happy for him to print it off.

He now needed to go there but would have to call on help if he was to have any chance of finding X. He didn't want to trouble Megan again. She'd already agreed to keep Jack amused in Prague while he was off riding Salamanca. He called Stony on speed-dial.

'I need to cash in that favour,' Danny said. 'Are you free first thing tomorrow?'

'Why?'

'I'll pick you up, say six in the morning,' Danny said.

'Hang on.'

'Good.'

'Have I got a say?'

'And don't wear any of your Hawaiian shirts – we're not there to be seen.'

'Where?'

'Also charge up your phone and bring it,' Danny said and then hung up. Stony owed him more favours than he could remember and this time he wasn't going to back out with some lame excuse.

As Danny stepped on to St David's Way, he was sorely tempted by a swift pint in the red-bricked Duke of Wellington at the top of Caroline Street, known locally as chip alley for obvious reasons. Drinkers were chatting and laughing at the outside tables. He felt like joining them, washing away his troubles, but knew only too well they'd still be there in the morning and he needed to get back, prepare for this evening.

He snaked the streets, passing the castle en route to the leafy Cathedral Road. He'd parked up near the cricket ground at Sophia Gardens. Danny put his foot down.

Seeing those moving images of Ely races somehow helped make it feel more real in Danny's mind; it actually happened, not just legends and fables of a bygone era.

Training losers week in week out, Danny could relate in some degree how Philip must have felt that fateful afternoon back in thirty-seven, watching from the owners' stand or the bar the titanic duel between the top two chasers of their time in Wales, if not Britain. But he could also relate to Samuel's anguish as his great mare succumbed to Johns' newly crowned champion Shadow Master.

He knew no one stayed in this sport without having a thick skin, an ability to take a leaf out of Rudyard Kipling's book and treat those two imposters just the same.' So what the hell made Philip act like a crazed maniac? He'd given up a life of glamour, status and wealth to go on the run or into hiding. When Danny's response would be: 'I lost a horse race, get over it.'

Danny pulled up outside Samuel House. He put the kettle on. He then went to the lounge and downloaded a GPS app for his smartphone. As he blew the steam rising from his brew, he looked down at the X on the screen marking his current location at Samuel House in the Rhymney valley.

He once again placed the tracing of the racecourse over the printout of the OS map. The final fence before the finish line – the

193

one in the triptych – could once be found at ST1476 on the OS grid. He typed that reference into the newly installed GPS.

X marks the spot, he thought. He knew the fence lay diagonally across the box. But there was some margin of error and Danny didn't want to be digging up council land for any longer than he had to.

Herbie would know precisely where to bury it and then find it. Although without as many landmarks, Danny had the help of Stony and Salamanca in trying to unearth the Samuel treasure.

CHAPTER 22

6.39 AM. HE RECKONED it was light enough and there would only be a few dog walkers and joggers out enjoying the crisp morning air.

Danny plugged his phone into a lead coiling from the dashboard of the van.

'Running low?' Stony said.

'It needs charging,' Danny replied. 'Let's check yours.'

Stony handed over his scratched Pay As You Go. 'Cheap, good. Battery, full.'

'Eh!'

'Don't want it nicked.'

'And why did it need charging,' Stony asked. 'We are staying local?'

Danny shifted up the gears.

'Danny?' Stony questioned. 'Why am I getting worried?'

Danny drew up outside wrought iron gates fashioned into Trelai Park'. A few bangs coming from the back broke the silence. Danny had slowly brought Salamanca to the boil for his Czech date. He was restless.

Danny eyed Stony and then the passenger door.

'You want me to get out?' Stony asked, unclicking his cabin seatbelt.

'Yep.'

'Something I said?'

'We're here.'

'You're not going to work Salamanca in a public park, health and safety would go ballistic, and why would you? That ground has nothing on the gallops at Samuel House.'

'Shush.'

'Talking too much I know,' Stony said. 'Nerves, it is.'

Danny unplugged his smartphone, eased himself from the van and led Salamanca out too.

He then handed the reins to Stony, who whispered in the gelding's ear, 'Don't be worrying yourself, won't be getting on this time.'

Guided by the GPS on his phone, Danny walked through the gates and across the parkland, closely followed by Stony and Salamanca. It was empty, as he'd hoped. Danny glanced over at the oaks as he walked. The flashing X on the screen was slowly edging to the corner of ST1476. He stopped.

'I'll take that,' Danny said, grabbing the reins. He scanned the park and noticed they'd left orange traffic cones out from the night before. Danny handed Stony the phone. 'Don't move an inch.'

'I wasn't going to.'

'Where's your phone?'

Stony fished for it in his sheepskin jacket.

Danny sprinted over to the football fields and stacked up two cones. He struggled back with them.

'Is this a treasure hunt?' Stony asked, showing the flashing X on the screen.

'You're getting warm,' Danny said and dropped the cones. 'Except I don't know whether it's treasure I'm looking for.'

'You're something else,' Stony said and smirked. 'You really are.'

'Enough talking,' Danny said. 'We won't have the park to ourselves for long. Drop one cone here.'

Stony shook the top cone free and plonked it down where he stood.

'A typical fence is thirty-six feet long.' Danny motioned for the phone and then mounted Salamanca. 'Looking at the oaks, an this map, can you take twelve strides in that direction and then drop the other cone.'

'There better be a pint in this,' Stony sighed. 'Or better still, a share of the treasure.'

Stony counted to twelve and dropped the other cone as he was told. He called back. 'What's this show us?'

'The final fence at Ely races.'

From the triptych, he knew The Whistler had attacked midway along the fence.

Danny noticed movement in the corner of his eye. It was a male dog-walker who glanced over hopefully out of nothing more than idle curiosity.

'Can you go over there and stand just off midway between these cones and say about nine yards that way. Take the phone and as soon as Salamanca completes his third stride from the landing side of the cones, drop it. Would normally say two strides, but The Whistler was a freakishly large mare by all accounts. Same as this fella.' He patted Salamanca's neck.

'It seems a lot of trouble to bury something out here,' Stony said. 'Why not use a safe like anyone else.'

'Safes can be cracked,' Danny said. 'These people knew the track better than anyone else. And remember they had markers to guide them; all we've got are an old drawing and those trees over here. Now remember, three strides then drop, yeah?'

'Go on then,' Stony sighed and got into position. Danny cantered Salamanca half a furlong and then headed back, aiming for where Stony stood. Danny subtly pulled on the reins as he approached cutting a path midway between the cones, marking where the fence once stood. Salamanca's stride and speed shortened as The Whistler's would have some seventy years previous. As they'd flashed past the cones, he heard Stony call out, 'Three, two, one.'

Danny looked back to see Stony drop his phone to nestle in the grass. Danny reined Salamanca in and returned to the cones.

Stony asked, 'Is this it?'

'It must be,' Danny said. 'Unless they've moved those trees in the last seventy years.'

'What now, then?' Stony asked.

'Nothing, yet.'

Danny jumped off Salamanca again. He'd located Stony's phone and checked it was on. He then pressed his boot down on the screen as if stubbing a fag out, until it was lost in the deep thicket of grass, away from the threadbare football pitches and prying eyes.

'Mind now, you'll break it. Haven't got another one.'

'I'm making sure it's hidden,' Danny said. 'So it won't get nicked.'

'But you'll never find it,' Stony said.

Danny opened his mouth but then shut it when a loud, 'Oi,' echoed from the distance. Danny spun round to see a park-keeper power walking their way. Beyond the railings, in a direct line with the park-keeper, he made out a silver Vauxhall Astra. It was the same model as the one parked up opposite Fred Myrtle's house. His suspicions were turning into reality.

Danny could see the figure wore a neatly cut black uniform, mouth now masked by what looked like a mobile or a handheld radio receiver. He wasn't keen to find out. He was acutely aware this was the recent scene of a murder that he'd witnessed.

With one swift motion he'd mounted Salamanca and offered a hand to Stony. 'Quick, get on. I don't want awkward questions from that jobsworth.'

'The horse hates me,' Stony said.

'But he likes me,' Danny said, 'that'll cancel it out. Now get up.'

Danny noticed the park-keeper had slowed to a walk. Was he unfit or didn't he want to catch them?

He'd somehow hoisted up Stony and they rode double on the bare back of the strapping eight-year-old. When he grabbed that thick lush mane and pushed forward with a sharp kicked in the belly, Salamanca didn't need to be asked twice. 'Hold tight.'

Stony groaned. 'The new hip's not insured.'

They went with a brisk gallop towards the park gates, covering the ground with ease.

'Whoa, boy, steady now.'

'We clear yet?' Danny asked.

'We've lost him,' Stony said, glancing back.

They slowed to a standstill by the gate. The keeper had turned and was checking the cones, clearly content that he'd scared them off his lovely fields.

They both dismounted, Stony feelingly.

'It gets easier each time,' Danny said, glancing down at Stony's hip. 'Soon have you riding out in the mornings.'

'See what you mean, he's a tank all right.'

Danny led Salamanca through the gap in the railings and up a ramp into the back of the horse-box.

'What about my phone?' Stony asked.

'Best left there, lost in the grass.'

'But the keeper.'

'Didn't see you drop it,' Danny said. He loaded up and pulled away.

'Well?' Stony asked, still puffing.

'Well what?'

'Are you going to tell me now?'

'You'll soon find out.'

'Better be,' Stony said. 'I hate surprises.'

'What about tonight?'

Stony sighed, 'I'll check my diary.'

Danny knew Stony didn't have a diary. 'Don't say you've had enough excitement in one day. Where's the Stony who used to ride ten at two meetings in a day?'

They flashed past Cardiff Castle on the one-way system making through the city centre. He went to drop Stony off at his modest two-up two-down former miner's house on Rhymney Terrace in the Cathays area of Cardiff. It lay among a curious mix of student digs and those elderly residents who'd resisted the generous offers from house-hungry landlords fighting over prime rental areas for the university during the gold-rush of the last property boom.

Danny swerved an old man holding a carrier bag filled with clumps of torn bread, surrounded by pigeons and seagulls. As he pulled the handbrake, he looked down the narrow street, made even narrower by cars double parked. 'This is as far as I go.'

'Guessing all this isn't entirely straight, then,' Stony said.

'What made you think that?'

'You've asked me to turn up in a park at midnight, doubt it's for a spot of night gardening.'

Danny tilted his head donnishly. 'Who said midnight?'

'Glad to hear it.'

'Nearer 3.30 AM. It gives us a few hours before sunrise and less risk of drunken clubbers staggering home.'

Stony groaned.

'You wanted some excitement in your life.'

'Excitement,' Stony said, 'not jail.'

'Don't back out now,' Danny said. 'Gentleman's agreement.'

'Since when have you been a gentleman?'

Stony stepped out of the cabin of the horsebox and walked away, shaking his head and legs as he went.

Driving back to the Rhymney valleys, he had time to think back, assess the possible repercussions of returning to the scene of Walter's murder.

His phone went. Probably Stony already wanting to back out, he thought. He clicked the phone on to hands-free.

'Hello Daniel,' said a voice, filling the cabin. It was deep and gargling, like the intruder's.

Danny swallowed. 'What do you want?'

'I have a mutual friend that would like to say something,' the voice said.

There was a long pause and Danny glanced at his mobile to see if he'd been cut off. He was now driving past the county buildings and then the chocolate brown carbuncle that was the Student Union.

'Daniel?' another voice asked, thinner than crepe paper.

'Fred? Is that you?' Danny asked, though it was a rhetorical question.

His mind shot back to when he left Fred's house. He was being followed by the driver of the silver Astra. That shadowy figure was now speaking to him. And it was the same voice as the intruder. He wished he'd crossed the road and confronted him.

Danny removed the silver stopwatch from his jacket and clicked it in motion. 'Don't bother turning his place over, you'll find no secrets there.'

'Then tell me, now! Or Fred here won't be getting another card from the Queen.'

'Killing Walter did no good.'

'But this time you will be framed and blamed,' the voice rumbled. 'And there's not a single thing you can do about it.' Danny made sure he shifted up a gear noisily, lifting the clutch early. The voice added, 'If you're coming, please hurry, place you at the murder scene when the police arrive, make their job easier.'

'What is this, revenge?' Danny asked, now on North Road heading for Gabalfa roundabout. 'What have I done to you?'

'It needn't have gone this far,' the voice said.

The voice clearly had something of Danny's to leave in Fred's house, unless he was bluffing. 'They'll have nothing on me.'

The voice replied, 'If you'd only worn gloves.'

Danny cringed as he recalled touching the door handles and chain, the door frame, even Fred's chair.

'Did you have a nice time at the park?' the voice asked. *The park-keeper!* No wonder he held back that morning, probably hoping for Danny to do all the hard work and then take the prize. You clearly know it's not about the painting anymore.'

The keeper had stopped where the cone fell. Had Danny hidden Stony's mobile deep enough in the grass?

201

The fate of a frail old man was in his hands but he felt helpless. He hoped that fright hadn't already finished him off. Something then came to him.

'See Fred's support machine,' Danny said. 'There'll be a solid red triangle flashing on the screen. It tells us he's stressed.' Danny shifted up to fourth gear. 'Trouble is for you, it also tells his medical support team who are now winging there way there.'

Danny glanced at the mobile screen again.

The voice snapped, 'There's still time to finish him, leave and place you at the scene.'

Danny saw a four-way set of lights up ahead and had an idea. For once he was glad they'd just turned red. 'You may place me there but not at the right time.'

He then stamped on the accelerator pedal and kept it there. The engine roared. *Hold tight in the back!*

Danny was pushed back into the foam seat as they hurtled towards the lights still on red. Cars on the A-road crossing his path had already cleared. He hoped there was nothing else on its way. His hawkish eyes flicked from one side of the road to the other. He grimaced and held his breath as they ran the lights, bracing to be broadsided by some oil tanker. He pushed his face closer to the windscreen and felt like saying 'cheese' when there was a blinking flash from the roadside camera.

He'd cleared the other side unscathed and emptied his lungs. There were a few beeps from behind. He was more concerned for Salamanca. He picked up his mobile. 'I'll be cleared of anything you try sticking on me.'

'Why so confident?'

'I've found the perfect alibi,' Danny said. 'Reckon they got a good shot of me and it'll be timed. Worth the three points on the licence don't you think?'

Danny checked the ticking stopwatch – the call had been going just over four and a half minutes. After what he'd witnessed at the park, he couldn't bank on the voice leaving quietly and didn't want to hear that the bodies of Fred and his nurse were recovered from 23 Racecourse Drive.

'His memory is little more than seven minutes,' Danny said. 'Go now and all this will be forgotten. They'll think he's got stressed about the death of his wife. Just get out!'

The line went dead. Had he done enough to secure Fred and the carer wouldn't suffer a similar fate? He knew the voice was a cold-hearted killer but he also had a brain and was out for his own gain. What good would come from another death on his already bloody hands?

Seeing a vacant bus stop, Danny slammed the brakes and pulled over.

Fuck me! He knew Franco could plumb the depths, but this?

He'd clearly got the police in his palm and, fearless of the law, there was no longer a line to draw. Only Franco's conscience to rein him back, Danny reckoned, if there was such a thing. But had he shaken up Franco enough to make him flee? He could only hope and check the newspapers tomorrow. Then no news really would mean good news.

How did he know? Was he tracking Danny's every move? Was Rhys the mole – his eyes and ears in the yard? They were rarely seen apart these days, Danny reckoned, thick as thieves that pair. With Rhys already planning to leave the yard, there was no longer any loyalty, other than long-term friendship and that had also fallen by the wayside.

He cranked up the handbrake and vented his frustration on the dashboard. Seeing a bus in his wing-mirror, he pulled away and returned to Samuel House. He led Salamanca to the stables where Kelly and Megan were arguing loudly, again. Danny pointed at Kelly, 'You, sort "The Tank" out.'

CHAPTER 23

NIGHTFALL COULDN'T arrive soon enough. Danny pocketed a hand-knife, then flung two spades and rolled-up black plastic sheeting taken from the barn into an echoing horsebox. He then set out for Trelai Park, picking up Stony en route in Cathays.

Stony shivered. 'Nippy out.'

Danny knew it was a mild Indian summer night. 'We'll be back before you know it.'

'Where to?'

Beneath the glare of the reading light, Danny shot a knowing look. Stony pulled the passenger door shut.

The one-way system was 3 AM-quiet as they cut through Cardiff city centre. He drew up alongside the black Trelai Park gates, now padlocked shut.

His hand rested on the cabin door. He stretched his lungs and cracked some tension from his neck. After he attacked that once sacred turf, he knew there was no turning back. Before he made the move, he tried to get inside Philip's head that distant night. Why would he want to bury the goods? It's a lot of bother just to save some family silver and would it even still be there? After all, he wouldn't bury it if he hadn't planned on returning at some point. Perhaps he did and Danny was about to dig for something that was long taken. Or maybe Philip merely buried it to spite sworn enemy Michael Johns, who was expecting it as payment for a bet. Philip would surely rather anyone have his worldly goods than Johns. Perhaps that's why he uncharacteristically gifted Herbie the watch and painting. If that was the motive, Danny was confident the secret would still be there.

As he pulled the sheeting from a stall in the horsebox, he felt a weird sensation brush over him. It was like history repeating itself. Two men dressed in black turning up at Trelai Park in the dead of night, some seventy years apart. Knowing Philip and Herbie were never seen again, Danny hoped that's where the similarities would end.

Danny helped Stony over the railing, passed over two spades and the sheeting. He then pulled himself over. They paced across the patchy grass of the playing fields, lit only by the yellow hue of the distant flickering city lights.

Holding his smartphone, he dialled Stony's number. The distant tinny tune made Danny quicken. As it grew louder, he knew he was getting warmer. He could now see a faint green glow on the ground. He picked up the phone caught up in the tuft of grass and stuck the spade there.

'When will you tell me what's going on?' Stony asked.

'The phone marks the spot.'

'So this *is* some treasure hunt.'

'Except I don't know whether there is any treasure.' Danny tugged the spade from the ground and broke up the top soil. He began to dig and then looked up, 'Do you want to know a secret?'

'Yes.'

'Get shovelling then.'

Before long they were shielded by hills of earth either side of the hole.

Clunk. Danny froze, now up to his waist in the pit he'd made.

'Looks like we've struck oil,' Stony said, voice raised.

'Keep it down,' escaped Danny's dry mouth in a breathy whisper. He stopped shovelling and brushed away a gritty coating of earth. He then shone the torch on the find – some black canvas sheeting, torn and holey. Danny drew the knife from his fleece and sliced the sheeting apart.

Cautiously he dipped his hand into the black hole, fearing it was a body bag. He felt something smooth on his fingers, picked up and straightened. He flashed light over a silver jug, dusty and peppered with soil spots. The ebony base was embossed with the words: The Whistler – Cardiff Open Steeplechase Winner 1936. Trainer R. Shaw. Jockey C. Moore. Owner P. Samuel. It's hard to fathom just a year to the day Samuel was handed this big win, he might well have torched his own grandstand, killed his star jockey and a good friend and vanished into thin air.

'This isn't it.'

'Don't joke,' Stony said, swiping the jug from Danny.

'This can't be the reason why he'd just vanish, giving up everything - the estate, his beloved racetrack.'

Stony had also grabbed the torch.

Danny wiped sweat from his face and snapped, 'Careful where you point that.'

He then began to pull other heavy silver pieces from their shallow grave: plates, cups, tankards, picture frames and candlesticks.

'You're telling me all this isn't what you came for,' Stony said.

'This is merely the starters. Philip Samuel was worth more than that.'

'I'll gladly take the starters and run,' Stony said and began to bag the silver. 'Do you know the market price of silver right now?' Stony looked over but Danny was lost in the hole. 'Feel free to join me, anytime.'

'Bag it up if you like,' Danny said. 'I'm digging deeper.'

'For what?'

'If I'm right, it'll be worth it.'

'You've come here, dragged me along, looking for something but you don't know what.'

'I'll know it when I see it,' Danny said. Another blade's worth of earth flew from the hole.

'Why do you always do this?'

'What?' Danny asked between breaths.

'Look for something more, never satisfied with your lot – this lot,' Stony said and looked down at the pile of silverware lying on the plastic sheet, waiting to be hoisted up by the four corners in a hammy sack. 'Can't be that many hours till sun-up?'

'More than enough.'

As Danny pounded the cool earth with the blade, he remembered the words Herbie told his son that night. 'The winner is where our fortune lies.'

Perhaps he'd hoped his son could profit from that clandestine burial somewhere down the line.

'If they're gonna bother to bury that lot,' Stony said and flashed some light on the silver, 'why not chuck this thing you're after in with it?'

Danny glanced over the lip of the hole and said, 'Why do the royals fly the princes on separate planes? He didn't want to risk losing everything in one take. They had metal detectors back then, you know. No one in their right mind would carry on digging once they'd found the silver, they'd be thinking like you.' Danny glanced at the silver haul. 'I reckon that was their decoy.'

'No one in their right mind,' Stony replied and gave a look. A couple more showers of earth shot from the hole. 'Did he return?'

'Clearly not for the silver but that doesn't mean he didn't,' Danny said and then kept on working the spade. When the blade struck something hard and dull, Danny dropped to his knees and began pawing away at the soil, enough to get hands around the object. He pulled it from the ground like yanking a root vegetable.

'What is it?' Stony asked.

Danny's hand ran over the smooth curvy object. He flicked on the torch and, seeing what he'd found, dropped it in the pit. It's a fucking bone.'

'Oh fuck, Danny. What the hell have you dragged me into?' Stony asked and stepped back. 'I can't take this, anything for the simple life. No way am I doing time.'

'Deep breaths, Stony. You're not going down. We didn't kill it, just stumbled upon it. Walter reckoned there was an excavation of a Roman villa round here in the Sixties. It could be from way back.'

'That's Philip Samuel,' Stony said. 'Got to be, no wonder he never took the silver, someone did him in.'

'Why didn't his killer take the silver then,' Danny said. He'd picked up the bone again and was studying it closer this time. 'It's not human.'

'Alien?!'

'Animal,' Danny said. 'It's the cannon bone of a horse.'

'You sure.'

'Certain,' Danny said. He recalled Ralph say his grandfather reputedly rode The Whistler into the valley mist and was never seen again, until now. 'It's The Whistler.'

'Who?'

'Philip's wonder-mare. She vanished that same night. Papers reported witnesses saying Samuel was seen riding off into the night on her.'

'Did he?'

'Not in this state.'

Danny continued to dig and came across a horse's skull. Between the eye sockets, there was a gaping hole. 'She's been destroyed, bullet between the eyes, swift end. At least he had some scrap of humanity.'

'He loved the mare I guess.'

'All to swerve paying some bets,' Danny said.

'Welsher,' Stony added.

'She'd let him down when it really mattered most in '37 poor thing.'

'Was this it?' Stony asked. 'The thing Philip didn't want metal detectors to pick up. The Whistler was the secret.'

'This can't be it,' Danny said. 'What value is a dead horse to anyone? No, this was just another decoy to put people off the scent.'

'Have you forgotten your days as a housebreaker: don't be greedy! Now let's bugger off.'

208

Danny stopped to get some cool, night air in his lungs. He straightened and pressed the small of his back, spade resting against his belt.

'At last I'm getting through,' Stony said.

'You go if you like, I'll be fine,' Danny said and then continued to excavate horse bones, everything from the cannons, to pasterns, to huge ribs.

'You're good,' Stony said facetiously. 'Like I can lump that lot on my own.'

Danny said, 'Shut up and let me finish here.'

He kept stabbing the ground, turning the blade like a food mixer to loosen the soil. The deeper he went, the harder it was shovelling the soil from the hole.

'Anyway,' Stony went on, 'since when have they struck oil twice in the same spot?'

'We're not looking for oil,' Danny said. He looked up and saw the black silhouette of Stony peering down.

'Any deeper and I won't be able to get you out.'

'That Herbie must've been one hell of a fit lad, all the years working on Samuel Estate and here,' Danny guessed. 'Can't see Philip getting his hands this dirty.'

'Say you've paced it wrong,' Stony said.

Danny slammed the spade down in anger and a clunk of metal on metal bounced off the pit walls. Danny stood and they both looked at each other; now more than the moon lit their eyes.

Danny's hands acted like a snowplough, removing all surface soil. He once again fingered a gap between the earth and a rectangular object. It felt cool on his rough fingertips.

'Careful, Danny, might be a landmine, remember it was an army base long after being a racetrack.'

'Then it wouldn't be deeper than the skeleton and silver.'

Danny carefully stood and held it up.

'Great,' Stony said. 'A lead box.'

'Get some light down here,' Danny ordered and studied the find. Stony appeared right. It was the colour and weight of lead.

'Open it then,' Stony said, 'we've come this far.'

With the hand knife, Danny prised open the lid. He tilted the inside towards the torch-beam shining down from above.

'Bet it's stuffed with banknotes,' Stony said.

'Hope not, they'd be worthless now, museum pieces not legal tender.'

'What is it, Danny?' Stony asked. 'What is it?'

'Paper,' Danny said and removed what looked like documents, all crinkled and yellowy. The beam of light was shaking ever so slightly now. It seemed Stony was now as keen to know what could be worth more than that silver bullion. Danny began to scan over the papers when he was distracted by a small white spot in the distance. It was too low to be a star and thought it might be an outside light of one of the houses beyond the ditch where a swollen Walter had been discovered. But he could now make out the dot was bobbing and growing. Had the park-keeper returned or had the police been called? Danny expected to hear, 'Put it down,' blast from a speakerphone.

'They've come,' Danny whispered. 'Kill the torch.'

Stony turned and it went very dark. Danny stuffed the documents down the back of his jeans and hoisted himself from the hole he'd made. He felt the turf until he'd found the corners of the ground-sheeting where they'd piled the silver.

'Let's get out of here,' Danny whispered.

He glanced over at Stony's silhouette against the strengthening aurora of light. He looked frozen, like a deer in the headlights.

'You wanted out,' Danny growled. 'Let's go!'

Stony sidestepped the hole and helped hoist up the hammock of solid silver pieces.

'Drop it and go!' a rumbling voice came from the dark. Danny's hand left the sheeting to shield his eyes from the blinking light splashed over his face.

'Who are you?' Stony asked.

Danny tugged on Stony's jacket sleeve. 'Do as he says.'

'I'm not leaving without something,' Stony said, clearly unaware of what he was dealing with. Danny feared his friend would also end up in the ditch and pulled him back when a loud crack filled the air. There was enough light to see the turf had scuffed up where the bullet had buried itself.

Danny said, 'They'll bury you! Now go!'

They both ran. Danny occasionally looked back and felt for the paper tickling his back. The dot of light swept the dig site and then died. Had they seen enough? Perhaps they were gunning for the silver after all or were they now pursuing Danny and Stony in darkness?

They clambered over the railing. Danny fired up the van and they revved away. He then dropped Stony off again, still grumbling they'd left empty-handed.

As Danny dropped the latch on Samuel House's oak door, he turned and sighed. In the harsh light of the kitchen spots, he felt exposed and vulnerable, looking out into the blackness of the courtyard. He pulled down the blinds. How the hell did they know he'd be at Trelai Park at that hour? Other than Stony, there was only one other person who could know – Megan.

He placed the papers on the kitchen table and cracked open a can of Carling.

Once they realised these papers weren't among the silver, Danny suspected he'd still be a wanted man. He'd already checked the camera and alarm system and looked in on Salamanca.

The crinkled cover sheet was from a solicitor: Maurice, Davis and Hart. Danny couldn't understand much of the legal jargon. When he turned to the next page, he spilt some of the lager. Jesus, Philip!'

Seems Ralph was right about his grandfather Philip losing the Samuel Estate on the turn of a card. He did indeed try to win it back from Michael Johns in the great match up of thirty-seven between The Whistler and Shadow Master. But Ralph was wrong about it being double or quits, much more was staked at that Ely race meeting seventy years ago.

CHAPTER 24

DANNY'S FINGERS drummed the desk. There was business that needed finishing before he jetted off to the Czech Republic that weekend. He'd done plenty of thinking overnight and felt sure he'd found the mole in the yard.

There was a knock.

'Come in,' Danny said.

Megan poked her head around. 'What is it? Jack needs changing.'

'Jack can wait.'

Megan appeared to pick up on the atmosphere and sat silently the other side of the desk. 'If it's my fashion mags, I'll keep them in my room.'

'It's you.'

'I don't–'

'You've been acting odd around me, nervous,' Danny said. 'And then flirty, no way am I going to fall into this honey trap.'

'It's not,' she pleaded.

'And I think I know why.'

'Don't do this,' Megan said, bottom lip quivering.

'It needs to be cleared up and–'

'I'm head over heels in love, all right!' Megan said.

'Arse over tit more like,' Danny said. He had recalled Rhys say she'd already got a partner. Perhaps her boyfriend was in on it, maybe she was seeing Franco. He was conspicuous by his own absence around the yard in recent weeks.

Or was Rhys two-timing Kelly?

She took a moment and then said, 'What's that supposed to mean?'

'Since you've arrived on the scene, everything has gone tits up.'

'Don't go blaming me!' she said. 'I've been slaving night and day, unlike the lovebirds Rhys and Kelly.'

'And your boyfriend? Who is he?'

'What boyfriend?' she said. 'Who told you that?'

'Rhys.'

Megan said. 'I wasn't expecting a gold star or a bonus for my work, but didn't see this coming.'

'Is it Franco?'

'No!'

'There was only one person who knew I was going to the casino *and* when I left in the middle of last night.'

'I slept right through till my alarm went off at six. I would never lie to you Danny. This is killing me.'

'If it's not you,' Danny said, 'then that boyfriend of yours, or one of his friends.'

Megan turned and made for the door.

'Where are you going now?'

'Anywhere but here. Don't get paid the minimum wage to take this abuse. Finally get a job, one that I love,' she said. 'And this happens.'

Her head tilted back slightly to stop wet eyes from spilling over. He'd done the same at his brother's funeral though it didn't work. She clearly wanted to appear strong, unaffected by this. It told Danny more. She seemed genuinely insulted that he could think that way about her. A tear escaped but she was quick to wipe it from her flushed cheek. Perhaps stress had made him go too far.

'Can I go now?' she mumbled.

From the other side of the office door, he heard a floorboard creak. Danny glanced at Megan and put a finger to his lips. He crept to the door and then flung it open.

He could hear leather soles slap the hallway tiles. Danny ran down the landing and leapfrogged the banister to land four steps down. He then burst on to the driveway.

Rhys was in Kelly's new Union Jack mini and was revving up to pull away when Danny leapt on the bonnet. He could see the shape of Rhys' head behind a windscreen made white by the cloudy sky. His head was moving side to side, as if to say don't make me do this.

'Rhys, you can stop this,' Danny said. 'I just need to talk.'

Rhys slammed his foot down and the wheels flicked up fountains of gravel as they sped away. Danny slid across the bonnet this way and that, but managed to grasp the windscreen wiper which bent in his hand.

Fearing for his life, Danny blurted out, 'I want on board!'

Rhys skidded to a stop, sending Danny flying off the shiny car, rolling to finish seven paces away. Danny picked himself up and checked for damage. He flicked away the bits of gravel stuck in the grazes on his knees and elbows.

Rhys got out and looked over but he seemed more concerned with his own business. 'You want in? That's what you said.'

Danny brushed off the last stone. 'Come back inside.'

'You haven't answered my question.'

'I want in. The yard is dying a slow death but I need to know more.'

Danny returned to the office, this time with Rhys in tow. Megan was changing Jack.

'Sit,' Danny said. 'Drink?'

'No.'

'Franco was a placer for you?'

'Only cos jockeys can't bet,' Rhys said. 'Eyebrows go up if I step in a bookie. Even if it didn't break the rules, no way they'd take a bet from a jockey, couldn't get much closer to the horse's mouth.'

'Where the hell did you get thirty grand? You were always pleading poverty round me.'

'It wasn't all mine,' Rhys said. 'We went half and half.'

'That doesn't answer my question,' Danny snapped. 'Where Rhys?'

'From winnings, the stakes were rolled on to the next winner. It works.'

'Something happens at each of these betting coups,' Danny said. 'You sign Franco's racecard. Except that is another of Franco's diversionary tactics.'

'I'm actually writing the time we should meet up later,' Rhys explained.

'Why before weighing in?' Danny asked and then dropped the paperweight in his hand. 'That's when Franco returns the lead to your saddle isn't it.'

'We don't disclose trade secrets.'

'Come on Rhys, I've seen you at it,' Danny said. 'You carefully pick horses that have a favourite's chance on form and swing the weight of balance in your favour. Explains the bulimia and shaven head. The lighter your riding weight, the more lead was packed in the saddle, the more that could be removed the bigger the certainty.'

'All right, Sherlock, you said you want in.'

'Franco was chosen for his financial backing and sleight of hand,' Danny said, 'As you're scribbling away, in the twitch of a hand, he removes and replaces the lead weight. Racecourse security is busy eyeing flare ups at the bar rather than an innocent race-fan asking for an autograph. The stewards will be busy looking over the race for any interference between runners. Neither would dream all this was going on under their noses.'

Rhys' face seemed to soften slightly, as if relieved their secret was out. 'We chose tracks where there was a long walk from the winner's circle to the weighing room, preferably away from TV cameras and roaming officials. Took just seconds, we'd honed the operation to military precision, like changing of the guard.'

Danny thought about that. Perhaps Rhys was running the whole show. Danny played on Rhys' competitive spirit by saying, 'Franco was taking the lion's share.'

'No, it's all my idea! I pay him a fee. I knew Franco was looking for a scam, a shortcut to easy money and he could offer me the skills and coolness under pressure I wanted. I mean, I was hardly going to ask you.'

'Why do I not believe you?'

'Ask him.'

'He's not going to deny that,' Danny said. 'You're taking a bullet for him, of course he'll back you up.'

'You just don't want to believe it,' Rhys said. 'The stable jockey taken under your wing and nurtured has turned out bad, on the fiddle.'

'Why are you telling me this now?'

'I know you'll never go gassing to the powers. A scandal this big would bring down Samuel House with me. We'd both be blackballed for life. And if you turn Franco in, I'll be the first to know. He's a bit player, an associate in all this. Trust me, he won't like being thrust into the limelight one bit. He has ways of finding names, even from the inside, and if Danny Rawlings is mentioned, it won't be just the yard's future you need to worry about.'

'That's blackmail.'

'Just making sure my arse is covered, that's all,' Rhys said. 'I wasn't asking you for anything.'

'So I'm protecting you from both sides, Franco and the BHA.'

'If you like,' Rhys said. Danny wanted to punch that smug grin from his elfin face.

'If I blew the whistle on either of you, I'm finished too. You needed a trainer who would toe the line and I'm it.'

'Does knowing make any difference?' Rhys asked. 'Just enjoy the ride, results are good.'

'Rhys, you're a fucking idiot.'

217

'It's the perfect crime,' Rhys said. 'I haven't hurt anyone.'

'Guess I don't come into it.'

'What about all the winners,' Rhys said. 'Some of them might not have happened if I'd ridden the correct weight.'

'You really haven't listened to a thing I've said over the years,' Danny snapped. 'No one gets hurt? Punters have been robbed, tabloids would have a feeding frenzy over this. Bad news sells. Do you really want to hammer another nail in the coffin of our sport?'

'Just another reason why this should never get out,' Rhys said. 'Anyway I can't take credit for masterminding everything. The switching lead was Kelly's idea. We were chatting one day about how easy it would be to fix races, with the right planning and plenty of bottle, and she came up with it out of the blue. Think she wanted to impress me. Little did she know I'm easier than that, would've shagged her either way.'

Danny shook his head, not from Rhys' shallow outlook, but because Kelly – a stable lass in every sense of the word and one that he'd trusted enough to head the staff – had betrayed him so badly.

'And she knew Franco from when she used to pop in for ice cream after school. He used to impress them with tricks. She knew he would be up to the job and willing to bend some rules.'

'Bend some rules? You've broken them.'

'That's your opinion.'

'But Megan's in the clear.'

'Barely know the girl. She seems more concerned with mucking out than me.'

She was clearly a better judge than Danny had hoped. He had a feeling there'd shortly be a vacancy for head lass and Megan wouldn't need interviewing this time. 'Was it because you were hard up?'

Rhys seemed to take great delight in saying, 'Nah, would've done this if I was rolling in it at the very top of the game.'

Meticulously betrayed and for what? Greed. Why? Because he could.

'Still want in?' Rhys asked.

'Get out,' Danny said.

'So what are you going to do now? Nothing stupid I hope.'

'Bit late for that,' Danny said.

'Don't go blaming Kelly in all this,' Rhys said. 'The plan was hatched before you'd promoted her. She was pissed off with it all. Told me the horses were all that stopped her from jacking it in.'

'I said to speak to me if she was having problems.'

'She hasn't had anything to do with it since turning head-lass, just so you don't fire her as well.'

'So you've still got a shred of decency in there.'

'Just don't want her to dump me.'

'You're unbelievable, Rhys. With friends like you … just get out! And don't expect any severance pay. Get your stuff together, anything you leave I'll post on, I don't *ever* want to see you again!'

'So that's it, the end of us.' Rhys' lips parted slightly. 'You know how this'll look.'

'It'll look like I'm getting shot of a has-been jockey.'

Danny went over to the window and looked over to the emerald green valleys.

'We either part ways, both still with careers,' Danny said, 'Or if either of us calls the other's bluff, we'll both end in the shitter.'

Rhys came closer and offered a hand. Danny turned away.

Before Rhys had reached the door, Danny turned back. Rhys looked over his shoulder. A flicker of hope lit his eyes. 'Yeah?'

'Don't treat your next boss the same.'

The slam of the door felt like a symbolic full stop, completing chapter in his life that had its highs but there was no happy ending. One that he'd like to forget and hoped no one else would discover, particularly some of the jittery owners in the yard.

Rhys left Danny to sit in a silence eventually broken by Rhys leaving Samuel House for the final time. More than ever, he was glad to be pencilled in for the Pardubicka ride, the getaway to Prague couldn't come soon enough.

He felt he'd been shafted by those closest. He sent Kelly a text: 'Need to speak, urgent.'

He hoped her motives were more persuasive, not just the fact she just wanted to get inside Rhys' britches. He was going to reveal Rhys was the one who grassed her up. Perhaps then she'd see the real Rhys.

Danny wanted Rhys to be punished for what he had done. As Rhys had smugly pointed out, the yard would be black-listed by owners if Danny ran squealing to the BHA but there was another way. He waited a day for Rhys to cool off and then called his number.

'I've changed my mind,' Danny said. 'You were right – it'll be good for all of us.'

There was silence. 'I don't believe you. It's too much of a U-turn.'

'Rhys, I can't see my desk for bills,' Danny said. 'And results haven't been great. When Turnabout sluiced up, didn't mention it, but I got a few phone-calls from new owners. I mean, if my horses win, I'm in for a cut of the bet for keeping quiet and I also get a winner on the board. I'm happy, the owners are in the dark but happy, you're happy as you've got a safe trainer on your side, we're all happy.'

Danny waited for Rhys to get back from conferring with a 'business partner', presumably Franco. 'We'll work on a trial basis and want full access to all the yard's runners. It's risky and we stick to the smaller tracks, less chance of getting caught out by security that way, see. If we get a sniff that you're up to something or even threaten to blow the whistle, it won't be just your career you'll lose.'

Danny hoped that those words had come from Franco and not his old friend Rhys. Either way, he reckoned it was an empty threat. They'd be prime suspects if they came after him, Danny reasoned, but then he remembered the fate of Silver Belle and Walter.

'We have a runner earmarked for Fontwell tomorrow if you fancy tagging along, seeing the masters at work,' Rhys said, tone lightening.

'Might just do that,' Danny said. 'Which race is it running?'

'The second, two-thirty, Brake Fast, forecast to start at even money or around there. Twenty grand will be on it, split between four bookies. You'll only get a share of winnings on those trained and offered up by you though.'

Danny felt it most natural to pause, as if considering his position. 'Seems fair.'

'Good,' Rhys said. 'We'll see you there, well, Franco will. I'll be focused on getting the job done. And from now on, I ring you on this Pay As You Go, don't want any phone or paper trails.'

'But you're my stable jockey,' Danny said, 'it's hardly going to raise eye brows.'

'These are the rules, I don't make them,' Rhys said. 'Anyway, no one will be looking into who's phoning who, now you're on side.'

Fontwell Park Racecourse. 2.28 PM.

Lost in the shadow of a topiary statue in the main enclosure, Danny stood patiently, holding a cotton kitbag. From the tannoy speakers, the racetrack commentator said, 'They're circling at the start, won't be long now.'

He was met by Franco, who, as he approached, slipped the signed racecard in his left pocket of the same brown raincoat he'd always reserve for race-day. Danny also noted Franco was leaning ever so slightly to the right. He now knew where to look.

'It's good you've seen the light,' Franco said and smiled. 'Welcome on board.'

'Don't know what took me that long.' Danny lunged forward and hugged him. He felt Franco back away but Danny made sure he was going nowhere. Franco appeared less keen than before to hold the embrace, as if he was a leper. No wonder as Rhys would be about to jump off for the race and Franco needed to be positioned near the unsaddling enclosure with a pen or a camera to greet his favourite jockey.

Danny's hand dipped into the torn right pocket and, having felt seven two-pound lead weights, he deftly fished out two, enough for the clerk of the scales to object. With one swift action, he'd lifted them to drop and settle at the bottom of the cotton kitbag. He whispered, 'All *good things* must come to an end.'

Franco released from the embrace and gave him a look. 'There's work to do – I must be in place before Rhys returns to the winners' circle. And in future, keep your distance, there are eyes everywhere.' He removed a racecard and pen.

Danny just hoped Franco couldn't sense he was four pounds lighter. 'Sure, right you are, boss.'

Danny tossed the lead weights into a thick bush nearby. Once again Rhys came home a clear winner.

Danny thought about leaving before the bing-bong of a stewards' enquiry but he wanted to see Franco and Rhys suffer how he had.

He stood well back. The crowd was sparse, probably why they'd chosen this midweek fixture. He enjoyed a clear view of Rhys, saddle slung over one arm, slow down as he waited for Franco to rush forward and do the dirty deed. Except this time there was no Franco, whose nimble fingers had clearly counted the lead weights and, knowing he was three short, fled the scene.

Not so cool under pressure after all, Danny thought.

Rhys was now looking around like a lost puppy. Danny could have felt sorry for him but he didn't. A course official tapped Rhys on the shoulder and pointed over to the weighing room. Rhys didn't immediately respond but surely couldn't stall much longer. He looked like he was on his way to the gallows. Danny wouldn't know what he would say to the clerk of the scales if he was in Rhys' riding boots. He was riding a stone light. There wasn't anything he could say.

Danny had seen enough. There was only so much suffering he could witness. He left the track with just three races gone and returned to Samuel House. That evening as he logged on to a racing website, the headline read, 'Jockey Rhys Thomas' licence revoked after weighing in light. Full BHA investigation pending.'

CHAPTER 25

SATURDAY 16.38 PM. Bristol Airport.

Given Salamanca's freakishly large frame and stature, and a propensity to play up under stress, Danny was granted special dispensation to accompany a travelling groom alongside his charge on the cargo aeroplane. The gelding had been good on the road, which was said to be an indicator, but, for Danny, leaving his stable star to travel alone would be a risk too far.

While on board, Danny tended to Salamanca's every need, regularly administering water from a bucket – a trough would get messy during turbulence – and occasionally pushing his big chestnut head down to clear the airways. For two hours, the eight-year-old hulk mercifully stood still and quiet in the cramped and noisy pallet thirty-thousand feet up.

All the worrying proved unfounded as the flight was smooth and the shallow landing prevented the need for heavy breaking when they touched down on a runway at Prague Ruzyne International Airport.

In Danny's mind, they'd already cleared the first hurdle. But he would only be completely relaxed once Salamanca lined up at the start. Then it would solely be in his hands.

A vet was arranged to push the three British raiders through customs and they were booked to go direct to the track in good time to settle in for tomorrow's Velka Pardubicka – the oldest sporting event in the Czech Republic.

He hailed a taxi to meet up with Megan and Jack, who'd travelled the more conventional route via passenger plane from Cardiff, in a four-star hotel in the Czech capital Prague, in the heart of Bohemia.

Danny could hear Megan unpacking all her make-up in the bathroom. Jack was jumping on the springy bed.

He parted the heavy red curtains and looked down on the Old Town Square framed by a mix of gothic, Romanesque and baroque buildings, their pastel shades gave off a fruity glow, basking in the low evening sun. Overlooking the busy cobbled square were the imposing twin spires of the fifteenth century Church of Our Lady before Týn.

Tourists also mingled around the ancient astronomical clock in the town hall tower and the centrepiece bronze Jan Hus statue which cast a lengthening shadow. He wished he could join them, see the real Prague and soak up its atmosphere and sights. He'd heard plenty of the nightlife and the famous local beers. In the tourist blurb provided by the hotel, Franz Kafka had said, 'Prague never lets you go … this dear little mother has sharp claws.'

But he chastened himself, he wasn't here for the fun of it, this was a business trip above all else and the clincher meeting was looming fast.

'Done,' Megan said.

'You don't need to paint your face you know,' Danny said. 'You're pretty as you are.'

Megan smiled. 'Thanks, Danny.'

'Got anything planned for tomorrow?'

'I don't know,' she said. 'Lose myself in my fashion mags at one of those cafes probably. Pretend to blend in, never been abroad before, apart from Ibiza last summer which is still a blur. See what Jack feels like, eh monkey. Got to get back for three-thirty, I'll be glued to the box for the big race.'

Danny looked on as Megan rushed over to Jack, arms out and then tickled his tummy. He fell back helplessly on the bed in fits of laughter.

Again Danny went back to the suitcase. It wasn't his passport or silks he was checking on but a Pringles tube he'd packed. He popped it open and fingers felt for the crinkled paper inside. A quick look in the trade press would reveal Danny was away from

225

Samuel House this weekend. He feared there'd be another break-in and there was no way he would leave the Trelai Park find behind. Not after all he'd been through.

When morning arrived Danny couldn't be sure if he'd managed to get any sleep. He then remembered at some point he'd woken moments before hitting the turf. He was reliving the Market Rasen fall yet he'd convinced his mind it was the final fence at Pardubice.

For a few seconds, lying there in the dark, he couldn't even work out where he was. When he realised, his stomach tightened into a ball. He couldn't even face breakfast, only just managing to force down a complimentary biscuit and bottled water left in the bedroom.

He wanted to get to the track without fanfare and took the train, confident he wouldn't be recognised. Even in Britain the only time he was stopped in the street was to ask for directions or to answer a questionnaire.

On the train ride to the track he tried to play catch-up with the sleep. Having once woken on a bus to everyone staring at him, he would normally worry he'd start snoring but right now he was simply too tired to care.

First thing he did when arriving was dump his things in the weighing room. Thoughts elsewhere, he brushed by the successful French jockey Jean Ricou, early thirties with dark chocolate hair, who turned and snapped, 'Careful, do that on the track and I'll snap you.'

He'd clearly remembered Danny cutting him up at Market Rasen.

Nearby, three-time Bulgarian champ Androuin Maillot came over. The smudges under his eyes were almost as dark as his hair, which was grey-flecked, yet he was probably no older than Ricou. He grabbed Danny by the forearm, 'I saw it. He bumped into you. It's a game he plays, get under your skin before we do battle. Ignore him.' He moved closer and added, 'It is me you should fear.' He then stood back and laughed.

German veteran Andreas Bosche had appeared from nowhere. He'd already changed into his work clothes, yellow and red chequered silks. He'd been allotted the peg next to Danny.

'Good luck out there,' Danny said.

Andreas looked over but didn't initially reply. He was busy strapping up his wrist. 'Think it should be me saying that to you, no?'

'I'm on the second favourite.'

'But didn't yours not get round at some small English track.'

'Yes, but–'

'Then I return your good luck unopened, think you'll need it more than me.'

'Thanks,' Danny replied flatly.

Local jockey Petr Kousek came over and rested a gloved hand on Danny's cold shoulder and whispered, 'Watch for the "in and out", gets most of you foreigners.'

He already felt out of his league pitted against this elite group of international jump jockeys and, like a new boy at school, he really didn't need these mind games. He felt a fraud in this company, an imposter stood in the shadow of greats. Thinking he couldn't feel any more inadequate, he then saw the shirtless Australian ace Ricky Walters' ripped and bronzed torso. He was sat there, back to the whitewashed wall, nodding away to something on his iPod and occasionally ruffling his blond out-of-bed hair. But Danny had his own ace up his sleeve: Salamanca.

With the promo photos taken, Danny turned and slipped out of his shirt. He began to button up his own silks, brown body, green sleeves and cap. Ricky was packing his iPod away and called over. 'Have you seen a ghost mate, because I think I have.'

Danny glanced down at his bread-white skin. 'No, just an Aussie prick … mate.'

'Hey, only kidding, mate.'

'Just don't know what passes for banter in this place. Thought the sledging was bad enough in the weighing rooms back home.' Danny shook his head. 'No offence, yeah? Stress does funny things.'

'Takes more than that to get me pissed off.'

'It's called a valley tan,' Danny said. They slapped hands. 'Couldn't find out much about yours?'

'Should have looked harder, course record holder at Caulfield in the spring, horse is bionic, jumps like a kangaroo,' Ricky said, oozing confidence. 'Mind, we've just got plain fences at home, none of the crazy stuff out there, sure to be a culture shock. But reckon we wouldn't have done the three-stop flight to come here for the fun of it. What about yours?'

'Flying the flag for Blighty. Reckon I can bring it home.'

'Nice to hear a Pom that's not whinging.' Ricky said. 'But aren't you overlooking something?'

'What?'

'Devil's Detail.'

'But he's Czech.'

'Was.'

Danny had a question when the speakers blared out for all jockeys to head for the parade ring.

Ricky said, 'Whatever happens, fancy a couple of beers in the city?'

'Sorry, here with my kid.'

'Another time,' Ricky said. 'Hope to bag a ride at Cheltenham one day, may be see you there.'

En route to meet up with Salamanca, Danny checked out the odds on the betting board near the Grandstand. There was a typically cosmopolitan feel to this year's race. Czech star Devil's Detail was 5/2, next best was Salamanca on 6/1, then came the emerging Czech talent Kafka ridden by Petr Kousek on 10/1, along with French ace Parisian Angel, who was on a hat-trick bid after two sizzling displays at Auteuil, while others up there in the betting were the 'Bulgarian Beast' Troyan Pass at 12/1, same as the German challenger Treasured Memories.

Jumps racing was one of the few sports in which the Australians had yet to make a big impact and Danny hoped their 20/1 unknown quantity Dark Horse wouldn't live up to his name in the hands of the cocksure Walters.

They had also flagged up the various nationalities of the runners and had GB beside Devil's Detail. Must be a glitch in the electronics, Danny thought, and was more concerned by the odds on offer about Salamanca. What an insult. Didn't they know what they were dealing with?

He was tempted to have a bit on but it had been two years four months and six days since his last bet on the horses and he knew there was already more than enough at stake.

Danny returned to the stabling area. Salamanca was there patrolling the box in tight circles, like a prize-fighter bursting to get in the ring.

He'd only just tacked up when he stopped to check his smartphone for emails, hoping to be lifted by good luck messages from colleagues at home. It felt like the whole world was against him here and it was hard to imagine any support, even from the UK. He opened the first, sent just minutes ago, but wished he hadn't. He steadied himself with the stable door as he read the sentence and saw the image.

At first he thought it was some sick joke or a prank from a rival jockey trying to get a psychological edge but then he saw the sender's name. He looked at Salamanca yet he saw nothing. He quickly blanked the contents from his mind with the hope of sorting it out when he got home, hopefully with a trophy in cargo. Now he had a job to do and nothing was going to derail him just minutes before the biggest career-saving race of his life.

After a parade in front of the stands, the field went to post without incident. Circling quietly beneath giant ad banners at the leafy start, Danny kept his head down, trying to regain the lost composure. He puffed his flushed cheeks. Soon muscles he didn't know he had would be crying out for the clean, warm air.

A small crowd had gathered by a sign there: '123rd Velka Pardubicka'. They appeared to be waiting rather more calmly for the off than those on the other side of the fence. The homework was done, tactics locked in. He knew the dodgy jumpers to give a wide berth, the form dangers to keep in range and, above all, the snaking layout of the course.

When a familiar rival drew alongside all those fastidious race-plans went begging. It was Ralph. His black and yellow bumble bee silks glistened in the autumn sun, goggles down over those emerald eyes. Having pored over the racecard, Danny knew those colours represented hot favourite, unbeaten Czech superstar Devil's Detail. The awesome chestnut boasted a sexy profile of seven wins from as many runs on home soil.

'How many arms did you break to get that plum ride?' Danny managed from his mothball mouth.

Ralph held Devil's Detail still and smiled. 'You wouldn't believe the current market price of silver.'

'You!' Danny said. 'I'd deciphered the triptych.'

'And I'm grateful,' Ralph said. 'The fortune has returned to its rightful owner.'

The silver was only a fraction of its value, Danny thought, and then hoped Ralph couldn't read minds.

'I've waited forty-two years for this. Now this majestic specimen can help fulfil my dream,' Ralph said and glanced down. 'And you really shouldn't ride that thing in the park.'

'The park keeper,' Danny said. 'You drive a silver Astra.'

'Make that a Ferrari now.' Ralph said. 'But this is about proving them all wrong – the doubters, the Samuels! Show I can succeed at something.'

'Don't count on it,' Danny said.

'Deny me this,' Ralph said, stretching the goggles away from his face to show the intent in those eyes. 'And expect your dear mistress and child to see Silver Belle sooner than you think.'

Danny heard himself swallow. 'You're full of shit!'

'Come now, Danny, best not get upset, not now,' Ralph said. 'I'll find a quicker method to finish them than that mangy mare; she simply refused to go, writhing in agony for minutes, legs threshing the air. Not pleasant at all.'

Anyone capable of killing a defenceless horse to meet his own needs was capable of anything. Isn't that how many killers start, Danny reckoned, torturing animals as a child, a wanton disregard for life?

'And there's nothing going on between me and Megan.'

'Funny, Sara seemed to think she's your mistress.'

'How would Sara know?'

'Oh yes, how is your marriage?' Ralph said.

Danny felt like lamping Ralph but he was only too aware of the TV cameras at the start and dotted around the course. Flooring the jockey of a Czech horse with the nation watching would make him public enemy one, as well as the first jockey to be disqualified before the race had even begun.

'You're pure evil!'

'Fighting spirit, that's good,' Ralph said. 'But you cannot win. You *must* not win!'

Danny walked Salamanca away. If it boiled down to a match, should he throw the race and let Devil's Detail by? If he couldn't allow himself to go through with the win, was there any point letting off? There was a long British campaign mapped out for Salamanca. Leaving early would also give him a head start in getting back to Prague to protect Megan and Jack. But would the starter allow this? No vet would pass Salamanca as lame, still bouncing with energy. He wasn't familiar with the rules and penalties over here.

Perhaps Ralph was bluffing. He'd fooled Danny all these months. But he simply couldn't pull out. He didn't want Jack to think Daddy was a quitter. He pulled up his goggles and slotted back into race-mode. But this time he was steering clear of the black and yellow colours now turning by the far rail.

Months of counting the weeks and days and now there were only seconds, ticking down to post time. When a bead of sweat tickled his wrist as he gripped the reins, Danny was glad of the leather riding gloves.

He sat still as they walked forward. Fear of the unknown – a foreign track in every sense – now gripped Danny, verging on stage fright.

With the Aintree Grand National already locked safely in the memory bank, Salamanca would no doubt relish tackling the thirty-one fences over the stamina-busting four miles one furlong. If anything, the variety in obstacles would help keep The Tank interested. But it was Danny's inner fears and doubts that were surfacing. A summer of talking their chances up, but this was where the talking stopped and all that bravado had sieved away. With expectation, comes fear of failure.

Could he cope with the disorientating switchback track or the stretches of plough? This was as much a test of Danny as Salamanca. But he couldn't back out now.

Salamanca was primed and cocked his jaw and flashed his tail to voice his disapproval as Danny kept a tight hold.

Danny saw a woman in a dark green blazer gripping a large red flag. The distant crowd fell quiet, no doubt keenly anticipating the spectacle of jumping and staying power over the next nine minutes or so.

Danny wasn't keen to bag an early lead, as much for finding someone to follow, just in case he'd take a wrong turn on this maze of a course. He noticed rival jockeys break from circling and were now organising themselves into a line of sorts. His arms and torso felt taut with anticipation.

A flash of red and the tape rose.

They're off!

CHAPTER 26

A CAVALRY CHARGE of twenty top-flight chasers made the short run to the first fence. For a few strides, Danny rousted along Salamanca, who had yet to find a decent rhythm, mindful of his lazy tendencies and they soon lay a handy sixth. The field had barely reached racing speed when the first of two neat hedges came upon them.

Danny afforded the briefest of glances across at Ralph just a couple of lengths ahead in second, going at it hell for leather. No wonder, as this railed hedge was one of the widest on the course, with four feet of foliage, and momentum was the key to clearing in style.

Danny eyed the white pole at the base of the hedge and pushed on. Salamanca's lead foot impacted just inches from the wall of fern. They'd got in too close but Salamanca was blessed with a clever front end and tucked in his undercarriage to flick through the top layer of twigs and leaves. Pushing with his powerful hind legs and rump, they flew through the air.

Salamanca cleared the fence with a couple of hands to spare and possessed the agility and power to land clear the other side. We're back in business, Danny beamed. The anxiety had melted into pure adrenalin but he needed to supress those excitable urges, it was a marathon not a sprint.

Danny looked both sides. He was now tucked in, getting some cover in the heart of the pack as the intact field careered into fence two. Viewing internet clips, Danny had grimaced at some spectacular falls here. He caught the flash of red from the ground staff's trousers, watching on from the safe side of the rails to his left. He pushed again, hoping Salamanca would repeat the first jump. He did. Hind legs coiled like a spring, launching from the firming ground and landing safe the other side.

What was all the fuss about, Danny thought, but he knew complacency was the downfall of many. Even a split-second loss of focus from either of them could literally be fatal. He grimaced as he heard a sickening shriek and then thud in behind. Danny again surveyed those around him. There was a rider-less horse to his left, herd instincts taking over, running freely with eleven stone seven pounds less on his back.

Danny could see the colours of all the leading protagonists. Probably one of the no-hopers bailing out before things got tough, he reckoned. Danny was riding short up Salamanca's thick neck which gave him more control but less leeway to adjust the length of the rein if they were to hit a fence. Danny was confident Salamanca's jumping would hold up.

Ahead, the modified water jump. Although small, he'd seen less experienced chasers make a splash here and his eyes honed in on the strip of aqua blue, not much longer than a horse length. Danny held his breath and ground his teeth as the strip grew wider. Three-two-one. Jump! Salamanca did, almost too well. He nearly ran into the backside of the lightly raced Parisian Angel, whose hind legs dragged in the cold water. Danny put the handbrakes on, reining Salamanca back. Serious interference at these early stages would eat into energy reserves. All those times they'd cleared the brook on the estate had paid off.

Looming large on Danny's flank was the 'Bulgarian Beast' Troyan Pass. He could've been Salamanca's full-brother. For once, he met a rival jockey eye to eye. Bulgarian champ Andrey Stoev was doing the steering though he had his hands full. Danny hoped it wouldn't set Salamanca alight, as he knew his charge loved a mid-race duel.

Ralph was sitting quietly the other side, travelling sweetly on the seven-year-old chestnut. Danny knew he'd need to coax a personal best from his yard's flagbearer to lower the colours of that one.

The field were now forced into a pecking order as they cornered right. Danny was fifth, chasing Troyan Pass' big shadow. He caught glimpses of the pink and purple quartered colours of rising Czech star Kafka up ahead, cutting out the early strong gallop, rider Petr Kousek clearly confident of his charge's ability.

To the right, the white rail was no longer a guide. The course opened up, large spaces. Danny saw Petr's hands start to move up front and strides later the pace was cranked up a notch. That left him edgy as he knew the upcoming fence was the largest and, round here, that was saying something, known locally as 'The Taxis Jump'.

The crackle of the crowd in the main stands had become muted. He caught sight of a huddle of press photographers dressed in green vests, some perched on stepladders, showing their hunger to snap the field as they attacked this towering barrier. Danny had learnt that only three times in the hundred and twenty-year history of the race was there no fallers here. And that stat proved prophetic. As he looked down to his right, Ricky Walters had been fired into the lime-green grass. He heard just a sickening thud. No scream or cry. Was he still conscious?

Danny supressed the natural urge to look back and check, there simply wasn't time. Ricky's mount Dark Horse seemingly had no answers to this biggest of asks, crumpling to the ground nearby, despite being dubbed the bionic kangaroo. He guessed the Aussie would be having that drink for medical reasons now. Danny looked away. There was no room for pity or concern. If that was him on the ground, only the medics would show compassion.

The run to the fifth, known as The Irish Bank, was all too brief. There was nothing like this in Britain, though it resembled something of the Ruby's Double at Punchestown. An up and over job. Shaded by the dense woodland off to the right, Danny asked Salamanca to up a gear as they approached the steep ascent. May as well go out in style, he thought.

He couldn't block out Ralph appearing bold on his right which piqued his enthusiasm. Devil's Detail was barely breathing, fluent action covering the grass like a hovercraft. Shame there weren't a few like him in the yard, Danny conceded.

Danny homed in on the bank, now just strides away. Despite his seventeen hands and brisk approach speed, Salamanca attacked it with relish, like a big fearless kid. Danny pulled on the reins and feet pushed forward in the stirrups, transferring weight back in the saddle as he stepped up the bank. The climb helped absorb some speed.

Ralph had stopped to a walk, as if admiring the view up there, but was more likely finding some balance for the equally sharp and treacherous descent. Salamanca had no such reservations and three staccato strides later, he'd leapt back on to the level, losing no fluency. Ralph had dropped back. He hoped that would be the last he'd see of him. But at least while he was involved in the race, Danny knew Megan and Jack were safe.

Another two loose horses appeared, eagerly chasing the leading pack. He hoped they'd drift away, as if there wasn't enough to contend with.

Kafka was still seemingly enjoying himself, the bright young spark, as he cut out the donkey work up front. They pounded the green-brown turf, patchy and balding at this section of the leaf-littered parkland.

Danny afforded a brief scan of those nearby as they disappeared from the stands, masked by tall, slim trees. Most had seemingly survived the early skirmishes, maybe four or five light, but that left fifteen or so still in the hunt.

For a beat, he hoped likely danger Treasured Memories had waved the white flag but it was wishful thinking as he was being held up, switched off out the back, for a late surge.

Danny gathered the reins and saw to his left Jean Ricou, who'd eased off the pace, presumably to give Parisian Angel a breather, like a service break, as this was a long journey.

'Get away,' he snarled and then spat phlegm which mostly flicked across Danny's goggles. Charmed I'm sure, Danny thought. The murky deposit was going nowhere fast and hindering his sight so he wiped the Perspex with the back of his gloves.

No way was he going to be bullied and he let out an inch of rein to edge ahead of the hat-trick seeking French rival on the approach to fence six, better known as Popkovice Turn, a railed hedge with a ditch. Danny reckoned it resembled Canal Turn at Aintree, only not as sharp.

Salamanca had only ever allowed one rider to give him the boss around. Danny felt privileged and thought nothing of yanking down right on the rein which acted like an instant trigger and Salamanca cornered well while others lost ground shifting wide.

He now found himself in fourth but he'd yet to clear the ditch, the point where British runner Supreme Charm, ridden by Robert Thornton, came down in 2001. Although only four feet high, there was a total of nearly fourteen feet of hedge and then ditch to clear. The dappled sunlight only added to the tricky sighting at this shady part. Danny knew from glossing up, it was no stranger to a pile-up. The Pardubice's version of Foinavon, Danny guessed, as he refused to let go of his breath.

They were due a bad jump. When things went this easy, Salamanca was prone to lose focus or lack respect for the course. As Salamanca's stride shortened, he felt like time had also slowed. Danny was now asking for a short one to negotiate it safely. Get over it any fashion possible, Danny hoped. No shame in winning ugly.

When his ride's front feet once again lifted up, Danny pushed back and the ground dropped away, like a plane's take off. Salamanca's lean fighting-fit belly rustled the birch, yet those sturdy front legs thumped the drying ground the other side, absorbing the impact, as if he had built-in shock absorbers. There was another yelp from behind, probably a straggler breasting this unforgiving fence.

By now Kafka had surrendered the lead to Troyan Pass. Stoev's capable hands had awakened the Bulgarian Beast, whose brutish strength and willingness to win carried him to the front. Perhaps it was him he should fear after all, Danny thought; their moment in the weighing room still fresh. It was his sixth ride in the race so he should know his way around.

After the slight scare at the last fence, Danny was happy sitting fifth and had plenty in reserve.

They now turned back and headed into the far straight. Plumes of milk chocolate brown dust were kicked up as the survivors pounded over a lengthy stretch of plough. It was as if a silencer had been put on the thundering hooves, cushioned by the powdery surface. It was no stretch for Salamanca after working out on the beach.

Danny ran a glove over his dust-coated goggles and then sensed Ralph, who'd gone strangely quiet over the last few, surge up his outer, coming back for more on the Czech star.

Their serious eyes met briefly. Ralph growled, 'Remember what's at stake.'

Danny didn't rise to it. The seventh fence was on its way. At first glance, this looked like a regulation hedge but, having seen footage, he knew it wasn't all it seemed. The landing side was difficult to negotiate, so when Salamanca hit the turf running, gaining a length on Devil's Detail, Danny beamed.

Then there was another stretch of dusty plough. Danny counted thirty-nine strides until back on grass again. The next on the menu proved well within range, a double hedge, separated by little more than three feet. It required a big leap and Salamanca supplied it. He seemingly wasn't spooked by any of this but there was worse to come.

Neither of them had experienced anything like the next challenge. Petr Kousek's words came back to haunt him, 'Watch for the "in and out", gets most of you foreigners.' And Danny was indeed now watching it. Next time they'd be confronted by this would be coming the other way, hence the 'in and out'. Also known as the Small Gardens, it comprised one hedge followed by a short road-crossing of no more than two strides and then another hedge. More like something you'd come across at Badminton. Shame they weren't pushed nearer, like the last one, as he was sure Salamanca could've cleared both in one go.

Danny's body clock sensed they were nearing three minutes, yet barely a third of the way to glory, still much to do. Danny's focus had become heightened. He hoped Salamanca was equally on his mettle. As, if there was ever a sequence of fences designed to catch a big horse out, this was it. It was more a test of agility than jumping.

Danny steadied the gelding. Going in too fast wouldn't allow enough time for the massive chestnut to lift for take-off in a bid to clear the second in quick succession. He saw Parisian Angel pass by, along with an outsider, as he put the skids on. No time to improvise.

Three-two-one. Jump! One-Two. Jump!

They floated over green but landed with a heavy thud. Danny yanked back, saving himself from being catapulted over Salamanca's bold head. Now more than ever, he had to trust Salamanca. He was merely a passenger on this runaway train. He growled through gritted teeth, no way was it going to end on this first lap. No surprise Troyan Pass also lost ground there.

Danny didn't panic. Everything was still going to plan. Salamanca had hopped over the second hedge without grazing a twig but was now relegated to sixth. But there were still twenty-three fences until heroes were made and lost.

Salamanca's ears were pricked, treating everything as if it were all just a game. Danny knew what was at stake. Ignorance was bliss.

He sought out Ralph's black and yellow silks. He was tracking a wider path, possibly searching for a lightning fast strip of ground. He seemed to be eating up the deficit. Danny was content sitting eight lengths off the pace, marking time for an assault late on.

Ahead was a caramel sea of plough. They'd close down the leading four, still spearheaded by Troyan Pass, which proved a mistake as both Danny and Salamanca were both forced to suck up the dusty kickback.

Despite the low visibility, Salamanca fearlessly strode through the dust clouds on this soft surface, a blessed relief from the jarring summer ground.

Next up for the fifteen still going was the English fence, a two-foot rail guarding a five-foot ditch and a four-foot green-brown block of hedge. It was Parisian Angel's turn to hit a flat spot, Ricou's arms were flapping wildly into this regulation fence.

For the first time in the race, Danny felt relaxed. Three-two. But Salamanca left the ground a stride early, a good six-feet before the railing. Had Salamanca's exuberance turned to foolhardiness? They soared through the air; Danny perched precariously on half a ton of horse flesh. But they began to lose altitude and the hedge came rushing towards them. Danny's hands gripped the reins and tensed his bent legs, preparing for the crashing impact. He grimaced at the rustle of twigs and dead leaves on Salamanca's hide but he just kept moving forward, living up to his nickname, parting the hedge and leaving a trail of destruction in his wake. Danny bit his tongue and sides of his mouth from the jolting mistake. Blood leaked from his lips but adrenalin masked the pain. He pinched Salamanca's big ears and ran a soothing hand down that thick chestnut neck.

Equilibrium was restored in just three strides but he didn't dare look back or down to see the damage. They won't be inviting us back anytime soon, he thought. There was a moment's respite as the field banked a gentle right, guided by white markers, into the middle of the course. By then he'd closed back up into a handy posi. Danny was relieved not to have yet resorted to the whip but did plant a couple of taps on Salamanca's neck just to make sure that lesson had hit home. It had. He leaped the second English Jump like a buck, one of many hedges running parallel with the infamous 'Taxis' fences.

Danny was confident Salamanca had rediscovered a rhythm of sorts. He spotted three riders, including Ricky Walters, with mind, body and dreams all bruised by crushing falls, now just curious bystanders on the other side of the rails, wishing they were still part of the action.

More plough as fences eleven and twelve came into sight, both daunting in size, yet forgiving. He hoped the memory of his penultimate fence howler wouldn't scar either mentally or physically. Salamanca still handled as though sound and that was good enough for him.

Directly ahead, Parisian Angel had barely lifted a leg, paddling through the fence rather than over. A spike of adrenalin awoke Danny to the potential danger of being brought down. But the French horse left the fence going the same gallop. Danny wasn't prepared to take any liberties and asked for another quick one. This was a decent place to make up some lost ground and Salamanca didn't disappoint. A fast, efficient, low jump. He was tailor-made for that fence. *You beauty!*

The twelfth had a drop on landing but, having dealt with The Chair at Aintree, this was a breeze for Salamanca. He now found himself in third, behind Troyan Pass and Kafka. Danny knew the latter was a doubtful stayer, which fuelled him on.

Where was Ralph? He hoped he'd fallen. That would surely let Danny off the hook as Devil's Detail's loss would be none of his fault.

The field banked right and they were quickly swallowed by shade from tall trees either side. Danny thought it wise to track the hoof-prints of Troyan Pass for the guided tour. His experienced jockey Stoev would surely know the best line to take, thereby reducing distance and finding the best ground.

Fence thirteen was another railed blocky hedge, four by four. Fairly regulation and Salamanca met it with laser accuracy. Had he found a home-from-home round here?

The sun-dappled grass was thinner here. Yellowing leaves clung to the trees. It suddenly felt cooler. His skin crawled beneath those brown and green silks. They were now joined by a loose horse that had strayed from another part of the track. A rudderless nuisance as they filed away from the cheering stands. They now headed in the opposite way from the Popovicos Turn as they twisted into line for yet more plough. Next up was a low set of timber rails hammered into the plough called the Popler's Jump. It wasn't a test for these jumping stars but it still needed clearing and if they'd mistimed the hop, the penalty was skinned shins, or worse. Salamanca cleared it with daylight to spare.

Knowing what lay ahead, he administered another couple of love taps to keep Salamanca sharp. There was a bank of trees off to their far left, appearing like green smudges as he rushed by. Danny had read this was where the Czech Zoleznik was brought down only to be remounted to provide a historic fourth win for legendary countryman Josef Vana.

Danny had lost his bearing somewhere on the first lap and was surprised to see the grandstand again. The field were now towed along up front by Parisian Angel and Troyan Pass in a two-pronged duel.

He felt like he was looking through sheer mesh. Again he ran a glove over his dusty goggles. Despite all the research, he couldn't recall what came next. His photographic memory was being let down by his short-term memory. When he saw The Drop, it all came back to him. It lived up to that foreboding name, similar to the Bank at the Hickstead Derby. With a slope of nearly seven feet to a small watered ditch at the base, it certainly wasn't a bespoke design for the hulking Salamanca, who careered along blissfully unaware of what lay ahead. This was something to get out of the way, rather than go for the Hollywood display. Danny pulled back, flexing his strong biceps, as he ratcheted up the handbrake.

He looked on as Parisian Angel winged it, negotiating the steep slope as though it were level ground, and took two lengths out of the field. Salamanca's stride began to falter. He'd never seen anything like this either on the track or up in the valleys. *Come on boy!*

Salamanca quickly regained composure and a couple of short paces on, he'd seen off the drop, balance and rhythm still intact. But the slowing meant he now sat a good four lengths off the leader in fifth, still no sign of Ralph. Surely even he could steer the mighty Devil's Detail into contention. Perhaps he'd fallen, but Danny hadn't heard any groans or boos from the crowd to signal the favourite had crashed out.

Danny began to feel the burn, as the field past the halfway point. Enthusiastic cheers from the packed and vast stands gave Danny an instant mood lift, like a marathon runner passing fans lining the road, and the pain subsided for now. Salamanca's big ears pricked again.

For a brief moment, his focus was stolen by the spectacle of all those people. Soon they switched to the other side of some advertising hoardings. A well-set wall grew larger. At three foot or so, it was shorter than the one at home, but this was thicker, extending six feet. Land on that and the horse and rider would know. As if Salamanca instinctively knew they needed to go faster into this, he began to pull. Danny let him go. Fired into the wall, Danny trusted Salamanca would get his feet up in time. They soared over the stonework, feet tucked up against his barrel, matching the prowess of the quartet ahead.

He heard another cheer from the crowd. What had happened? He didn't have to wait long for the answer as Ralph swept into vision.

As the remaining runners turned away, Ralph cut the corner, forcing Danny to race wide. A blue strip in the turf came rushing towards them: The Big Water Jump. There was over thirteen feet of shallow aqua-blue water to clear.

When Ralph produced Devil's Detail all wrong, the Czech chaser did well to only get his hind feet wet. Ralph seemed to be proving the weak link in that partnership and a few strides on, he clearly hadn't recovered from the mistake as well as his mount

243

had. His weight had now lurched badly, like an old building in an earthquake. Devil's Detail now appeared rudderless and, with Ralph clinging to stay on, the pair was drifting over on a collision course with Danny, who had little room or time to manoeuvre. As gravity's pull took over, Ralph reached out and grabbed Danny's britches. It was Danny who was now shifting off balance. He looked across and then down.

'We're in this together,' Ralph cried, looking up with fiery eyes. His right foot was wrapped up in the stirrup iron and Devil's Detail's head was up, reefing and hollering, as much of Ralph's weight was supported by the reins bunched in his right hand and Danny's leg.

Clearly not even a wild horse was going to drag him off and, as these two smart steeplechasers ran in tandem, the likes of Troyan Pass, Kafka, Treasured Memories and Parisian Angel were shrinking up ahead.

Salamanca was being anchored back. Danny had to make the tough choice whether to release that anchor or draw it up. It was survival of the fittest out there and Ralph clearly wasn't up to it. But no way was Danny going to let him ruin both their chances.

They were doing little more than a canter now, as if pulling up, yet both were still full of running. More from self-preservation than goodwill, he gathered the reins in his right hand, reached down with his left and heaved Ralph up by the collar of his silks. Not yet fully balanced in the saddle, Ralph grabbed Danny's hand, whipping his glove off to land somewhere on the plough. Danny wiped his sweaty palm on his silks and bit the other glove off. It felt odd with just one, like wearing one sock.

Before Danny had reorganised himself and, without even a thank you or a touch of his black cap, Ralph had surged ahead, urging his Czech champ to shift back up the gears.

Danny knew Salamanca had it all to do but there was still enough track and fences ahead to make things happen.

Danny had a flash of Megan and Jack glued to the hotel lobby TV, along with most of the hotel staff watching the race unfold. He hoped he was doing them proud.

He was relieved to see the third and easiest of the Taxis jumps, known as The Small Taxis for obvious reasons. With some rhythm and momentum gone, this represented an ideal confidence restorer. Danny guessed he'd lost over ten lengths from the altercation and went after Ralph. Perhaps if he focused on winning this private battle, the war would take care of itself.

Long shadows reached across the track here, making it harder to get a good sighting of the fence as they crossed a brief stretch of plough.

Danny knew he couldn't touch a twig from now on and asked Salamanca for one of his specials at this easy fence. Three-two-one. Salamanca made it appear even smaller, mocking the fence's place on the course.

The leaders were just a blur in his fuzzy goggles and as he drew alongside Ralph, he shouted, 'What's next?'

Ralph didn't reply. Perhaps he didn't hear, or chose not to hear.

Danny eased off slightly to let Ralph edge ahead. He could see Devil's Detail make a beeline for fences twenty and twenty-one. It was the Ins and Outs approached from the opposite way. Danny's heart sank. Of all the fences to tackle twice, he thought, recalling the hash Salamanca had made of them last time.

He thought about playing it safe and settling for the minor money but it wasn't in his DNA. He urged Salamanca on to meet the first of the railed hedges at full flight. He nailed it. Step-step. Jump! Another faultless leap at the second hedge saw him surge ahead of Ralph again. Now he had to believe he could reel the leading pack in. The pursuit was on.

He could see the gap closing on the fourth Kafka with every stride. Next was a dry ditch some ten feet across and three feet deep. It was all about speed this one; a long jump, rather than a high jump. Danny asked for maximum speed, rowing along with

245

all his strength after two cracks of the whip. His arms began to feel heavy as if moving through water. Salamanca left the ground just inches from a wooden take-off rail and skimmed over the gaping hole, momentum carrying them forward on landing.

Salamanca's nostrils flared. He was blowing as hard as Danny now, huge lungs servicing a heart to match and muscles that put Ricky Walters' to shame. Come on!

Czech hope Kafka was now treading water after setting the early pace though that rising star would have other days. Danny overtook as if he were passing trees, moving into fourth just seven lengths off the leading trio. Next in his sights was the German Treasured Memories, who'd made an eye-catching forward move. He hadn't the time or inclination to check what had happened to Ralph, praying he was lying in that ditch, just like he'd left Walter.

Salamanca flicked over the next routine fence like a hurdler. He was motoring along at full gallop. Nothing and no one was going to get in their way. Danny felt the brush of warm air blow over them. Like a champion swimmer, he kept his head down as he pushed forward, coming up occasionally to check alignment for the next obstacle, a railed hedge four feet in depth. Another skip from Salamanca sent them skimming over the loose greenery.

Less time in the air the better, Danny thought. He heard a gasp from the crowd. He hoped it was either in awe of Salamanca's jumping or at a rival's mistake. Good news, either way.

He looked up and was glad he did. Doubtful stayer Treasured Memories was backing a hasty retreat and was in his flight path. Danny yanked left on the reins and Salamanca managed to deftly sidestep the legless rival. Now Stoev aboard Troyan Pass was his next in his sights.

With no more plough to cover, he whipped away his goggles in one seamless motion and gave Salamanca's rippling rump another smack, a firm reminder he had to earn his keep. He could now get a clear view of Troyan Pass's thick legs. Gone was his raking stride, now merely plugging on at the one pace. He was easy meat, Danny felt, as he homed in on the Big English Fence. This was a hedge and a ditch combination but often caught Pardubice virgins out with its landing being a foot higher than take off. Danny had seen the fence design and wouldn't be fooled. He fired Salamanca into the fence, aiming for a low one. If he'd asked for height, Salamanca's weary legs may knuckle landing steeply, not expecting higher ground the other side. He chose right, brushing away twigs and leaves without losing any speed.

He was now just a few lengths off Troyan Pass when a ten-foot ditch needed clearing. No easy task on fresh legs let alone at this stage of the race. He used the white take-off barrier as a guide. *Three-two-one*. They soared over what felt like the Grand Canyon but they made the other side with a good two feet to spare. He wanted to whoop with delight but had no air left.

He powered by Troyan Pass, who'd seen enough and was dropping away. The Bulgarian Beast had been tamed by the rigours of the Pardubice track. As Danny grabbed second position, Stoev glanced across and shouted, 'Get him, for me.' Clearly no love lost between the fiercely competitive Bulgarian and Frenchman.

Danny found himself in silver medal spot, with only Jean Ricou's Parisian Angel to beat. He was now expectant rather than hopeful he could pick this inexperienced rival off as and when he liked.

The adrenalin kept his muscles from seizing. There were no words of encouragement, just the blind trust between man and horse.

Salamanca thought nothing of reaching maximum physical capacity, treading the knife-edge between triumph and disaster. With every breath, forty litres of oxygen stretched those huge lungs, massive heart now pumping four times a second. Nothing manmade could compare to this wonder of nature. Approaching nine minutes of physical and mental torture but there was still four to negotiate and the upcoming Havel's Jump was a tester, a railed hedge six feet in depth followed by an eight feet ditch.

Danny felt there was a real possibility they'd breast the hedge before slumping in a heap in the ditch. He knew after this there were three standard regulation fences seen anywhere in Britain, so drew a lungful and fired his charge into it. They rose, hit the fern, and then began to descend, Salamanca's front legs reached for the green stuff on the landing side of the ditch.

Danny tugged on the bunched reins and the hooves landed on the tufts of grass overhanging the lip of the ditch. Danny now sat back, almost reclined as he pulled Salamanca, who began to skid and knuckle on the grass.

Salamanca bravely fought off gravity and Danny's weight to stay up. He hadn't lost much ground on Parisian Angel, who was starting to meander like a drunk. He could hear the hoof-beats resonating in the air and the machine-gun jets of air from Salamanca's large flaring nostrils, desperate to get oxygen to service his fatigued muscles now working overtime.

But Danny's fragmented thoughts couldn't piece together why, with three still to jump, the crowd's volume had turned up to max, cheering wildly as if they were near the finish line. Perhaps it was local tradition. When he saw Devil's Detail drift into sight again, moving with the swagger of a champion-elect, Danny knew the answer. His worst fears had been realised. There was a moment when their eyes met.

What a fucking monster, a freak of a horse, Danny thought, now seeing why that pairing was well matched.

Danny's cheeks felt prickly and hot as he kept blowing hard. Being a part-timer against these seasoned pros, he was asking his body to go beyond anything it had faced before. He was now working on fumes but he suspected Salamanca had something left to give and he couldn't let him down though he suspected Devil's Detail had even more in reserve.

With muscles cramping, he felt trying to organise Salamanca would do more harm than good. So he switched to autopilot as

248

they cleared the third last, allowing Salamanca the freedom to tackle this regular fence on instinct. His trust in that instinct was rewarded by a textbook jump, making up a length on Devil's Detail, with both bearing down on Parisian Angel, whose petrol needle must've been hovering on empty.

Nearly there, Danny thought, don't give up. He was thinking more of himself than the out-and-out stayer between his numb, shaking legs.

Devil's Detail and Salamanca surged past the French star as if he were a pacemaker. After nearly four miles, they had the race between themselves. Salamanca's iron will countered the class of the unbeaten rival, Danny believed. And he fancied his jockeyship could tip the balance their way but had he the energy to deliver? Two to go.

He let out some rein and kept pushing and pushing and pushing. Ralph still had a fractional lead as they both scraped over the second last and, galloped on as if wading through treacle, closing in on the final fence. One more, he thought, but would Ralph go through with his threats? There was a big prize for second, Danny knew, which would surely soften the blow.

Ralph looked across, frowning. Cracks were appearing in Devil's Details armour. Again, he started to drift on a collision. Danny reckoned a strong gust would knock him sideways right now and tried desperately to get ahead of his ailing rival. He caught a glimpse of Ralph's right hand pulling down on the reins. He was deliberately coming over.

Did he fear that was their only chance of stopping the rally of Salamanca?

They were now just inches apart, with Danny's boot brushing the belly of Devil's Detail. If this was the Boat Race, the referee would now be screaming into the loudspeaker.

All Danny could hear now was a loud ringing. He eyed the line of thick birch looming large. He leapt. Mid-air he felt his left leg being crushed, Salamanca's body was baulked sideways, as the two came together with a jolting blow. Danny yanked hard right on the reins to prevent Salamanca from landing on his side. He then heard a shriek as Devil's Detail kissed the turf and Ralph was pushed up his neck.

Danny's legs pressed against Salamanca's barrel in a vice like grip. If Salamanca was going down, he was going with him. But, despite the jolting knock, enough to floor most normal chasers, Salamanca had the foresight and skill to find a leg as the ground came rushing for them.

Survival instinct enabled Danny to coax out the last ounce of strength to rein him back and they kept on going. He couldn't hear the crowd's gasps or their subsequent cheers. He looked over but couldn't see any dangers, just trees and blue sky. Just yards from the line he could afford the luxury of easing down to a walk. *They'd done it. They'd actually done it.*

Danny wanted to laugh, but just brought up phlegm and bile. He cleared his mouth and then flopped forward and hugged his hero. His lip was still bloody. No words were spoken. Arms wrapped tightly round that lolling neck, shiny with sweat. All the months of traversing the valley contours had finally paid off.

He was surviving on adrenalin. Whether it was from shock or exhaustion, he didn't see the TV camera crew come rushing over as he slowly slid off to lighten Salamanca's load.

The woman presenter asked a question but he couldn't hear anything for the ringing and the crowd. He nodded but even that made him giddy.

CHAPTER 27

WHILE POSING for a huddle of press photographers and struggling through a local TV interview, which lost something in translation, his mind was whisked to Prague on the desire to share this success with those that really mattered – Jack and Megan. He was surprised that without thought Megan's name came to him. Spending much of the summer with her probably had something to do with it. She'd clearly made more impact on his life than he'd thought.

Danny's reverie was broken when asked if he would try to emulate the legendary Josef Vana, who rode six and trained seven winners of this race.

Danny answered, 'Let me enjoy this one first.'

He took to the presentation stand and, being the owner, trainer and rider, was showered with prizes, including gold brooches, while shaking hands with the mayor of Pardubice and representatives from the Czech Steeplechase Association. And then, Danny was handed over a large cheque inked with 4,550,000 Czech crowns, which converted into £170,000 and made that final lung-bursting lap worthwhile. Danny held it up for the cameras, but what good would it be without those closest to him?

He touched his cap and then waved at the cheering crowd but he wanted more than anything to leave the track for Prague.

Tradition had the first five riders home up there for the ceremony, presumably as it was a colossal achievement just to get round. But Danny only noticed three other jockeys.

He asked the runner-up Androuin Maillot, 'Where did Devil's Detail come in the end?'

'Fourth, I think.'

Ralph clearly didn't value that achievement as much as others.

Salamanca was led away to the stabling area. Transport had been arranged to fly the champion back first thing in the morning.

Danny was glad to weigh in, escape all the fuss. But he had to stay on for more press and publicity stuff, which dragged on for what seemed like hours. He'd promised a handful of autograph hunters that he'd be back but when he entered the changing room and fished in his kitbag, they were now furthest from his mind.

Where was the hulk of wood attached to the hotel key? He kept searching his stuff, turning over a sweater, shirt, socks, antiperspirant, bottled water, plasters and rolls of strapping. He now knew it wasn't there but that didn't stop him looking again. It had to be there.

He picked up his phone to call Megan, warn her to get out and stay out of the hotel. There was another text, this time from an unknown sender.

Go enjoy the celebrations. Deserve everything you get. I'll take care of Megan and Jack. R.

Leaving the track, Danny saw one of the journalists who'd held out a Dictaphone in his interview and dipped his pocket for the device. He suspected he'd need a recording of what was about to take place for the police. This was his black box.

Danny's legs were stiffening up as he sprinted to the platform on Pardubice train station. He jumped on board the Prague-bound train. He released the top button of his green and brown silks, damp with sweat and tucked into white britches, tanned by dust from the plough fields.

He shrugged off the inevitable gawkers and pointers; let them think its fancy dress. Neither was he in the mood to admire the Bohemian countryside flashing by, as he paced the carriages, working off some pent-up anxiety, growing every time they'd stop-start at empty platforms. He could've made quicker progress with Salamanca still under him.

He stared at his mobile. Should he phone one-five-five to alert the Městská Policie – the city police? Would they believe him or even speak English? Perhaps her mobile would be on? Surely that would be the first thing Ralph would seize.

Danny felt it worth the risk. Maybe Ralph was full of empty threats and Megan had indeed gone to the café quarter with Jack and her magazines.

On the fourth ring, Danny felt his heart quicken. It would have gone to messaging if she had switched it off and she'd normally answer it by now. It fell silent. Was he being redirected?

'Megan?'

'Oh ... hi Rufus, it's been a while,' came down the line, definitely Megan. 'How are the kids?

'Megan it's me.'

'Yes,' she said. 'Little Jack's fine. We must catch up.' It then fell silent.

Danny recalled Megan's dog was Rufus. Panicked she'd clearly called upon that at random. If this was code, something wasn't right, but she thankfully made it clear that Jack was fine.

Danny pressed the phone to his ear. He could now hear the slow rhythmic brush of air. Was it Ralph? Had he picked up on another layer to Megan's reply and pushed her aside?

Danny didn't speak, just hung up. He didn't want Ralph to know it was him and that he was on his way though he could do nothing about the rumbling train.

As they finally screeched to a halt at the cupola-shaped Praha Hlavni Nádraží – Prague's main station – Danny pumped the carriage door lever until the safety release allowed him off. He jumped and ran along the concourse. He was blinkered from the sumptuously decorated Art Nouveau lobby made of steel and glass, and its many statues looking down on the milling travellers.

When he snaked the crooked cobblestone lanes, the towering spires of the Týn Church, which rose above the rooftops, were his North Star. His heart filled with dread at the scene he might find. Tightening thighs meant he was struggling to lift his legs.

253

His progress was stifled by the historic Charles Bridge spanning the River Vltava, as he slalomed half-a-kilometre of bustling souvenir stands, portrait artists, street musicians – animatedly playing banjos, trombones, trumpets and acoustic guitars – entertainers and puppeteers, all a slave to their arts. Beaded threads of gold rippled on the meandering brown-green waters below.

He swerved a crowd of tourists pointing digital cameras and mobiles at Death striking his bell from the town hall clock. Danny hoped that wasn't a portent. He guessed it had struck the hour. 6.00 PM.

He wasn't religious but he was now pleading with a god, any god, they'd still be safely in refuge behind locked hotel door number one-three-two. He turned into the now familiar Old Town Square.

He scanned the busy tables shaded by the pyramid umbrellas outside the string of cafés hoping to see a young woman with child. He ruffled the waistcoat of a waiter but was soon shrugged off, seemingly freaked out by Danny's flustered demeanour, manic eyes, glistening face and stuttering speech. There was no time to explain his predicament with charades, so he sprinted over paved stone to the hotel lobby.

A thick red carpet below a matching canopy of the hotel entrance muffled the slap of his leather soles. The doorman had barely time to open his mouth when Danny breezed by and spun through the revolving door, knocking off balance a fat man laden with cameras and a Prague sightseeing map.

Danny brushed past guests and leapt a pile of cases as he careered across the marble foyer and skidded through shutting elevator doors. A white-haired woman wearing a floral skirt and smelling of peach blossom looked at Danny as if he were a mad man. He didn't care.

There was another chime and the lift voice said, 'Second floor.'

He squeezed through the parting doors and sprinted down the corridor.

As his knuckles hovered by the fisheye below the 132, he collected his thoughts and composure. He knocked. 'Room service.'

There was silence within, not even a stirring. But being on her own in a foreign city, Megan probably wouldn't respond if she hadn't ordered anything. He clicked on the Dictaphone in his pocket. He turned to face room one-three-three across the hallway, back straightened by the wall. With his left hand, he squeezed the handle and pushed. Through the slender gap, there was darkness. Had they gone out?

With a finger he pushed the door wider, still facing the opposite wall of the stuffy hallway. He felt like an FBI agent, primed to swivel into the door mouth with a revolver outstretched. But all he had about him were his wits. He edged closer to the doorframe, heart thumping his ribcage. Bracing himself, like a sprinter on the blocks, he spun on one foot and peered in.

His hawkish eyes were first drawn to Megan and Jack, both perched on the bed, facing him. They wore matching *I ♥ Prague* t-shirts. They didn't even turn their head, let alone get up. There were tissues strewn over the carpet. He then noticed the rest of them were stuffed in their small mouths.

The snowy TV screen was flickering silver-white, turning their faces into apparitions and the glass of the wall pictures shone like headlamps. It was peaceful, almost serene, yet everything about it was wrong. The bed was a tangled mess of sheet and duvet, pillows at its foot. They would've been made by this hour. He could picture the struggle Megan had put up to protect Jack.

'If you've laid a finger on either of them, I swear I'll kill you.'

'I doubt you'll have much say in the matter.' Ralph stepped from the dark, waving a pistol. 'Do you?'

Danny saw the lidless Pringles tube by one of the pillows. 'You've got what you came for, now go. Why all this?'

Ralph held the secret of the triptych in his hand. The crinkled documents, now curled from being hidden in the tube, were worth far more than any silver. 'These are the deeds to Ely Racecourse and the estate, both held in the name of Philip Samuel. This is what my grandfather paid the ultimate price for. Yet you dared to steal them from under my nose that night,' Ralph said. Danny could make out a smile.

'Philip lost the estate to Johns on the turn of a card and then stakes the racetrack as a double or quits on The Whistler beating Johns' Shadow Master in the '37 Cardiff Open, except Philip lost again,' Danny said. 'Those deeds belong to the Johns family.'

'That's not what's inked on these,' Ralph said. 'Those bets were merely gentleman's agreements, these are hard facts. To think, all these years I'd been searching for the lost fortunes *in* Trelai Park, little did I think it *was* Trelai Park.'

'But it's just playing fields,' Danny said.

'Which isn't protected,' Ralph said. 'With this proof, it will be a simple land claim for my legal team. And not forgetting the housing estate beyond will soon be mine.'

'No way would it stick in court,' Danny said. 'Not after all these years.'

'Want to bet?' Ralph said. 'Or perhaps not, that was the reason behind Philip's downfall.'

'I'll go to the police.'

'What with?'

'I saw you kill Walter.'

'But can you be certain?'

Danny glanced at Megan. He could make out her soft cheeks were burning red.

Ralph added, 'If you can't and you were there, how could a jury call it beyond reasonable doubt.'

'It was that gun used,' Danny said.

'You're really not selling it for me to spare your life.' Ralph glanced down at the bed. 'Or theirs.'

'If this is a grudge about what happened on the racetrack, don't drag them into it.'

'And the alley that night,' Ralph said.

'But–'

'You left me for dead in the skip. Is that what you were about to say?' Ralph said. 'Or were you too drunk to remember?'

Megan started to whimper. The TV lit up Jack's bubbly nostrils and a shiny toy truck lying on the duvet.

Ralph unbuttoned his shirt enough for Danny to see a blue padded vest.

No wonder there wasn't a pulse, Danny thought. 'But you came after me, with my wallet.'

'Most of your blows either struck my torso or were merely glancing. Your drunk, blind swings made little impact. You're not as strong as you like to think.'

When Ralph ran to him that night, he'd claimed Danny had dropped the wallet outside the casino. But Danny had found Megan's photo in the alley. He'd kept it in his wallet to spite Sara. Danny must have had his wallet when they fought, placing Ralph at the alley. He was angry for not figuring that at the time.

'How did you get the ride on Devil's Detail?' Danny asked, giving them all a few more precious seconds' stay of execution.

'The silver was auctioned online. There were some rare pieces I believe. It fetched two hundred thousand in total. Mercifully Philip had a better eye for antiques than betting. He hid them well.'

'Why the Pardubicka?'

'I can also blame that on you,' Ralph said. 'My dream was to win the big race I never could as a professional. Finally silence my doubters.'

'The Samuels you mean.'

'I took your advice and bought abroad but then you deny me.'

'So now we're getting to what this is really about,' Danny said. 'I've ruined your fantasy.'

'Shut it!'

'Made sure you bought the best, didn't you,' Danny said. 'Doubted your own skills in the saddle?'

'Just shut it!'

Danny had finally landed a blow that hurt Ralph.

There was a click from the gun's safety catch.

'The police will come.'

'I think you'll need them before then,' Ralph said.

'How can you live with yourself?' Danny snapped. 'Killing Walter for nothing.'

'Far from it,' Ralph said and stepped forward. 'You see Philip would rather see his fortune go to anyone than his own son, my father, and, years before Philip lost the bet on The Whistler in '37, he made his trusty groundsman Herbie sole beneficiary to the entire wealth in his will.'

'I knew once I'd deciphered the triptych, Walter, being the only surviving Morgan, would read the papers and come out of the woodwork, trying to claim his rights on the fortune. If I couldn't destroy the will, I had to destroy the sole benefactor.'

'Don't you feel a shred of guilt?'

'Who said anything about guilt?' Ralph replied. 'We all possess the ability to kill if the motives are strong enough.' When he saw Ralph bend to pick up a biscuit from an uneaten pile on Jack's lap, Danny stepped forward. 'Take a battered wife or a bullied child who finally snaps.' Ralph broke the biscuit in two. 'Remember the alley that night. The thing is, you can be an ex-jockey, but you can never be an ex-killer, it stays with you.'

'But you survived.'

'You didn't think so at the time,' Ralph said. 'Is there a difference between our actions?'

'Just let us go.'

'It's a bit late for that,' Ralph said. 'We're not the most dangerous species on this planet by being nice. Say something happened to Jack here, I'm sure you would be inclined to do harm to whoever hurt or killed your child, no?'

'You wouldn't.'

'While you were celebrating on the podium, I was in the town of Pardubice, I chose to take some souvenirs on my way, a couple of local specialities,' Ralph looked down at Jack, who was wailing for his father, and added, 'now I cannot imagine Daddy being so thoughtful. Unless I'm mistaken.'

'I had to get back, stop some sick fuck from getting his kicks.'

'Do you know what Pardubice is known for?'

'Enough of the games.'

'Gingerbread,' Ralph said and then bit into biscuit he held. He then offered the other half to Jack.

'Don't, Jack.'

It was then he noticed their cheeks were puffed and their chins glistened with spit.

Danny pleaded. 'For God's sake, let them breath.'

'God gave them nostrils.'

Danny ran through his options. It didn't take long.

Ralph added, 'So that's Jack sorted. But what to get Megan?'

'What else is Pardubice famed for?'

'You're a fucking nutjob. A psycho.'

'Come now, Danny,' Ralph said. 'Play along.'

'Let them go!'

'No? Well I'll tell you, it's Semtex.'

Danny shook his head. This wasn't happening. He then noticed Ralph's right eye twitch. He recalled why Ralph hadn't moved on to the poker tables in the casino that night. He was bluffing.

'Don't worry Danny, your bit on the side hasn't been putting on the pounds. I took the liberty to strap the gift to her waist. She wears it well, don't you think.'

Danny said, 'I yell fire, the concierge will react.'

'You do and the concierge will need to react,' Ralph barked and pulled out a mobile phone with his free hand. 'I press this button and we're all charred meat. My life has been a string of disappointments, this afternoon no different. What the hell, Danny, why not go out with a bang?'

'Do what you like but don't take us with you.'

'Make another sound, and I'll have you picking up bits of Jack's brain, understand?'

'The man is just playing a game, Jack,' Danny said. 'Everything is fine, we'll be home soon. I'll buy you a bike for being good.' But no words could clear the tension in that room.

'Your daddy's wrong child,' Ralph said. Jack was now bawling. He had clearly picked up on the atmosphere. 'You see, he's betrayed me, been a very bad man. And you know what happens when you're bad, you get punished. I was punished when I was your age, hit until my eyes puffed up so I couldn't see any more, hit until my skin bled and I had no more tears to shed. Even from my earliest memories, far too young to know any different, my father beat me. He thought to peel away the rubber surface from a table tennis bat to leave hardwood, very hard wood. He slapped me, again and again, until his face was as red as my arse, left me to pick at the splinters. I used to cry myself to sleep, not from the cuts or bruises but from guilt.' His voice now shook with supressed fury. 'With every smack of that wooden paddle, he'd shout at me, say I'd been bad and I'd let him down, their one and only son. I'd never live up to the family name.' He fastened a weary gaze on Danny. 'And it *was* a name back in the day. I was robbed of my childhood, and now your daddy tried to rob me of the payback for all those years of misery, my inheritance – the one thing that kept me going.'

'That's not Semtex,' Danny said with as much conviction as he could muster. 'With those deeds, you have every reason to live. Why end it all now you've got what you want? This is all an elaborate bluff.'

Ralph had no immediate answer. 'I can kill you.'

'Then none of us will get out alive. I can hear sirens already. Police are armed over here.'

Ralph said, 'I'll take the fire escape.'

260

Danny felt he wasn't getting anywhere and changed tack. 'But the deeds are worth nothing without my say-so. You see, I bought the freehold to the Samuel House three years ago. You read the small print. Philip tied the land of the estate to the land occupied by the racetrack, something about security if the business went tits up. Whoever owned one, owned the other. The current name on the Samuel House deeds is Daniel Rawlings. You need me as much as I need you. We could both become very rich out of this if we agree this out of court.'

'And you accuse me of an elaborate bluff.'

'Can you afford not to believe me?'

Ralph lowered the pistol and loomed over the bed. What was he going to do? Had Danny pushed Ralph over the edge? His alert eyes followed Ralph's spare hand as it pulled a penknife from his breast pocket and flicked it open. The blade shimmered.

As Ralph pulled the balls of tissue from their small mouths, both panted to feed their racing hearts. He cut the hand-ties with clean swipes of the blade.

Megan didn't immediately get up. Was she frozen by fear, or waiting for orders or didn't she want to leave Danny alone? Perhaps revisiting his childhood memories helped Ralph have a change of heart.

'Move!' Ralph said. A bruising yank of her arm and she was up.

'Megan, get Jack outta here.' When she didn't react, Danny added, 'Go, for me. I can handle this.'

'Do as he says,' Ralph said, 'before I change my mind.'

'Can I at least say our final goodbyes?' Danny pleaded. 'It's the least I deserve.'

Ralph nodded. Danny edged forward at an angle that masked his right hand. He slipped out the Dictaphone that had been quietly whirring in his pocket and, as he gently hugged Megan, slipped the device into her jeans. 'He whispered, 'Go to the police with this.'

Megan backed off and mouthed, 'What?'

261

'You'll understand.'

'Enough,' Ralph said.

Megan gripped Jack's hand. Danny knew his chance would soon arrive. The second Ralph turned his back he'd pounce. Now! But Danny had taken just one step forward on the plush red carpet when Ralph either sensed or anticipated the move and spun back to face him again, gun held at arm's length. Its eerily still shaft just a few feet from Danny's face.

'Don't even think of it,' Ralph said quietly. One soft step at a time, he led Megan and Jack to the door. Megan glanced over her shoulder but she said nothing. Her solemn eyes, glassy with tears, told Danny all he needed to know.

He winked and managed to stoke the embers of a smile. But she'd already been forced from the room to fall in a heap in the corridor. As Ralph moved the *Please Do Not Disturb* sign to the outside handle of the door, Danny darted sharp left and picked up Jack's toy truck from the rippled duvet. Ralph turned. Danny masked the truck with the front of his hand, resting in his curved palm and shelved there by his fingertips. He mirrored the pose with his other hand, trying to look natural as possible.

Danny edged forward, now level with the TV screen, still silently flickering away. His moist fingers tightened around the truck, like a boa constrictor.

'Stay-where-you-are,' Ralph said, motioning with the gun. 'This is nice, just the two of us again.'

'Very cosy, shall I ring room service?'

'You won't need it.'

'What's this really about? That you failed again on the racetrack.'

'You didn't heed my warning.'

'I helped you back up, would've been game over for you, it nearly was for me, only Salamanca had the class and stamina to recover.'

'If you beat me, I'd wreak revenge and I'm a man of my word.'

'You gonna go hunt Andreas and Jean down for finishing ahead as well?'

'They didn't baulk me at the last fence.'

'You veered into me,' Danny said. 'Both of you were punch-drunk. What race were you watching?'

'Enough!' Ralph cried. 'You'll rue the day that mirror broke. At least you won't have to suffer the full seven years' bad luck.'

That gave Danny an idea. He drew upon Franco's art of deception and sunk his right hand into his jeans pocket.

Ralph said slowly, 'Hands where I can see them.'

This afforded Danny some licence to make his move. As he removed his right hand as a distraction, Ralph didn't immediately react to Danny lifting his left hand and, with one sharp shift of weight, slam-dunked the metal toy into the TV set. With an echoing crash, the truck was eaten by the screen. Once the sparks died, the room fell pitch black. Danny could make out cushioned footsteps. They grew louder. He sidestepped and felt the brush of the duvet. Danny's eyes had yet to fully adjust but suspected Ralph held no advantage there. He knew, however, once the cover of darkness had lifted, Danny was a dead man walking.

'I'll sign over the racecourse land,' Danny said, 'on one condition.'

'You have nothing on me,' came from the dark. 'and once I reclaim Trelai Park from its caretaker, the local council, I'll be wealthier than any Samuel before me. Why should I bow to you?'

'Megan,' Danny said. 'She has a recording of all that was just said.'

'I don't believe you.'

'Can you afford not to,' Danny said. 'You should've kept the voice disguiser.'

'No, no conditions! I'm controlling this. I'm the only winner here.'

Greed still coursed the Samuels' veins, Danny thought. He hoped it would be their downfall once more. 'Then something has to give.'

Danny lunged towards where the voice came from. His shoulder hit something hard and then fell to the ground in a tangle of limbs. In the sparse light, Danny made out the glint of the gun now lying on the carpet beneath a bedside chair.

He scrambled to his feet but was held back by Ralph, who then stood and grabbed one of Danny's fatigued arms, slamming his palm on the wooden table, by the TV.

Danny looked on helplessly as an arcing shimmer of light from the penknife came down and sliced through his hand and then the veneer of the desk, pinning him there. Danny yelped. His free left hand reacted by grabbing the knife handle before Ralph had chance to twist it. He could feel the warm liquid surround his hand like a moat.

The blood wasn't spurting from him in time with his pulse, suggesting an artery hadn't been severed. He was now shaking and felt weak. Ralph grabbed Danny's hand, now glistening in the sparse light and thrust it into the alcove of the TV. Danny bit back the searing pain as he made a ball with his fist, fearing he'd touch a stray live wire. His hand was forced deeper.

A mains shock would be the end, Danny feared, now ready to pass out.

Knuckles now an inch from a tube still warmed by two hundred and twenty volts, Danny hissed, 'You'll be shocked too!'

Ralph suddenly eased his pressure. There was a stalemate, hands held in the cavern of the TV. Danny was first to make a move and withdrew his hand, whipping up his balled fist to meet Ralph's chin. Ralph staggered back.

'Should've finished you in the alley,' Danny said.

'We're born killers,' Ralph said.

'Except I'm provoked,' Danny said and lunged again, grappling him to the floor, Ralph's head knocking a plant stand to land softly on the carpet. Ralph shook Danny off.

A shadow flicked across the room over to the bedside chair. Would Ralph find the gun?

He could see the shadow silently return. Ralph's silhouette was now blocking part of a thin line of light seeping through a crack in the curtains.

Danny held his breath and pulled his silk sleeves down over his wrists to stem the flow.

Target in his sights, he charged forward. His strong arms and shoulders took Ralph with him, like a snow plough, to the window. Their heads struck the single pane of glass which shattered in shards to the pavement and canopy below. Passers-by crouched or raised their arms to cover their heads. Danny grabbed Ralph by the neck; more to stop himself following the glass than to starve Ralph of air. But Ralph had now pushed Danny bent backwards over the windowsill. Danny could feel fangs of jagged glass rip through his silks but not his body protector. He tensed his lower back muscles just in case; he'd seen someone demonstrate lying on a bed of nails once. When Ralph's gun came into view over his stomach, Danny feared this was it.

Danny glanced down, blood flooding his head. The added oxygen sharpened his mind. His fingernails snapped as he clawed into the paintwork of the window frame. As his torso hung over, suspended mid-air, he felt the odd sensation of leaving his stomach behind, like when cresting the rise of a Big Dipper.

Down below, he caught the shape of Jack, who was now cocooned in a blanket, with Megan shielding his eyes. She was screaming something, looking up. They stood beside the red awning directly below. It was all Danny needed to find that extra energy burst.

He heard the distant police sirens and the rattle of the room's door handle. He couldn't hold on any longer, grip loosening on the window frame.

Whether it was hysteria or the body's way of releasing endorphins to mask the pain or had he just come to terms that this was the end, but Danny began to laugh.

'And you think I'm a psycho,' Ralph snarled.

Danny recalled the thick red carpet beyond the awning and left hand whipped up to grab Ralph's jacket. 'We're in this together!'

He then let go of the frame with his right hand and allowed himself to fall back, Ralph let slip the gun, as if shocked. He heard it thud off the awning below. But his grip on Ralph never wavered, as if holding a life jacket; no way was he going to die and let that scum live on. He resisted the urge to shut his eyes and hope. He needed to see the awning rush towards him as they turned over in a tangled mess, like panicked skydivers unable to release the chute.

For the briefest moment, he felt a dreamy floating sensation.

They sliced through the air and then the canvas, which bowed as it briefly broke their fall. But their combined weight ripped open the awning and both struck the red carpet with a dull thud. Danny was no stranger to being fired into the ground and knew how to land. He extended his legs and feet out to soften the blow, strong arms pillowing his skull. Better a broken leg than a broken head. He then rolled to a standstill.

Both lay there, splashed by light through the ruined canopy above.

Danny could see his sleeve, now matching the red carpet. He began to fade away, as life left him. No way was he going to let that happen. Not with Jack there. Daddy wasn't a quitter.

With all his might he kept his eyes open and saw the hotel doorman's black jacket, then his face. He looked as confused and shocked as Danny felt. Megan's face was next into the fuzzy picture.

Danny shook his thumping head and struggled to his feet. He looked over at Ralph, who was hobbling towards the pavement. His left leg didn't look right as he staggered lamely past a growing crowd. Seeing what spurred Ralph on, Danny began the chase.

'Let him go!' Megan shrieked.

'He's not escaping, there's a gun,' Danny said, which dispersed the crowd enough for him to leap forward and shoulder Ralph to smack the concrete slabs, just an arm's length from the weapon which had bounced off the canopy like a trampoline.

He felt life fading from him and could only remember Megan sobbing as she cradled his head. 'Why do it?' she whispered.

'Guess you were worth saving,' Danny croaked. He looked up as she blinked her wet eyes.

'Just keep your eyes wide and stay with me.'

'Check your pocket,' Danny said. 'If I don't make it, give to police.'

'Don't be silly, of course you'll make it. I'll have you tangoing before the week's out.'

They both smiled.

He then coughed up some blood. He glanced over at Ralph, who groaned as he lay strewn, perfectly still, but for a slowly moving chest.

Hearing the sirens now just yards away, Danny felt like passing out too, as he knew there would soon be plenty of awkward questions. With Ralph alive and witnesses rubbernecking around them, he was certain they'd be answered.

CHAPTER 28

HE'D WORKED through the last of the outstanding bills. His desk and conscience were now clear. Though that was a great weight off, his shoulders dropped slightly when he looked again at the email he'd initially opened in the weighing room of Pardubice. He was entranced by the grainy image on that tiny screen. The picture had been sent by Rhys and showed Sara and Franco kissing passionately outside his ice cream parlour. The text above read: 'Thought you'd want to know. He's taken both of us for a ride.'

Danny didn't need convincing it was real and not some photoshopped act of spite. Rhys' primary motive for sending was to reveal Franco for the traitor he was, not to punish Danny. Franco had, after all, deserted Rhys outside the weighing room.

Maybe at some subconscious level Danny wanted it to be real, help ease their decision to call a day on their marriage.

The snapshot made it painfully clear why she needed time and space by herself. The suicide bid was just an act, an excuse to shift any guilt or blame on to Danny, one that had Franco's grubby fingerprints all over it.

Danny knew little about how relationships work. Whenever his car broke down, he could fix it. When his marriage broke down, he didn't know where to start. He never felt he could fall out of love with Sara but when she said, 'We need a break from each other' he didn't feel shocked or disappointed. He barely felt anything. Did that mean he didn't feel anything for Sara?

If he was being true to himself, their marriage had stalled soon after Jack was born. He always thought having kids would bring them closer together.

He looked at their wedding photo on his desk and couldn't face it. He put it in the drawer and then took out the stopwatch which lay beside the Dictaphone he'd borrowed from the journalist in Prague.

There was a quiet knock on the office door. He put down the watch. 'Yes?'

Megan entered. She wore a flowery dress above the knee that hugged her shapely curves.

'You look pretty, where you off?'

'Oh, nowhere,' she said and looked away. 'A girl doesn't need an excuse to dress up.'

'I'm not complaining,' Danny said. 'And thanks.'

'For what?'

'Everything,' Danny said. 'Sticking by me when … well, others haven't. Don't know where I'd be without you.'

'Don't be silly.'

Danny had never seen Megan this shy. 'I'm complimenting you. It's out of hours, you don't have to think of me as your boss twenty-four seven.'

'What are you saying?'

Danny felt shitty about the way he'd taken out his stress on Megan when she was nothing but a help.

Knowing she had a partner, he didn't allow himself to think of her in that way. More like the sister he never had. She wouldn't be interested in someone the wrong side of thirty, he felt certain.

She suddenly moved in close. Her cheeks turned pink. The whites of her eyes grew as she stared intently up at him.

Danny swallowed and then said, 'But your partner? Rhys overheard you on the phone.'

She smiled, 'Dance partner.'

'So you're single.'

'It depends who's asking,' she said, 'Because for months now, I've only had eyes for one person. When I told you I was head over heels in love. What I was about to say but couldn't–'

There was a heavy silence.

'Just say it.'

'It's you, okay? I love *you*!' she said, wide eyes seeking the slate tiles. 'Now what are you going to do?' Her bottom lip started to go.

'You're nervous.'

'I don't want to finish your marriage; Sara's pillow is barely cold. I care too much for you to do that.'

'Two can play at her game,' he said and kissed her.

'This isn't a game, Danny.'

'I know it's not.'

It was only then it dawned on him how much he adored her. She was good for him. She made him feel younger, more positive. A fresh start.

He held her hands still as they stood by the office door. He asked, 'You're shaking.'

'I've dreamt about this moment, I get nervous when I want something so bad, scared I'll mess up and lose it.'

He looked deep into her blue eyes and felt a whole new lease of life. 'You won't lose it.'

She laughed. 'Just had a blonde moment.'

'Are you naturally blonde?'

Megan bit her lip and then said playfully, 'That's for you to know and … well–'

She grabbed Danny by the hand and they rushed along the landing, stopping outside the guest bedroom. She looked up to him. Her cute face was beaming. Her eyes sparkled with life, vitality and youthful exuberance that had been absent from Danny's for too long. She then shut them tight. She kissed him on the lips. It felt so good, like being a teenager again; he tried to forget that she was.

She ran her soft hand down his forearm. The touch of skin on skin, something he'd been deprived for much of the past couple of years, felt like a static shock.

He noticed her hand trembling. 'What's wrong?'

'It's just you're older.'

'Thanks.'

'Not in a bad way, I didn't mean old, there is a difference.'

'Experienced is the word I think you're after.'

'And I'm worried I won't live up to, well,' Megan said, her voice was now shaking. 'It's all because you mean that much to me. I want it to be special for both of us.'

Danny's finger pressed her soft lips. 'It's who you are. I remember your interview, nothing wrong with being nervous.'

'But I wasn't that nervous about the interview, didn't dream I'd get the job see?'

'You looked it.'

'The nerves only came when I saw you.'

'Didn't look that scary, did I?' Danny asked and then smiled.

'You know what I mean,' she said and kissed him again. 'Do I have to spell it out?'

CHAPTER 29

THERE WAS a spring in Danny's stride, loved up from the night before. He paced deeper into the darkening tunnel cutting through the woodland. While he hated this place and hadn't planned to return, he felt duty bound. He couldn't fathom where the bones of Herbie were laid to rest. It then came to him – the clearing.

All he could hear was the swish and rustle of the green canopies above and clomp of his leather soles on the earthy path as it grew cooler and gloomier. The jutting stump of a beech made him stop. No Salamanca to worry about this time.

Danny stepped into the clearing. He went over to near where he'd found the stopwatch. The pile of bones was still there. Last time Danny was here, he hadn't dreamt they might be human and not animal, particularly with the foxes circling. He picked up a large, curved fragment, clearly part of a skull. He swallowed. Poor Herbie.

He was about to collect up the remains to give a proper send-off when he spotted something glisten in the morning sun.

He must've been too entranced by the stopwatch to spot it last time. He dug it out from the knotted grass and pieces of bone. He held it up close to his face. At first he thought it was a gold nugget but when he looked even closer, he could see it was tooth-shaped. He held it tight and returned to where he'd found it. There were other enamel teeth. Ralph had talked with disdain about his father's distasteful lust to show his wealth and that gold tooth was a means to get one over rival Michael Johns. When fortunes turned, it's a wonder he didn't have it removed and melted down.

As Danny now held it in his moist palm, his fertile imagination swept him back to that misty morning over seventy years before. Walter saw Philip and Herbie pace up-valley until lost by the peasouper. As Philip had taken the lead, Danny just assumed he was in charge. But you don't have to lead to be in control, a rifle in the back would see to that.

Herbie was the murderer not the victim that morning.

Ralph revealed Philip had changed his will to make Herbie sole benefactor in his will. But there was every chance Philip would outlive Herbie who, being the only other person to know where they'd buried the fortune, saw his chance to take the lot and run.

That didn't explain why he never returned to the racetrack for his reward. Herbie had given up his family, his job, everything he'd ever worked for. Surely he'd go collect.

Danny then recalled the racetrack closed not long after. Points of reference like the final fence and the grandstand were gone. He wouldn't even tell where they'd disturbed the ground; they'd removed the top layer of soil in order to level the ground for playing fields and the housing estate.

With no GPS, there was little chance Herbie would strike lucky on land which was large enough to now cover Trelai Park, the housing estate and four schools, even if he had a rough idea of the burial site. He couldn't make repeat visits for risk of capture as, by then, he would be a missing suspect in the disappearance of Philip and the racecourse fire.

Danny placed the last of the bones he could find in a shallow grave he'd meant for the body in the skip. He dropped in the gold tooth and the stopwatch, returning them to their rightful owner. It seemed Philip wasn't so much the villain of the piece after all. He deserved some kind of proper burial. He had done more than most to bring racing to the area. Perhaps that was Philip's ghost he'd seen in the wooded copse backing the stone base of the old Samuel House. His troubled spirit unable to rest until Herbie was exposed as a murderer.

Danny would rather believe it was his heightened imagination seeing things that weren't there. He'd have to gallop up there most mornings and the horses would pick up on any anxiety. And probably Danny convinced himself it was a park-keeper when in fact it was Ralph wearing black and talking into a mobile and not a radio. Given the setting, his mind and memory had made the rest up.

From an early age Ralph believed Philip was a cold killer and had convinced himself it was in his DNA. Certain the apple fell close to the tree, he clearly felt he had no choice in the matter. It almost gave Ralph a licence, a get-out, to act the way he did, sure in the knowledge it was nature over nurture. That 'I was born this way mentality' couldn't remotely justify what he did to Walter and Silver Belle and he would surely have carried on.

Danny suspected Ralph was more the product of what sounded like a brutal upbringing by his father. Either way, it was no excuse at all, as Philip wasn't the cold-hearted killer Ralph thought or, in some perverse way, hoped he was.

He'd never fully know or understand what went on that night. Perhaps jockey Charlie Moore caught them burying the fortune and threatened to raise the alarm. Shame there was no one willing to raise the alarm while he was burning alive locked in the stewards' room.

Philip was dead, Herbie was without a fortune or a family, Charlie was ashes and a popular racetrack had shut its gates and for what? Greed.

He removed a newspaper clipping from the zipped breast pocket in his jacket. He unfolded the paper and, not knowing the Lord's Prayer, he felt Philip, if he was somehow listening in, would want to hear this. He read aloud: 'BHA gives Green Light for New Cardiff Racecourse. Ely Racecourse will rise like phoenix from the flames when construction shortly gets under way on Trelai Park – the sight of the old course which held its last fixture in 1939 – and will become Wales' fourth racecourse.'

'Gone, but not completely forgotten,' he added. 'Much like the racetrack, until now.'

He patted the Dictaphone shape in his jacket. Fearing another break-in, he kept it on his person at all times. He was sure Ralph wouldn't come after it. He was doing more than okay out of this deal. Danny knew one day the recording he'd taken in that Prague hotel would make Ralph pay for what he did for Walter and Silver Belle. It was all about timing as to when he would parcel it to the police. He'd wait until the track was built, had enough support from sponsors and supporters to survive, even if the owner Ralph had to go away for several years at Her Majesty's pleasure.

He then returned the damp, cool soil back into the hole and stamped it down. He hoped he was burying his problems along with Philip. This was private land and as long as he owned Samuel House, it would remain a secret, hidden away. After the Czech payday, he didn't expect to move from such an idyllic set-up anytime soon, though, learning the fate of Ely Racecourse, nothing was a certainty. Philip couldn't have dreamt the leading track in Wales would eventually fade to just a distant memory.

His feet skated over the earthy mound until fully concealed by dead grass and weeds and brambles, as if nobody had ever stumbled across this remote clearing.

With the money and prestige of Salamanca's win and a thriving local track in the making, the future of Samuel House looked a good deal brighter now.

Even saying those words Samuel House now stuck in his throat. Perhaps it was time for a change, a fresh start. Would have to update these, Danny thought, looking down at his rather bedraggled fleece embossed with the gold stable logo.

He shivered in the warmth. This place gave him the creeps and he wanted out, so he hastily retraced his path through the woods.

With conscience clear, he glanced back for one last time and thought, Silver Belle Stables has a nice ring to it.

Printed in Great Britain
by Amazon